E·ST·E·L·L·A

E·S·T·E·L·L·A

Alanna Knight

Macdonald

A *Macdonald* Book

First published in Great Britain in 1986
Macdonald & Co (Publishers) Ltd
London & Sydney

Copyright © Alanna Knight 1986

All rights reserved

British Library Cataloguing in Publication Data

Knight, Alanna
    Estella.
    I. Title   II. Dickens, Charles, 1812-1870.
    Great Expectations
    823'.914[F]   PR6061.N45

    ISBN 0-356-12072-4

Photoset in North Wales by
Derek Doyle & Associates, Mold, Clwyd
Printed in Great Britain by
Redwood Burn Ltd.,
and Bound at The Dorstel Press

Macdonald & Co
London & Sydney
Maxwell House
74 Worship Street
London EC2A 2EN
A BPCC plc Company

For
SUE FLETCHER

The Nightmare lurked at the place where time and memory began, emanating from the sinister marsh lands, and bringing into Satis House the evil presence of grotesque creatures who had risen bodiless from their graves to destroy me. Why then did I awake weeping, my infant heart aching with pity and terror and later with the greater agony of loss? Why indeed, for what had such beings tearing at one another's throats like wild beasts with human voices, to do with my very civilized, genteel life with Miss Havisham?

Part One
Satis House

The Nightmare and the Hulks.

A slice of plum cake and a pair of creaking boots.

And hunger, the pangs of gnawing emptiness, I can recall vividly to this day. I would have suffered anything, undergone any trial, borne any tribulation for that piece of plum cake, the largest I had ever seen and Bessie Maydie's reward for undergoing the hearty ablutions necessary for my presentation to Miss Havisham.

'I dare say you can take care of this.' She might as well have entrusted lamb to wolf as that slice of plum cake to a hungry child determined to demolish at the earliest this bribe to follow Mr Jaggers' brown shining boots, redolent with polish, into the strange house's upper regions.

Did he and the housekeeper fear a small female child's reactions to that bizarre room where all clocks had stopped twenty years ago and a bride, a woman now old, but still clad in the tatters of her wedding gown sat before the ruin of a wedding banquet only the creatures of the darkness had secretly enjoyed?

'Are you afraid of spiders?' demanded the Grey Lady as I stared at the ghostly table with its festoons of cobwebs.

For answer, I shook my head and as a gesture of defiance

11

to all spiders, took a bite of cake, so rich and delicious that it made my jaws and ears ache and my eyes water.

'Mice then?'

'Tell Miss Havisham the truth, and you shall have more cake,' boomed Mr Jaggers.

Cold and hungry still, if more plum cake went with pleasing the Grey Lady then nothing would be too much trouble for me to admire.

'Are you afraid of me, then?' Her smile, rarely exercised, bore remarkable resemblance to a grimace, revealing teeth like long yellow fangs against the grey veils.

'Speak up, child,' roared Mr Jaggers, rocking back and forth and sending the boots into a clamour of supplication.

I looked Miss Havisham straight in the eye. 'No. I am not afraid of you.'

'Well done, well done.' Miss Havisham was obviously pleased as Mr Jaggers pushed me forward. Plum cake and I were momentarily involved with grey veils, skilfully extracted and sent back downstairs to a triumphant symphony of creaking.

Through the green baize door hidden by the old dusty staircase, in a kitchen with cheerful fire and cat curled before it, Bessie already carved the next succulent slice of cake. Lawyer Jaggers' demand for a basin of warm water set me a-trembling. My skin still red and sore from Bessie's ministrations indicated that I had done very well by ablutions for some days to come. I watched fearfully as the lawyer solemnly conducted a searching investigation of basin and snowy linen in the manner of one examining incriminating evidence. Satisfied, he vigorously doused his own hands and face before turning his attention to where I tried to make myself invisible in the fervid hope of being overlooked.

Was it only those great heavy eyebrows and slab-like tombstone face that made me afraid, or the threatened return of that dark misery from whence I had come? However, with a pat on the head, and a stern recommendation to good behaviour at all times, he creaked his boots out of the house.

My sigh of relief came too soon, for even as the door closed, I learned that for pleasing the Grey Lady and accepting the plum cake there was a price to be paid.

'Kind Miss Havisham is now your Mama,' said Bessie.

'He is not coming back for me?'

'Bless you dear heart, no. And you'll be happy with us. As for that gentleman,' she said, nodding towards the door through which Mr Jaggers and his boots had made their exit: 'As for that gentleman, he would be the last man on earth to allow a respectable orphan child to be adopted into a house where hands and faces are not washed regular,' and advancing upon me again with determination, 'I never saw his like for soap and water.'

With a sigh, I submitted to her ministrations, the ways of the grown-up world were quite beyond me, although I was certain sure that Kind Miss Havisham was not my Mama and that I had never seen her before in my life ...

Allowed to play in her spectral world, with events in my forgotten life more dreadful than mice or spiders, I felt neither revulsion nor alarm, but privileged indeed. I soon learned, but without any understanding of its true significance, my role at Satis House. Miss Havisham's lessons were directed towards the cure for love: 'From one who has suffered'. And I discovered, in the manner that wars are waged between Heads of two nations opposing each other, that my duty was to chant a catechism of hatred for all men, since one of their kind had betrayed Miss Havisham's love and broken her heart. Men, I was encouraged to regard as my mortal enemies, vile cruel beasts, without hearts. Her lessons contained bewildering examples of wronged women from Biblical days to the present.

As I recited or read out loud, she would pay particular attention to my voice: ('Higher, dearest child. No, no, a tone lower if you please.'). Afterwards, I must show her how well I did in deportment, practise my curtsies and winning smiles: ('Too wide, just the merest glimpse of teeth, dearest child'); gentle caresses: ('The merest touch, a butterfly wing – never below the wrist on naked flesh, or above the elbow for that would seem familiar and might be deemed encouragement. Your *hands*, dearest child'). Even my mother by adoption could find no good word for my hands, large and strongly formed and quite at variance with my slender limbs. I hated them and was glad at an early age, of Bessie's knitting as a method of concealment. When I was older, I resolved to take refuge in gloves.

Before I was considered competent to exercise the full measure of my heart-breaking skills on the male species, as personified by Pip, the blacksmith Gargery's boy, Miss Havisham offered me a maid of my own age. 'To practise your lessons on, for that will give you confidence when the time comes for greater things,' she explained, and ringing the bell for Bessie, announced: 'Summon the Small Person.'

This recruited whipping girl's name was Jolly. Never did name so belie its owner, for her wretched orphaned life in the local workhouse had been the very antithesis of merriment. But the words 'Summon Jolly' would have hung like lead upon Miss Havisham's lips, an offence to her melancholy and an imminent threat to the spectral surroundings in which she chose to live.

In the Small Person's presence I was encouraged to perfect my small cruelties: At the slightest misdemeanour, the merest fumble of a cup or drop of a spoon, I was commanded: 'Nip her arm sharply for that. Box her ears – harder. She deserves to have her hair pulled. Go on, child. Don't be afraid of her.' And I, vile unfeeling wretch, never gave second thought to the Small Person's bravely suppressed tears. To my own everlasting shame many years were to pass before I even knew her first name, and memory no more records her presence in the kitchen than Bessie's cat before the fire.

During those early years, except for my almost daily lessons with Miss Havisham, memory prompts that Bessie fitted more adequately with the role of mother by adoption. For the housekeeper was stout, merry and, with her abundance of shining red curls, youthful as her mistress was grey, middle-aged, thin and melancholy;

trusting and caring as Miss Havisham was suspicious and miserable.

On fine days we took our shopping baskets and walked down the High Street with its leaning gables that drooped like eavesdroppers on our conversations. Sometimes we climbed the hill to the ancient ruined Castle so skeletal that it seemed to have been gnawed away by giant insects and defeated even my ready imagination to recreate it as a cheerful home. Bessie would insist that I breathe deeply, get the fresh clean air into my lungs, and gazing over the Medway, would regale me with her young days 'up North' where she had been a mill-child. The conditions of child workers she described, made me glad to be free to take a good many deep breaths and be grateful that orphaned, I had escaped a like fate.

'How did you get away, Bessie?'

'I escaped, in a manner of speaking.' I always wanted to hear more but she became reticent, saying only that after a bad accident she met Miss Havisham, travelling in Derbyshire with her father.

'She was a different lass in those days was your dear Mama, always laughing. Her papa, Mr Havisham, was a rich brewer' (the ruins of the brewery stood in the grounds of Satis House), 'her mother died when she was young and there was nothing he would not do for his only daughter. He spoilt her dreadfully, and often she was very naughty and wilful, too, a wrong 'un, she could be sometimes, just like yourself, Miss Estella, and a bit of a devil at times. But she could be very lovable and kind when she wanted to. We took to each other right away when we met in Derbyshire and as her maid had recently married, when she asked me to come south to London with her, I never gave it a second thought. All I had left of kin was a married niece –'

At this stage I would ask: 'Tell me about Mr Arthur.'

It was from Bessie I pieced together the fabric of a life I could not remember, the life my mother-by-adoption would never discuss with me. Bessie, however, had no such scruples.

'Just suppose, you might well be Miss Havisham's niece.'

Mr Arthur, half-brother by her father's second marriage, had introduced her to his friend, the absconding bridegroom. She never spoke to him afterwards but when he married (a lady of good but disapproving family and no fortune) and both fell victims to the cholera, Miss Havisham with a rare display of magnaminity, (according to Bessie's hints) thereupon refused to allow her only niece to vanish into the convenient oblivion of the workhouse.

'And wouldn't it be the most natural thing in this world for your dear Mama to put the matter of adopting such a bairn into Mr Jaggers' hands.'

Later, it occurred to me as odd, that the child of parents she hated should have been chosen as her instrument of revenge. But then who would doubt Bessie's word? Everything about her seemed vigorously alive and honest, although at the best and most exciting parts of her narrative, she had a habit of closing her lips firmly and laying a forefinger against her nose, hinting at Great Secrets too weighty to be entrusted to the infant mind. But I was eager to accept Bessie's story which delighted me with its ring of tragic romance and hints of noble birth.

'Where did my mother's family live?'

'Oh, a long ways from here,' she said vaguely.

'In a castle?' I asked eagerly.

'Perhaps.'

With, alas, rather more regret for the loss of such a background, even a dispossessed one, than for parents I could not remember, I was content to ask: 'Will you take me to it?'

'Bless your heart, it's too far for a little girl to walk.'

'Further than the village?' I persisted.

'Bless my soul, yes. Even Bessie couldn't walk that far. Which reminds me,' she added with the rapid change of subject I learned early to associate with embarrassment and topics considered indelicate or dangerous, 'you will need a warm scarf for this afternoon.'

A great believer in the powers of fresh air Bessie was very insistent that my lungs and small legs be exercised in unison. Her friend Mabby lived 'down the village,' the poor

relation of 'up-town' where Satis House was situated. It
was quite a step for short legs, but I was told to take deep
breaths, and there was little else to concentrate on since
the scenery consisted of the long unrelieved monotony of
the marshes.

The short-cut through the churchyard was our approach
to Mabby's cottage, a detour not to be undertaken lightly.
Lurking mists bore uneasy resemblance to ghosts who had
left their tombstones, some of which were so encrusted by
moss they suggested green topcoats, the frightening
half-buried remains of headless humans.

The horizon was flat and grey by day, streaked black and
red at sunset, a desolate place fitting admirably with
Biblical accounts of lands smitten by plagues of
unpleasant variety. Bessie's friend, about whom memory is
quite blank, was the possessor of two grandchildren, and
my arrival, a special treat, arose out of Bessie's misdirected
kindness, for it mortified and worried her exceedingly that
Miss Estella lacked companions of her own age, the advent
of the Small Person Jolly having proved a complete
disaster and waste of time.

Acute social awareness marked those first interchanges
between Mabby's grandchildren and myself. They recognized contempt in my eyes and I, generations of servitude
in theirs.

'Get along with you. Play with the nice little girls, do,'
hissed Bessie, impatient for exciting grown-up gossip, as I
clung doggedly to her side.

'I don't wish to play with them.'

'Now, don't be a wrong 'un, there's a dear, Miss Estella.'
There followed whispers of tempting and substantial
bribes awaiting back home for my good conduct, and
sulkily accepted.

As the three of us trotted obediently outside, I found
something repellent about that foreshore. Even on a sunny
day, the shadow of the great square black ship moored off
shore, with its tiny barred windows, cast a gloom over the
imagination. Its presence defeated all ideas of joyously
scampering about, laughing and shouting in childish play.

'That's the Hulks, the prison ship,' said the elder girl. 'Our Pa's a Constable and he caught an escaping convict single-handed at Christmas.' A pause for my astonished admiration. Receiving only indifference, she asked sharply: 'Well, what does your Pa do?'

'My father is dead,' I said loftily. 'But he was a great man, very wealthy and powerful with many servants and a carriage and he lived in a castle.'

There was a moment's silence – respect, awe or disbelief, before the younger girl said: ' 'Spect he's gone to heaven then like our Ma.' The thought of my illustrious though somewhat fictionalized father sharing a Heaven for the privileged with these urchins' kin suggested a deplorable breakdown in the system of celestial justice.

'You're an orphan, then?' The elder girl managed to endow the word with raggedness and scorn.

'Indeed no. My Mama is Miss Havisham.'

'She can't be a Miss if she's your Mama,' was the relentless reply. ' 'Taint allowed.'

'She is my mother-by-adoption and a lady of considerable wealth and influence.' As will have been observed, even at ten years old I was already the complete mistress of evasion.

'Is that so? They put people in the Hulks for telling lies, don't they, Sis?'

Sis nodded obligingly. 'And sometimes the convicts escape and then a cannon is fired to warn people that they are wicked and dangerous and cruel.'

'The fellow our Pa caught had broken into the blacksmith's forge and stolen a file and a pork pie,' was the triumphant adjoinder.

I was about to take her to task upon the validity of such an absurd connection when she leaned forward and hissed: 'Our Pa says it's people who tell lies, right from being children who end up on the Hulks. There now.'

I was heartily glad to return to Bessie and as we passed by the blacksmith's forge on our way home dusk was already gathering, an hour which did nothing for the marshes' appearance. Add the fierce red light, the ring of

18

steel, the hammer blows, all transfigured into a demonic scene of brimstone and hellfire, preached by the minister each Sunday.

At Satis House, coincidence was not yet over. I learned that I was to expect another playmate, a greater challenge than the Small Person, the little maid whom I had soon bent to my will.

'How would you like a boy to practise your lessons of life upon?' asked Miss Havisham.

'I should like that very much.' It was another lie and I was rapidly qualifying for the Hulks and transportation to the Colonies.

'You have chosen well. Now is the moment to try out your powers; for a natural beauty can learn to be a natural temptress. I have sent for the blacksmith's boy.'

I shuddered even more. The prospect of a boy sickened me with fright. Boys were tough and a lot stronger than girls. Unlike the Small Person, a boy might refuse to be bullied and might well hit me back and that could hurt. A blacksmith's boy, emanating from the forge with its glaring light, would possibly be a demon.

Expecting a red-eyed imp, I encountered instead a boy who was half a head smaller than myself although we were of an age. He had fair curling hair and eyes of periwinkle blue that crinkled when he laughed; but solemn, their proud unflinching gaze lent dignity and sensitivity to the poverty of his dress.

Poor Pip. I can still see him across the years, with his coarse heavy boots, several sizes too big for his thin legs. As he shuffled his feet unhappily, I watched them with ill-concealed amusement. Surely such boots had never been intended for him but had reached the blacksmith's abode through several generations of previous owners, poor children who never had anything which was theirs alone, except perhaps the privilege of starving to death and dying early.

'Philip Pirrip. But you may call him Pip.' What an absurd cloddish name. I watched him scornfully, eager to criticise. He met my glance steadily. Confused, I was the one to lower my eyes.

'Pip becomes him well, for he is very small for his age.' And I allowed my gaze to linger contemptuously upon his shabby ill-fitting clothes, despising the stammering politeness in which he answered Miss Havisham's questions. When she had us play cards and I beggared him, as he fumbled and spilt the pack, I said loudly:

'He calls the knaves Jacks. And what coarse hands he has, this stupid clumsy labouring boy.'

But Pip said nothing, his eyes unwavering on the cards. 'She says many hard things of you, yet you say nothing of her. What do you think of my Estella?'

'I don't like to say.'

'Whisper then.'

Perhaps he fancied her to be deaf, for in a whisper that could be heard clearly across the room, he said: 'I think she is very proud.'

'Anything else?'

'I think she is very pretty.' (Oh, how that pleased me.)

'And?'

'I think she is very insulting.' (Beastly boy.)

I was about to leave the room in high dudgeon, but was restrained by Miss Havisham's hand on my arm. She chuckled, and asked:

'Anything else?'

'Yes. I should like to go home.'

'And never see her again, though she is so pretty?'

Pip stood up and looked her straight in the eye with that steady unnerving gaze. 'I am not sure about that, whether I would like to see her again. But I should like to go home now.'

'And so you shall, boy. But first play out the game.'

To my chagrin he won that game. Miss Havisham looked at us, from one to the other and back again, weighing the unworn satin bridal shoe in her hand, as if she might consider giving it to the victor.

'Equally matched, equally matched.' And with the weird smile that set her eyes rolling back in her head, lids trembling: 'Equally matched,' again she sighed. 'This makes it better, better than I had dreamed.' And tapping her stick on the floor. 'Another game, another game.'

'I do not want another game. I want him to go home.'

'Another game, Estella,' I quailed at such firm tones and knew I must obey.

One glance at the cards I held told me I had lost. Scattering them angrily I stood up: 'Mine is the winning hand. A waste of time to play.'

Miss Havisham clapped her hands. 'Well done, my dear. Hate him, hate him, with all your heart.' And turning her head, she dismissed us both: 'Now take him away, let him have something to eat before he leaves.'

I felt his eyes upon me as I picked up the candle and he followed along the corridor and down the stairs, but although I knew I had cut him to the quick, insulted, degraded and cheated him, he said not a word. And I was conscious of unwilling admiration for the burning pride with which he had picked up the broken pieces of his self confidence.

I opened the door into the yard, with an imperious flourish: 'Out there, boy. You are to wait out there.' And I went below stairs to the kitchen, that pulsating heart of generations of earlier Havishams, now the kingdom of Bessie Maydie, with warm welcome and food and laughter too.

'Are you not bringing the lad inside out of the cold?'

'Of course not, Mama says he is to roam there and look about him while he eats.'

Bessie tut-tutted sadly over the vagaries of her mistress. 'What's amiss with the lad eating indoors I'd like to know.' She grumbled, handing me a large plate of bread and cheese and a pot of light ale.

He was not where I had left him. For a moment although I knew the gate was locked, I suspected he had seized the cowardly opportunity of leaving by clambering over the wall. I felt angry, cheated too, that he would never come back. I would never see him again. Much later in my life, a day was to come when I recalled that extraordinary feeling and knew why it had cut so deeply.

I found him sheltering from the stiff wind beside the

brewery yard and put down the food and drink on a stone, as I would to a strange dog, without a word. I walked scornfully away, for I saw he was crying, and his tears shamed me, where anger and blows would have only made me hate him more.

It was a very cold day and I wanted to go back indoors to Bessie's warm kitchen, but that would have shown weakness, so I must march about where I could be observed by the blacksmith's boy, as one strong and impervious to bitter weather. At length I sauntered back, saw the empty plate, and jingled the keys like a goaler to let him out.

He looked at me proudly. 'Why don't you cry, you boy?' I said viciously.

'Because I don't want to.' Again that stinging glance that looked all the way into my soul. And it suddenly seemed to me that here was an enemy worth having, but oh such a friend he would make too. For with such a friend one need never fear the world.

'You want to see me again?' I said sounding lofty.

'I don't think I do.'

I pushed him towards the gate. 'Liar. People who tell lies go to the Hulks.'

'Who says so?' The question was cautiously asked.

'One of my very good friends whose father is the Constable who rescued, single-handed, the dangerous convict who escaped at Christmas. Indeed, from your forge,' (I made the word 'forge' sound as common as I could,) 'you must have heard the cannon fired when he escaped.'

He smiled into the distance. 'Indeed, I did. We all did. We were at dinner.'

'Well, then, the Constable should know,' I said triumphantly.

Again he smiled and looking over his shoulder, whispered: 'Not as I know, miss.'

'Indeed? And what could you possibly know?'

'Just that I aided and abetted that very same convict in his escape.'

The absurd boast made me angry and with an

exclamation of exasperation, I pushed him out of the gate, and locked it behind him.

'Your dear Mama is waiting for you,' said Bessie. 'That seemed a nice like lad, what I saw of him from the window. Were you tormenting him, Miss Estella? You're a wrong 'un, you are, sometimes, a right little devil.'

And leaning on tiptoe, I kissed her cheek because we both knew she didn't mean a word of it. As I ran from the room, she called: 'And remind your dear Mama that the water's hot for her bath, for she's liable to argue with me that six days haven't passed by since last time.' It was obvious to me at an early age, for I was always an observant child, that Miss Havisham could never have survived all those years in Satis House alone, without someone to care for her. She had been brought up as Bessie would call it, 'bone idle'. The preparation of food was a mystery to her, any of the domestic virtues had long been considered beneath her. However, she had to be fed and clothed. She also had to be bathed. In more practical terms, although the illusion be maintained for all the world, and in particular Mr Jaggers and Pip, of a heart-broken recluse for whom all time had ceased twenty years ago, the human body could not be so arrested.

Bessie was a stickler for cleanliness which she regarded, I suspect, as at least one step ahead of Godliness. And without dwelling upon the indelicate, I realized when I came to womanhood that Miss Havisham still functioned as did others of child-bearing years. Had she neither bathed or changed her body linen for a quarter-century, then life in her dust-filled, cobwebbed shrine to lost dreams, would scarcely have been tolerable. And although Bessie's polishing and scrubbing ceased by Canute-like command just short of the upper floor, she took care that the upstairs bath was brought forward each Friday evening on the stroke of nine, and there before a roaring fire overlooked by the ghostly banquet, to the quivering terror of every mouse and spider, she superintended her mistress's ablutions.

My mind still on Pip's visit, I found Miss Havisham in

her dressing-room and perhaps that was the first time its oddity struck me forcibly, as of seeing it through a stranger's eyes. My mother-by-adoption sat in her arm chair, in her usual pose of an elbow resting on the table, leaning her head upon her hand. The faded torn bridal gown, the faded worn face. She wore her usual jewels about her neck and rings on her fingers and toyed with other costly gems that lay on the table beside her. The dresses, velvets and furs still only half-packed, lay scattered about the little room, the hankerchief, gloves and a Prayer book positioned in front of the looking glass.

A week passed and I was tortured by secret doubts about Pip's return. I hoped he would come, but at the end of six days I was so miserable that I almost hoped for both our sakes that he would not. But come he did and regularly until Miss Havisham had him apprenticed to the blacksmith Gargery. Only then did the visits to Satis House become more infrequent and we both had our separate ways to walk. I cannot remember the details of all his visits, only a pleasant sensation, something akin to indefinable memory of a summer's day when nothing much happens but the recollection of the sun's warmth on bare arms and the feeling of well-being remains: the knowledge that one was happy and carefree without knowing the reason why or being able to pinpoint events.

Only one day stands out in memory. My own pride when I watched him knock down Miss Havisham's visiting relative Herbert Pocket in the brewery yard. As I watched Pip help Herbert to his feet and dust him down, with self-conscious grins and a solemn handshake exchanged, for the fight had been Herbert's idea and Pip had agreed reluctantly, I remembered how I had tormented Pip about the convict he had helped, while he refused steadfastly to comment, saying only, 'I gave my word.' Uneasily I now believed he had spoken the truth. Such courageous action was typical of his nature, raising the vanquished, whether Herbert or an unknown wretched convict. Oh, how I longed at that moment to seize him by the hand and lead him downstairs into Bessie's realm of hot crusty loaves and apple pies. Instead, I merely kissed his cheek as reward, that most supreme condescension.

To all the world I would have declared that I was winning the game of being a breaker of hearts. I soon discovered that although I could make him blush for his coarse clothes and manners, in the matter of knowledge, Pip's was the superior role. This I found hard to bear. He went to the village school, to which Gargery paid the princely sum of twopence per week for his education, earning Bessie's praises, 'That lad'll go far. You just mark my words, a natural scholar born, that's what he is. There'll be no holding Master Pip.'

Her words hurt, making me both jealous and angry. For at home, tutored by Miss Havisham and later as a Young Lady at Dame Clarissa's (whose fees were a great deal more than twopence a week), my own education showed little reason for anything but gloom.

Pip's great love was history and when he heard the story that Satis House had come to the Havishams through King Charles the Second, who had stayed under its roof and formed an attachment for the Mistress Havisham of the time, he proceeded to tell me much more than I wished to know about Oliver Cromwell and the reasons why the first King Charles had lost his head.

'It was a cold February day, just like this, and the poor King worried in case the people watching should think he was shivering from fear and not from cold. A gallant loser, don't you think? How did Satis House become linked with the brewery?'

'Miss Havisham's father was very rich and very thrifty. Since there was a lot of land going to waste, he decided to build his brewery on the premises, so to speak, where he could keep an eye on it.'

'Have you never thought that Satis House is a strange name?' I supposed so and he said: 'Satis is Latin for enough. It means when it was given that whoever had this house could want for nothing else. Do you want for nothing else, Estella?'

'Of course I do. I want jewels, and a carriage and a rich husband.'

'You are a little young for that.'

'But I shall find one when the time is ripe, never you fear.'

I was pleased at the hurt look on his face, for I knew that he loved me but considered that I was far above him. 'That would make a fellow very industrious in life, Estella. It would make having a fortune well worth while.' He always managed to twist my cruel remarks to his own advantage so I said shortly:

'I want no common jumped up fellow for my husband, he must be well-bred. I shall marry a noble Lord.'

'I trust that you never have cause to discover that there are other noble qualities more worthwhile than the possession of a title. Besides, Lords might not wish to marry with young ladies who live in haunted houses with eccentric old ladies. There are many people hereabouts take the opposite side of the street after darkness falls.'

I was angry again at his superior way of twisting my words and making me sound foolish, especially when I knew he spoke truth, for the general air of delapidation and a preponderance of rusting padlocks might well scare off the unwary.

'As for those iron bars on the windows, if I didn't know you, gentle Miss Estella, I'd fancy there were prisoners locked up suffering unspeakable tortures. And as for these flagstones,' he touched them with his toe, 'see how grey and uneven they are. Don't you fancy sometimes that they hint at Gothic burials hastily performed at dead of night?'

'Pray, don't be ridiculous. Such thoughts have never entered my mind.' But they had and as it was growing very dark, very quickly, I left him at the gate and hurried thankfully to the part of the house devoted to the living, where I found normality expressed in the sight of Bessie taking a tray of baking out of the oven.

Only once was I ever afraid awake in Satis House. Not in

Miss Havisham's spectral domain, but on a windy autumn evening which caused the candles to gutter and splutter. I had been to a party given by one of Dame Clarissa's Young Ladies, a newcomer whose father was a jumped-up poor clerk and who therefore, like myself, was not greatly sought-after. This particular occasion did nothing to add to her popularity since, overplump and greedy, she had made herself very sick by sly application to the sweetmeats long before the guests arrived. Hers must have been the shortest birthday party on record as her mother dismissed us angrily, as if we were personally to blame, and carried her daughter upstairs, protesting and screaming to bed.

I walked home along the High Street and it was already growing dark when I opened the kitchen door. There, reflected by the dim firelight a strange man, with a completely bald head, nodded fast asleep in Bessie's chair by the fire. Not only sleeping in her chair but wearing her best woollen wrapper, while before him on the kitchen grate my Bessie's decapitated head, red curls and all.

Even as my screams rang through the room, the bald one awakened and leaped towards me.

'Don't touch me. Don't touch me,' I screamed.

'Estella, dear love, stop at once.' The voice, the hands and arms belonged to Bessie. 'It's me, dear lass. Come along now, don't be scared. It's only your old Bessie.'

The familiar voice halted my terror, for Bessie it certainly was. Bessie, as bald as the eggs laid by the hens next door. Bessie, who had taken the opportunity of my absence to wash and dry the red curls, which were in fact, a marvellous wig.

'There, there, my precious. You mustn't fear old Bessie.' She sighed. 'Tis a mortal cross I carry for I lost all my hair when I was twelve years old in an accident in the factory and half my scalp as well. My hair was long and it got caught in a machine.' She closed her eyes, shuddering at the memory. 'It never grew again,' she whispered. 'I was lucky to be alive afterwards, they said.'

'Is that why you never married?'

Many had been the tales of the suitors she had rejected.

Now she smiled. 'It is. Men set great story by a woman's crowning glory. They do love bonny hair and I never could face the prospect of letting a husband share my shameful secret.'

Young as I was, the words of protest were forming as I tried to tell her that she was wrong. That any man worth having would have only loved her more when he knew that terrible story. As I did.

Ignoring the purpose of my adoption by Miss Havisham, Bessie ensured that my childhood was happy and as normal as the circumstances permitted. It was she who was in favour of my going forth into the world to be educated. Thankfully Miss Havisham responded to this suggestion without too much opposition, readily persuaded against the disruptive and gossiping presence of a governess in the house.

By a stroke of good fortune, Dame Clarissa's Academy for Young Ladies stood nearby the Cathedral. The impoverished gentlewoman, alarmingly small and so rotund that she gave the impression of rolling rather than walking, short of breath and long on moral tales, preached the daily lesson to be learned off by heart by discerning females:

'Remember always that the minds of young ladies are delicately balanced and too much learning, indeed, any attempts to over-stimulate their brains may lead to disastrous consequences, nay, even fatal ones. Besides being calculated to ruin their matrimonial prospects, should they survive this catastrophe.' To this horrible threat was added: 'Remember always that the minds of pure young ladies go in perpetual danger of being – sullied –' the word whispered with a nervous over-shoulder glance, as if her warning might already be too late. 'Sullied,' she repeated, 'and by what? Too much knowledge, of course.'

We were further advised to beg no more than the merest acquaintance of the Three Rs, our mental energies concentrated on matters of deportment and etiquette, plus agreeable accomplishments such as a modest indulgence in water-colour painting and polite French conversation. These gentle activities, she assured us, could do no possible harm and would be guaranteed to leave our matrimonial prospects quite intact and unsullied. For those who were so gifted, piano music and the singing of sentimental drawing-ballads stood high on the curriculum. The nobler more gentlemanly aspects of history were our daring excursions into culture. And since history was, in fact, a mighty rough business suspect of contaminating the female mind, we were restricted to a daily recitation of the dates of the Kings and Queens of England, with a few famous battles beginning with Hastings and ending discreetly with Waterloo.

The day ended as it began: 'And what important piece of knowledge have we acquired?' demanded Dame Clarissa.

'That the ideal of every young lady is to be amiable, inoffensive, always ready to give pleasure and be pleased,' we chorused in one voice.

Small wonder such ambitions brought a perplexed frown to Miss Havisham's face, whose sole purpose in adopting a female child was as her instrument of revenge upon all men. Such training could hardly guarantee the granite heart of an avenging angel ready to destroy all men, to break their hearts and have them wither at her feet.

Unaware then of my destiny, I did my lessons on the well-scrubbed kitchen table while Bessie's knitting needles clicked vigorously in constant competition with the crackling fire and a kettle that sang forever on the hob. She taught me early to knit and instilled into me that my life would be incomplete without 'something on the needles'.

When June approached, I wished to be like the other Young Ladies and celebrate with a birthday party. But none of the pupils had thus far rushed forward eagerly asking to be my friend. I walked alone, envying those who went in twos, arm-in-arm, heads close, giggling over their secrets. Wary of being 'talked about' as 'the mad Miss Havisham's ward' and sensitive regarding my orphaned state, I was distant and aloof.

Matters were not helped by parents or relatives of the Young Ladies, who claimed to be entirely conversant with the extraordinary goings-on in the upstairs of Satis House, or were ready to supply what they did not know by the simple exercise of ingenuity and speculation. I soon knew that Pip had spoken truth and I was regarded with the same caution as a witch who emanated from a haunted house.

One day I asked Bessie whether she had ever seen a ghost in Satis House?

'Who on earth gave you that idea, I'd like to know. Well, let me tell you there's none of that nonsense in this house,' she added sternly. 'Your dear Mama wishes to live in a grim fairytale land, but that is not for the likes of you.'

'Why does she wish never to see any friends, never go out into the sunshine?'

Bessie sighed. 'Maybe you'll understand some day when you're older. But meanwhile, think of her as being something of an actress, playing a part in a play.'

I understood that. 'Will the curtain ever come down, Bessie?'

'It will, lass, like as not, one of these days.'

Bessie's words consoled me and I dreamed that a party would put everything right and transform me instantly into the most popular girl at Dame Clarissa's. My mother-by-adoption however, was as disinclined to give her consent as the other Mamas were disinclined to let their precious darlings venture into 'That House'.

Bessie, however, was determined that party I should have.

'In the kitchen, says your dear Mama,' she wailed with a wringing of hands. 'It's the best I can do to persuade her and what their Mamas will say to that, I tremble to think.'

I thought of little else. It seemed that the day would never come, that some national catastrophe, earthquake, outbreak of fearful disease must occur, but that June morning dawned as radiant as if the angels had just painted it across the world.

For half an hour beforehand, I shook every clock not

firmly fixed to wall or bracket. Was that really the time? The hour of arrival came and I haunted the front door, specially opened for the occasion, its brasses shining. Why was there no one in sight? They had forgotten. But at last they began to arrive, staring round them fearfully as we descended through the green baize door into the kitchen. The intakes of breath, the gleaming smiles told of enjoyment today and stomach aches tomorrow, but I could see also that they were considering what a useful friend Estella Havisham might be after all, in the new light of Bessie's cooking.

At last someone suggested 'Games'. Hide-and-seek was the popular request, a ruse I firmly believe on the part of the more adventurous to explore the forbidden territory 'above-stairs'. Their curiosity was amply rewarded by the vision of a grey-haired lady in torn bridal gown, sitting before a ghostly banquet ravaged by time and the overtures of ...

'MICE!'

'SPIDERS!'

Screaming, they hurtled from the room, tumbling down the dusty stairs to the ruin of elegant gowns. Refusing to be consoled or silenced by currant buns and lemonade administered by Bessie, yelling for their Mamas, their cries were enough to terrify Miss Havisham, who did nothing to help a steadily worsening situation by appearing like an avenging angel on the landing. Peering over the banisters, brandishing her stick at them, she mouthed curses which did not quite fit the role of 'poor dear Estella's invalid Mama'.

As with all scenes of violence, even a bout of good-natured fisticuffs between Pip and Herbert Pocket, the Nightmare inevitably followed. The two mad creatures fighting, screaming, scarce-human. Another scene more monstrous and terrifying; the victor searching the darkness where I hid, striking my face with a bloodied fist. I awoke screaming ...

Where then did the Nightmare belong? In the months between my parents' death and my adoption I was convinced that some dire misfortune had overcome me, so terrible it evaded conscious memory. Even in daytime I could not think of those heart-stopping moments as 'only a dream' as Bessie would have me believe. When I awoke sobbing, to find her comforting arms, I wished her to see it too, to understand the magnitude of my horror.

'There, there, my pet. You must have strayed into the servants quarters of some inn that your parents took you too. Vagrants, gipsies and thieves, frequent such places. That's what you saw and they frightened your wits away. Never worry, you won't ever see the likes of them again in real life. Think of it, you'll be a young lady soon,' she ended, evasive as ever.

Although I was perfectly happy with my mother-by-adoption I sometimes thought it odd that I never dreamed of my real parents, never saw their faces. And why in this house of old portraits, were there none of them? Nor did I altogether believe Bessie's comforting explanation about the nightmare or understand her nervous advice:

'Don't tell your dear Mama, my precious. It will only upset the dear lady, for she has troubles enough.' In other words, how could she be expected to understand anyone else's nightmare when her own life was a long uninterrupted evil dream from which she had never awakened.

With the passing years, I made a few timorous friendships with Young Ladies who lived in the genteel villas about the town. Occasionally I came home in a state of rare excitement at having been invited to tea. The invitation was seldom issued a second time since I was unable to reciprocate. Miss Havisham retained an excellent memory of that one ill-fated birthday party; female companions of my own age were forever forbidden across the threshold.

However, I had all the other necessities: affection, comfort, food, well being, clothes, all I took for granted as a dweller in Satis House, and had any been withdrawn, I should have moped exceedingly. In spite of the materialistic outlook bred in me, to say nothing of still distant role of avenger, for which I was in constant training, as the years passed, I grew increasingly fond of Pip, my only true friend.

'Fond.' I use the word with caution, for I knew nothing of stronger emotions. As Pip's visits were irregular, each time he seemed to present yet another version of himself, a shadow as it were growing out of the future of the man he was to become. And even I could see a very presentable man in the making. Each time we met the shadow appeared to have taken on greater substance, added extra inches. Although he was never to be very tall, he had grace of movement and a look of solid strength. He also developed a droll humour that made me laugh exceedingly, a state of affairs much preferable to those moments when his very soul regarded me out of his eyes. On such occasions I felt impelled to warn him of his danger, even if that meant risking my guardian's displeasure by thwarting her well-laid plans.

For my instructions were clear, I was to make Pip my adoring slave, and the price he was to pay for this privilege: his broken heart. In truth, the role gave me a certain feeling of power. I knew by the time I reached fourteen, that my appearance was pleasing. I received many compliments from acquaintances to confirm what my mirror told me, concerning the possession of personal beauty. As I grew taller Miss Havisham no longer frowned over my less-than-perfect hands although I took refuge in wearing gloves whenever possible.

'A little princess, that's what you are,' sighed Bessie. A princess could not have been prouder.

'A breaker of hearts,' added Miss Havisham with a grim sigh of satisfaction for her own labours in this remarkable achievement.

To my still unformed mind, it seemed of no more significance than being a competent breaker of eggs in Bessie's kitchen.

Here, I must bring in an account of my short stay in France, at an establishment recommended by Dame Clarissa as an excellent finishing school for her Young Ladies. Four of us who could afford the fees were escorted by an elderly French couple, friends of Dame Clarissa who acted as couriers on such occasions. Together we crossed the Channel, all sick as dogs on the steam packet, our remaining high hopes and delicious excitement further shattered by the miserable *pension* and the greed of Monsieur and Madame Chauvez, eager to get their hands on our English pounds for as little effort as possible. My stay was shorter than had been intended, more disturbing than my mother-by-adoption ever dreamed.

The would-be breaker of hearts, the princess of Satis House, had also to endure in the household of Madame Chauvez, as doubtful tribute to my personal charms, not only the attentions of a spotty eighteen-year old son but also those of his portly father. Both of these odious creatures regarded my presence as an object for their disagreeable attentions and possessed between them as many pairs of hands and arms as the more worthy spiders of Satis House possessed legs.

I had been given a room of my own and was sharply aware of the disadvantages as many times I awoke to stealthy footsteps in the corridor and trembling watched the handle turn. Prudently I always locked my door and shuddered to think of what would have been the result had I not done so. Madame Chauvez was neither blind nor deaf and their blatant attentions convinced her that Mlle Estella was intent upon seducing her innocent son, her *cher* husband. I must leave immediately or she would be forced to ask my guardian to remove me and reveal the reasons for so doing.

I needed no second bidding to escape and wrote to Miss Havisham that I was bitterly homesick. Fortune was on my side. When my letter arrived, she was slightly indisposed and, according to Bessie, wept. Her dearest child was to be returned to her without delay by the same elderly couple who now, having heard Madame Chauvez's story, regarded me with a mixture of apprehension and embarrassment.

My return was followed by an immediate encounter with a distinguished young gentleman. In immaculate neck-cloth, handsome greatcoat, and shining riding boots, I could be forgiven for failing to identify at first glance, the blacksmith Gargery's boy.

There was a pause as we appraised one another with growing delight. Then Pip walked over swiftly and bowing took both my hands, held them in a warm strong clasp. Smiling but unspeaking we remained thus, as if time in that strange room had ceased for us too. At last, I raised my eyes, looked deep into his and in that one unguarded moment, a curious feeling overwhelmed me: that I stared into the well where all truth lay hidden. And if I read correctly what was written there and stayed with Pip at my side through life, then I need never fear again. After the sordid disaster of my stay in France, here I was being offered protection, security. I felt quite suddenly faint, light-headed and delirious, as one poised on the threshold of some amazing discovery that was to change for ever the course of my life ...

'Are you not amazed, Estella, at the sight before you? But there is more, much more. Tell her, Pip, what you have just told me.'

'I have received wonderful news,' said Pip softly, his eyes still holding mine. 'I have great expectations of a fortune – on one condition, that I retain the name of Pip and do not seek to know the identity of my mysterious benefactor. I am to come into a handsome property, Estella, and to be removed at once from my present sphere of life and learn to be a gentleman.' His voice was bewildered and he shook his head often like a man who has bad news – or learned that he has just come into a fortune.

'Mr Jaggers is to be my guardian until I come of age.'

Mr Jaggers? Our heads turned simultaneously towards Miss Havisham, with one idea.

'Who is this benefactor?' I asked sharply.

Miss Havisham shook her head as Pip turned again to me. 'That, Mr Jaggers is not at liberty to disclose. It is to remain a closely-guarded secret until that person chooses to reveal it first-hand to me, by word of mouth.'

In the small silence that followed our eyes again sought my mother-by-adoption, who regarded us enigmatically and asked suddenly, as if bored with the subject: 'Well, Pip, do you find Estella much changed? And will someone please retrieve my cane?'

Her acid tones broke the spell between us. Our eyes looked away, embarrassed, to search for that more mundane object. But in the years ahead, when life lost its meaning, its hope and coherence, how often I was to relive that instant of time and the image of Pip preserved within its sphere.

'I thank you, Pip, and now an answer to my question. She was proud and insulting and you were to go away from her. Do you remember?'

For the first time, I found her teasing of Pip unwholesome, detestable. It degraded both of us and I had no wish to see this young gentleman – for so he now appeared, belittled, stripped of his elegance before my eyes. I found myself willing him to retain that glimpse of honest purpose, of integrity and manly strength. But the old uncertainty was gathering in his eyes, as he looked at me helplessly while my guardian demanded that I tell him of my experiences in Paris.

'Did you not think she would have many admirers, Pip?' A nod. 'Tell him about them. Go along, dearest child.' Her laugh was shrill triumph. 'Leave nothing out, for he will wish to know every detail – everything. How greatly you were adored. Ah, these Frenchmen, Pip, so gallant, they make our countrymen appear the merest clods.'

I wondered how she would have reacted, or Pip for that matter, to the story of ever roving hands, of a locked bedroom door. I found myself gazing with new unclouded eyes, reluctantly finding no desire to please her but only revulsion for what she had become. The whiplash of her tongue, her shrill crows of glee as she patted and nudged my arm seemed endless, and I was heartily glad when Pip with considerable dignity decided to take his departure.

'You cannot go yet. I forbid it. You must walk in the garden with Estella. I insist. Put some roses back into her pale cheeks, cheer her with your gallantries, Pip.'

Gallantries? Poor Pip. Such pressure was bound to make

even a Casanova speechless, I thought, watching the blacksmith's boy again take up residence in his haunted eyes. He was polite, enquired after Paris, and Notre Dame and the Tuilieries, which he and Herbert Pocket were hoping to visit.

'We now have lodgings together in Barnard's Inn. Herbert is with a shipping insurance company.'

'And what are you studying with his father?'

'I am to have general tutoring only. According to my benefactor's instructions via Mr Jaggers, I am not to train for any profession except to hold my head high with other young gentlemen in prosperous circumstances.'

'It is quite extraordinary this change in your fortunes. Have you the least idea who this mysterious benefactor might be?'

He nodded, smiled. 'Of course. Have you?'

'There is only one person in the world – and in my mind –'

'And she is known to both of us,' he added eagerly.

But although we agreed that the mysterious benefactor could only be Miss Havisham, there was something nagged at me, something in her almost bored denial that was out of character and rang a false note.

'Well, well,' I laughed. 'What changes the years have brought. Over there, is the very spot where you fought with Cousin Herbert and gave him a bloody nose.'

Pip laughed. 'I little thought he would one day be my dearest friend.' Regarding me head on side, he said softly. 'I remember that you kissed me afterwards.'

'Did I really?' I asked, knowing perfectly well. 'You astonish me.'

He nodded eagerly. 'My mind goes even further back. I can recount every meeting we ever had together here at Satis House. The very first when you brought me meat and drink to eat at the back door like a beggar ...'

'And so you pretended you had helped some wretched convict in his escape from the Hulks, just to impress me.'

'You never believed me, but it was true, every word of it. I gave my word, but it can't do much harm to admit it now, for I don't suppose that promise did the poor wretch much good. I expect he is dead long ago.' He sighed and gave me a long mocking glance. 'But oh, how I trembled for your disdain in those days.'

'You are very changed now. No one would make you afraid now, especially a silly vain girl.'

'I wonder.' He looked at me intently. 'Perhaps now more than ever, Estella. Now when there is much more to be gained or lost than food and drink.'

Fearful that he might be about to kiss me and that my response might betray my guardian's trust in me, I said hastily:

'I remember telling you that I had no heart.'

'Is that still the case, Estella?' he asked gently.

'Still.' How indifferent I sounded.

He was silent for a moment, regarding me. 'I doubt that exceedingly,' he said softly. 'No one so lovely could be entirely cold and cruel. Such beauty could not exist without a heart.'

'Oh, I have a heart to be stabbed in, or shot at,' I said carelessly, 'and if it ceased to beat then I should cease to be. But I have no softness, no sentiment —' And while I continued in this vein to defend my lack of heart, he did not seem put out but continued to regard me smiling in a puzzled way, biting his lip, as if there was something he tried to recognize or fathom, some likeness he tried in vain to place, and I wondered if another rumour presently rife in the neighbourhood had reached his ears. That I was Alicia Havisham's secret love-child and the reason why her shocked and horrified bridegroom had deserted her on their wedding day.

The bantering conversation between us had ended abruptly. I was aware that the overgrown neglected garden had turned chilly, the dark bushes rustled, menacing. I wanted our interview to end on some happier note, ashamed of my old self and wishing to be remembered more kindly. 'Let us make one more round of the paths and then go indoors. You shall not shed tears for my cruelty today. You shall be my page and I shall lean upon your shoulder.'

I found the warmth of his touch comforting as we walked now talking of impersonal matters, the identity and sweet perfume of the pale hedgeflowers, and of a bird who sang its elegy, close and secret, unseen above our heads. In the growing stillness of evening, a gentle harmony descended between us and I hoped that my guardian and Pip's benefactor were one and the same and that this was her mysterious way of deciding our future. Had she chosen us for each other? Glancing at him in that moment, in his new role of a young gentleman with great expectations of a fortune, in a dizzy rush of feeling quite new to me, I thought I would be happiest of girls if such was Miss Havisham's will, whatever indifference I might be forced to pretend, to please her.

When we returned to the house, the spectral upstairs rooms were bright with pale light from chandeliers, glittering uneasily over the ruined banquet. For the first time I saw this scene as unhealthy, a corpse too long unburied. Something in me rebelled and I longed to tear open the shutters and let the daylight in. Ring down the curtain of unreality and put an end to the charade that had lasted more than twenty years. Even as I considered the enormity of such an action, Pip had resumed his original role of pushing my guardian around in her wheelchair. Round and round that old circuit we tripped. Silent, listening to the melancholy echo of our own footsteps, all three busy with our own thoughts, and saying nothing at all.

As I prepared to leave them to dress for dinner, Miss Havisham said: 'No, Estella, you are to remain for a moment more.' And as if I had not been present, she turned to Pip. 'Love her, love her, Pip. If she favours you, love her. If she wounds you, love her. If she tears your heart to pieces – and as it gets older and stronger it will tear deeper – love her, love her. I adopted her to be loved. I bred her and educated her, to be loved. I made her what she is, that she might be loved.'

And when Pip, too embarrassed to reply, avoided my eyes, she continued: 'Look at her. Is she not beautiful, graceful, well grown into womanhood? Do you admire her?'

'Everybody must who sees her, Miss Havisham,' he replied with admirable restraint.

And then she said a strange thing, her voice ringing loud, as she stared at that unworn bridal shoe she caressed against her heart. Pointing to the ruined banquet: 'I will tell you what real love is. Blind devotion, unquestioning self-humiliation, utter submission, trust and belief against yourself and against the whole world, giving up your whole heart and soul to the smiter – as I did.'

How her words stayed with me, echoing long after I left Satis House and following me down the years, to a time still mercifully veiled that made nonsense of all her fine hopes and plans to raise me without a heart that could be broken by any man.

Soon after my return from Paris, Bentley Drummle entered my life, almost as if he had been waiting to make his entrance at my most vulnerable moment. I was riding on the green with several of the Young Ladies, our equestrian activities watched over by Dame Clarissa twirling her parasol on a bench nearby.

'Estella!'

'Why, Cousin Herbert!'

How can I describe the man at his side who was to have so great an impact upon my life? The first meeting sounded no warning. I remember only that beside Herbert who was slight and pale, Bentley Drummle looked for all the world as if he had stepped down from one of the heroic paintings I had so admired in the Art Galleries of Paris. The wild and savage warriors of a bygone civilisation, mighty conquerors like Ghengis Khan whose strange looks might well have been the model for Bentley Drummle, an English gentleman, with as I learned later, expectations of a baronetcy in Shropshire.

Black hair and eyes, a sallow complexion with brooding heavy-lidded gaze; a large man, whose slightly ungainly physique suggested power. He walked like a wrestler, forward on the tips of his toes, moving his head slowly from side to side, as if he was on the defensive.

A strange meeting indeed. Herbert kept up a tide of chatter and I learned that the tall saturnine gentleman shared Pip's tutoring with Mathew Pocket. I naturally assumed that all three were companions, but this was not the case, although Herbert seized every opportunity, dear loyal friend that he was, of throwing in a good word for that 'excellent fellow', his absent friend, Pip.

The extraordinary thing was that Drummle, after the first polite bowing over my gloved hand, gave me no further indulgence. Not even when we parted did he deign to look my way in the interests of politeness. And throughout that short interview, his attention was one of utmost detachment. I might also add, of boredom.

This was indeed a new and intriguing state of affairs for Estella Havisham, already recognized by male acquaintance as being worthy of a second glance. Could I be losing my looks so soon? Was I, who had not yet exerted to the full my charms at past one-and-twenty, already *passée* in the eyes of discerning males? The thought gnawed at me fiercely. True, I did not specially like Herbert's boorish companion, for liking is founded upon stronger meat than a bowing over hands. But I had to confess, unwillingly, a secret attraction to his outlandish looks.

I had by no means dismissed him from my mind when my guardian reluctantly decided that, having kept me with her as companion since completing my education at Dame Clarissa's Academy, I was to proceed immediately to Richmond. In the house of Mrs Matilda Brandley, her one-time close confidante and girlhood friend, I was to be 'brought out' and presented to society. There I discovered that my activities were no longer limited to breaking men's hearts only, for the urgent matter of finding a suitable husband was also in the wind. I was somewhat confused. Was my marriage to be regarded as my mother-by-adoption's ultimate triumph, that I should be responsible for also breaking some poor unfortunate husband's heart? Alas, she was never to see that desire fulfilled. Long before my marriage was at an end, Alicia Havisham rested peacefully in her grave.

Pip was to escort me across London to Richmond and when the coach from the Blue Boar at Rochester deposited me at Wood Street, Cheapside, I found him anxiously pacing back and forward outside the coach-office and exhibiting every indication of a man who has been there for some time. I was delighted to see him again and while we stood in the Inn Yard and the luggage was brought down, after complimenting me on my appearance in my furred travelling dress, he asked what took me to Richmond.

'I am going to live at great expense with a lady there who has the power, or says she has, of taking me about and introducing me, and showing people to me and showing me to people.'

'I suppose you will be glad of variety and admiration.'

'Yes, I suppose so.' I was so comfortable with Pip, at that moment I had little desire to encounter strangers.

He laughed. 'Estella, you speak of yourself as if you were someone else.'

'Where did you learn how I speak of others?' I asked haughtily. 'I must talk in my own way.'

'Must you, Estella?'

Pip was the possessor of a charming voice, perhaps his most attractive feature. Now its tone was gentle, seductive and for a moment our glances lingered uncomfortably. Quickly I changed the subject to how he did with Mr Pocket.

'I live quite pleasantly there, as pleasantly as I could anywhere, away from you.'

'You silly boy.'

In answer, he took my hand, raised it to his lips.

'Will you never take warning?' I sighed. 'Or do you kiss my hand in the same spirit in which I once let you kiss my cheek?'

'What spirit was that?' he asked smiling.

'Indeed, I cannot remember but it must have been some worthy cause.'

'If I say hurrah to that, may I kiss the cheek again?'

'You should have asked before you touched the hand.
But yes, if you like.'

He liked. With a calm indifference I did not feel, I glided
away from him. 'Now according to Miss Havisham's
instruction, you are to take care that I have some tea,
before conveying me to Richmond.'

I remember little about that tea except that it was
dismal and unappetising. We got into our post-coach, and
turning into Cheapside rattled along past under the grim
grey walls of a grim grey building. I was told that this was
Newgate Prison.

'Wretches,' I said and the contamination that seemed to
emanate from its evil inhabitants and atmosphere of
wrong-doing took my mind back to my first impressions of
the Hulks long ago. 'I wonder if your convict is skulking
behind those walls.'

Pip shuddered. 'I sincerely hope not. Even to think of
him so near fills me with loathing.' As our coach hesitated
to negotiate a cart which was in difficulties with a frisky
horse in its traces, Pip considered the prison gates.

'I dare say there is one face familiar to us both, busily
engaged behind those walls.' And to my puzzled
expression, he added: 'Mr Jaggers, of course, for he has the
reputation of being more in the secrets of that dismal place
than any man in London.'

'I suspect he is more in the secrets of every place.
Perhaps he even knows what became of your convict.'

'He's not my convict, Estella. He scared the wits out of
me with his terrible threats of what dire misfortunes of an
alarming bodily nature could overcome a small boy who
refused to help him. All I contributed to his plan of escape
was a file for his fetters and a pork pie for the inner man.'

'Why didn't you turn him over to the law officers?'

Pip thought for a moment. 'I have often wondered that
myself. He was such a woeful, pathetic sight. Even though
he terrified me, I could no more have set the Constables on
him than on some poor dumb animal in a trap.'

'Mr Jaggers would be outraged by such misplaced
gallantry.'

Pip smiled. 'I expect my convict, as you like to call him, is dead long ago, but he is still our secret, Estella. I have no intention of ever telling Mr Jaggers. I suppose you have often met?'

'At uncertain intervals, ever since I can remember.' His presence was always fearful to me, his solemn visits threatening disasters even to my childish mind and I always sighed with relief when he drove off and the simple tenure of our lives resumed unchanged. 'What is your own experience of him?'

'Once accustomed to his distrustful manner, I have done very well. I have even dined with him at his private house.'

'That I fancy must be a curious place.'

'It is a curious place.' At that Pip fell suddenly silent but I saw him looking at me from time to time with a puzzled frown, in the manner of one who seeks to remember something of importance.

'Is anything wrong?' I asked.

'Of course not. Why do you ask?'

'You look strange, that is all.'

'No – no. Nothing. Nothing. Look – over there.' And he became sociable once more, pointing out landmarks of the great city of London which were almost new to me for I had never left Rochester until I went to France. When we passed through Hammersmith, Pip showed me the house of Mr Matthew Pocket and said that as it was no great distance from Richmond, he hoped that he should see me sometimes.

I was delighted at the suggestion. 'Yes, you are to come when you think proper. You are to be mentioned to the Brandleys, indeed you are already mentioned.' He was clearly pleased and asked if this was a large household. 'Only a mother and daughter. But the mother is a lady of some station in life, I believe, though not averse to increasing her income.'

'I wonder Miss Havisham could part with you again, so soon.'

'It is part of Miss Havisham's plans for me, Pip. I am to write to her constantly and see her regularly, and report how I go on – I and the jewels – for they are nearly all mine now.' Even to my own ears, I wondered why my voice sounded sadly depressed and lacking in enthusiasm.

Our destination was situated by the Green. A substantial grey and cheerless house with an air of grey and cheerless bygone days, echoed by a sorrowful bell with a very rusty voice, whose summons brought forth a bevy of grey-clad cheerless maids.

As they wrestled with my boxes, I thanked Pip and there was suddenly no more to be said for the door was quickly closed upon him. I was led upstairs to my bedroom and looking out, saw that he stood watching the house anxiously as if he could not tear himself away or hoped that by lingering, he might yet be of some service to me. And I knew that although his expression was concealed by distance, he wore the very soul of his longing, naked in his eyes.

'My dear Estella, welcome. Welcome.' Mrs Brandley and her daughter had entered. A little dainty fluttering bird-like woman with a plain daughter creeping relentlessly past thirty, that dread milestone for an unmarried lady without looks or the necessary fortune to compensate their unfortunate lack. Maud was sallow as her mother was pink and white, aged and dull as her mother was youthful and flighty. Indeed, at soirées and concerts, it became immediately apparent that Mrs Brandley's impact upon the male population was quite devastating. Apparently she still presented a more attractive matrimonial objective than Miss Brandley and most men given a straight option would not have hesitated to choose the sprightly widow rather than the sullen daughter.

Mrs Brandley's 'salon' entertained a constant tide of daily visitors and weekend house-guests. A place for the *ton* to see and be seen. The back of the house faced on to lawns sloping agreeably down to the river landing stage, often wreathed in fog and a trifle damp. It was a cheerful enough place inside, where the mother had more to say than the daughter, who missed no opportunity of reminding me that my presence was tolerated on

45

sufferance. Her manner was disdainful as if conferring a great favour when she would infinitely prefer to be showing me to the door. I was not ill bred enough to retaliate on the necessity of my guardian's money for their present comfort.

As for Mrs Brandley's conversation about clothes and balls and cards, that soon palled, as did her tinkling laughter and her utter dedication and determination to be young at all costs which set my teeth on edge.

'We must be on our toes at all times, my dear Estella, give of our very best. We must never be tired or cross. We must never give way to frowns, frowns are for age, but smiles are for youth.' Such were her oft-expressed sentiments when one gave way to lassitude. The party face and manner which she wore in happy expectancy of unexpected visitors by day was presumably only discarded in the shrouded hours of the night. There existed no moments of quietude or thoughtful introspection. In her presence, one was there for the sole purpose of being talked at, postured for, bragged for.

I found my patience sorely tried. The strange circumstances of Satis House and my lack of popularity at Dame Clarissa's Academy had contributed toward the nature of a recluse. Enjoying my own society, I found myself in constant rebellion at being a mere exhibit in Mrs Brandley's matrimonial showcase. An exhibit on sale to the highest bidder, for marriages were based on dowries and hard-headed calculations, and Romance belonged between the printed sheets of novelettes rather than the bridal bed. Let it be so, since emotions of passion presented certain difficulties for one bred without any heart.

As for Maud, despite her thin frame, she was extremely greedy, revoltingly eager to stretch out her hand and seize the largest slice of cake, or sweetmeat, for which she would turn the plate round and round in a vulgar manner matched by a carefully measuring eye. Her mother remained suitably blind to such behaviour as she tried to secure my wandering attention with some absorbing topic, such as the high price of lace in the local shops.

In this stultifying atmosphere, the presence of Bentley Drummle at one of Mrs Brandley's usually tedious soirées, was an exceedingly agreeable diversion. Impressed by his expectations of a baronetcy and my determination to marry a Lord, I smiled and postured, striving to remember all the elaborate rigmarole of instructions my guardian had so carefully laid down for a breaker of hearts.

Dismayed, I discovered that the target of my attentions seemed to favour the dour Maud with his conversation, while she permitted what was almost a smile to crease her countenance. With a stretch of imagination, one could almost say she basked and glowed. Then taking quite unfair advantage, Mrs Brandley swept down upon them and the radiance of the mother entirely eclipsed the daughter. Poor Maud, I felt an unexpected kindliness towards her as she took a backward step from the circle of her mother's beaming presence. Had I stumbled upon her secret, I wondered. Did Maud entertain requited longings for the stern Mr Drummle?

He was not intended for her. Even as the thought crossed my mind, Mrs Brandley was ushering him towards me, her manner purposeful.

Extending my hand, I found myself oddly tongue-tied. 'We have met before.'

He stared at me, frowning. Horror of horrors, what humiliation. He had forgotten entirely.

'It was with Herbert Pocket at Rochester – we were out riding,' I explained blushing.

'Oh, that.' Ungraciously dismissing the incident as of little importance, he suddenly remembered his manners: 'I seem to recall something of the sort.'

So that was the way of it? 'The occasion was, as I remember, in August, – a lovely sunny day –' I stammered. It was imperative that he should remember each precise detail.

'Hmm,' he interrupted, and as I blundered on, observed him agitatedly looking over his shoulder in the manner of one who desires instant flight. There was no escape for the poor unfortunate man as Mrs Brandley gushed over us:

'Mr Drummle, sir, you will oblige me by escorting Estella into dinner.' Trapped we regarded each other desperately. 'I hope Estella is telling you all about France. She stayed with Monsieur and Madame Chauvez –' and to me, in a tone of reverence: 'The Chauvez are great personal friends of Mr Drummle.' The conversation was in his hands and she regarded him wide-eyed, rapt and expectant.

Clearing his throat and much put out by this confrontation, he murmured: 'Mere business associates, actually.'

Perhaps prompted by this frail link, to make amends for our forgotten earlier encounter, he turned to me in the manner of one determined to make an effort to be gracious. Offering his arm, he gallantly led the way into the conservatory. 'I trust you found the Chauvez family in excellent health,' he said heartily, as we advanced towards the table.

It was a cold blustery evening. The cold collation spread on a white cloth amid tinkling crystal, frowned upon by curtainless windows which also seemed to shiver, served to remind me uncomfortably of Miss Havisham's wedding feast in its heyday before the spiders and mice moved in. The glazed cold meats, the chicken and ham, the turkey and lobsters had a funereal appearance and the banquet before us more resembled a lying-in-state than an occasion of cheerful social refreshment. As for the heavily decorated desserts, the ices and jellies, there was a toothache in every bite.

'Permit me to help you to a little roast fowl. Some greens perhaps. Some lobster – no?'

Armed with our plates he led the way to a sofa overhung by indoor plants that the nervous diner might have been pardoned for considering with great caution, after paying due attention to their fat glossy leaves and suspiciously predatory looks. Having seated me comfortably and speedily, Mr Drummle began to eat with such uncommon interest and vigour that again I was overwhelmed by the bleak despair of my own insignificance. In vain I searched my mind for some means of diverting his attention back to me. How to compete, how to come between a man and his food? That small matter was absent from my guardian's curriculum, a salutory warning that breakers of hearts lost their powers when confronted with the brute needs of the male stomach.

Believing all was lost, my pride was saved by the unexpected arrival of a young gentleman, extremely thin of face, body and hair, who had been casting admiring glances in my direction all evening. Now he hovered, plate in hand, beside the empty seat next to us.

'May I be permitted to join you, sir?'

Mr Drummle hardly vouchsafed a frown as he returned to his more urgent task of dismembering the roast fowl, but his non-committal gesture indicated permission.

Politely the young gentleman awaited my approval.

'Do please join us,' I said winningly, patting the sofa beside me and then with my warmest smile, I proceeded to devote my attentions to the newcomer. Yes, he lived in Richmond. Yes, he did ride in the Park. Had he not seen me in church on Sunday?

As Mr Daintree appeared considerably more interested in our conversation than the gastronomic delights being offered, our plates were neglected until I became aware that the rasping sounds of cutlery, the sole signs of life from Mr Drummle's third of the sofa, had ceased. Much to my delight, I observed a look of thunder had descended upon his brow. Could he possibly be jealous?

Restricting his observations to a muttered 'Hmm', he scraped his plate in a vigorous manner that threatened immediate destruction of its pattern of roses. Satisfied that no morsel had escaped him, my conversation with Mr Daintree was sternly interrupted with the invitation to accompany him in search of dessert. Obliging meekly, I offered the now rather forlorn Mr Daintree, left in sole possession of the sofa and predatory plant, the consolation of my sweetest smile.

After the food came the dancing. Like many big solid

men, Bentley Drummle was light upon his feet, giving the matter of the quadrille the same undivided attention he had devoted to eating, and with even less inclination for the light-hearted chatter that our partners enjoyed. Indeed, I might have been a statue he held, for all the attention he paid me.

I was left feeling rather small and dismal by the end of the evening. I had failed Mrs Brandley in her plans regarding Mr Drummle. Worse, I had failed myself. My first lesson, my entrée into polite society – dear, dear.

'Mr Drummle has asked to be permitted to take yourself and Maud riding in the Park tomorrow,' cooed Mrs Brandley. 'He has obviously found you most agreeable. Most agreeable, my dear,' she repeated with considerable satisfaction, while I looked across at poor Maud with her dowdy hair and her dowdy sullen face.

'Oh no,' said Mrs Brandley, shrewdly interpreting my look. 'My daughter is not the object of Mr Drummle's interest. She has known him since childhood. Is that not so, Maud my dear, you are not in the least interested in Mr Drummle, are you?'

Mutely, Maud nodded and turning away busied herself with the welfare of the potted plants dangerously wilting after so much contact with human food and cigar smoke. Relieved, delighted that Drummle thought me interesting but sad for Maud, I wished with all my heart that some man would find her attractive and agreeable too. But at the same time, I was glad that it was not Bentley Drummle who did so.

Anticipating our next meeting with great eagerness and much in the way of rehearsed topics of conversation, I found that he seemed both cold and indifferently disposed towards me. All my small attempts at light conversation fell horribly flat. But why should I concern myself about one man? After that first supper party, there were admirers in plenty, as behind the scenes Mrs Brandley spread the word that I was ward to the wealthy Miss Havisham and had expectations of a great fortune. My price tag was high. The admirers came to inspect the goods being offered. In all shapes and sizes and ages of mankind they descended upon us. The very young, to middling young, mature to downright elderly. There were even hopeful old widowers hiding in their ranks, on the lookout for a little extra capital to comfort their declining years, with the added attraction of a girl, young, healthy and strong enough to act as companion and nurse. Tall and short, fat and thin, bald and hair-in-abundance, moustached or clean shaven; there were precious few who bowed over my hand whose names I could remember.

'Moths and many kinds of ugly creatures are attracted by the flame of a candle.' I remember my words to Pip when hearing of my success, he accused me of heartless flirtation, and I can still blush at the memory of my supreme self-gratification.

Then suddenly one perfectly ordinary evening at the Brandley's dining-table, my sharpened senses became aware of an atmosphere subtly charged between Drummle and myself. There were other diners that night in particular a pair of very attractive twin sisters home from the Italian Riviera, but supper over, Bentley Drummle hastened to my side and offered me his arm. Through the conservatory, he ushered me into the garden with its twilight wraiths of mist from the river. Moths there were, I thought, but in search of brighter flames.

A pale moon had arisen above the trees and an owl's melancholy hoot warned that autumn was almost here. Now I was aware of Bentley's face far above me too, its black hollows where the moonlight did not penetrate turned it into something sinister, spectral. I must confess that I shivered, and not entirely from cold, when he ran a finger down my cheek, tracing it slowly from eyebrow to jaw and then cupping his hand around my chin, he said:

'Estella – Estella. How the devil did you come by such an outlandish name?'

'I have not the least idea. I expect my parents favoured it.' I said excited by the touch of his hand.

He frowned. 'Perhaps they chose the exotic name to go with your marvellous hair,' he said teasingly.

I smiled, liking this attention. 'My hair, sir? Why, you are too complimentary.' Had I been a dog, how my tail would have wagged at such kind tones. 'A wild mane, I am afraid,' I sighed, 'that positively refuses all elegant and civilized styles.'

He toyed with the curl on my shoulder. 'It is gipsy hair and fits the name Estella perfectly.'

'How so?'

'Why, Estella is a gipsy name. Did you not know that?'

My pleasurable sensations faded. I did not like gipsies or the hint that there was some connection, however remote. The Nightmare, absent so long, raised its head and began to creep stealthily over my horizon.

'I expect they favour the same names as other folk,' I said.

'More exotic than Sara, or Maud, or Agatha?' He shook his head. 'It means 'little star' and it fits you to perfection, my dear.' Bending down, his face was at that moment obliterated by his nearness. My eyes snapped closed as his lips, very thick lips, warm and sensuous in such a stern unyielding face, gently brushed my own.

'Gipsy name or no, Estella Havisham, you are a very exquisite creature. And I intend to have you. Remember that. You are to be mine.'

This remark which set so many carillons of joy ringing in my poor head, was abruptly ended as Mrs Brandley and the rest of the party erupted into the garden.

Drummle refused to be sociable and took his departure almost immediately upon the thinnest of excuses. I could see by Mrs Brandley's downcast face and accusing expression that she was dying of curiosity, fighting the temptation to ask: Had we quarrelled, had I displeased him in some way? I prepared for bed in a positive haze of delight. One day I should be Lady Drummle living in a castle, and it had all been so terribly, terribly easy.

Next morning when I awoke, I believed I had dreamed the whole episode. It was far less real than the Nightmare which had chosen to visit me again that night. The two women in their eternal fight to the death, watched by the child who was myself. And the victor I knew with one death on her hands and the red-murder light of madness gleaming in her eyes, was already reaching out to the hiding place where I crouched, shivering in terror. I awoke, sick and afraid, knowing that I should walk warily that day, tormented with fears that a secret door might spring open and carry me a prisoner, to dwell forever in that nightmare world.

I supposed Bentley Drummle's remark about the gipsies had occasioned the evil dream, for another piece of the jigsaw slipped into place. The woman who attacked me with bloodied fists now had hair, a streaming black mane, easily recognizable from my looking-glass as my own.

Several days passed as I waited eagerly but in vain for Bentley Drummle to call, and pursue the conversation begun so light-heartedly in the garden. I had decided that the extraordinary man had been flirting with me, or had imbibed too much wine that evening, when I received a letter from Satis House.

'My dearest child' (wrote my mother-by-adoption), 'Mr Bentley Drummle has written to me asking that he be allowed to address you with marriage in mind. He has informed me of his sincere regard for you. As I think you are aware, his background is next-to-noble, he stands to inherit the baronetcy when his grandfather Sir Hammond Drummle of Drummle dies. I urge you, dearest child, to accept his proposal promptly and with gratitude, for I have selfishly kept you by me for too long already. I do not expect, if you paid due heed to my instruction that you are in the slightest danger of giving your heart to Drummle, or to any other man. I further entreat that you continue to be guided by one who has suffered greatly, regarding marriage not with any emotion of sentiment but in the practical light of a transaction of business, never forgetting that the most successful marriages are based upon Property and the establishment of the Family. These are matters, bearing in mind your early training and expensive education at Dame

Clarissa's Academy, with which you will doubtless find yourself wholly competent. Come and visit me as soon as you can. – Your affectionate Mother-by-adoption, Alicia Havisham. P.S. Mr Drummle will also be welcome on such occasion.'

While he was announced the following afternoon, I was still in a state of dazed disbelief at this volte face from my guardian. Until I received her letter I had been certain that her plan, as Pip's mysterious benefactor, was to bring us together in marriage. Now it seemed that I was wrong and so, alas, was Pip. I entered the drawing-room calmly, and read to him the first sentence of Miss Havisham's letter.

He smiled delightedly, a rare occurrence: 'My dear Estella, it is all absolutely true. I have long been conscious of your regard for me and it was but a matter of time and seeing what other contenders for your hand lined the field – so to speak – before I proposed.'

Would he care to visit Satis House with me?

'I understand Miss Havisham to be a recluse and I am happy not to intrude upon her at the moment in what might appear as vulgar curiosity. Later perhaps, when the wedding arrangements are finalized, I will call formally.' Pausing he cleared his throat delicately. 'I understand arrangements for your dowry are already in the hands of Miss Havisham's lawyer, Mr Jaggers, who is known to me, of course.' He went on to inform me that matters concerning the merchant bankers with whom Sir Hammond was associated would keep him in London. He could be reached at Cadogan Crescent, where he resided with his mother.

Preparing to leave, at the door he hesitated. 'If I may be permitted one final word. I have no desire to see Mr Pirrip's glowering face sitting opposite me when I visit you. Be so good as to inform him that it is my wish his visits to this house cease immediately.'

I was truly fond of Pip and after consideration decided to remain deaf to Drummle's instructions, trusting that Mrs Brandley was also in ignorance of my betrothal. My motives were quite selfish, I was reluctant to banish Pip a moment before it was necessary, especially when he could be useful to me. I gave myself the rather different reason, when conscience twinged, that he would be hurt more deeply by never seeing me again. I regarded him as my oldest and perhaps my only true friend, and although I continued to deceive myself that I acted in the best interests of his happiness, the truth of the matter was that the spoilt child Estella might appear before him in her true colours, as one thoroughly degraded and mercenary.

I saw no reason for abandoning the many delightful social occasions where Pip escorted me, for in the season Richmond was well patronised by operas, concerts and plays. And when there was no outside entertainment worth seeing, he would read to us in the drawing-room, where Mrs Brandley heaped high praises upon his fine voice: 'You should be an actor, Mr Pip, really you have missed your vocation in life.'

But Pip gently laughed aside such an absurd idea. Often as I listened to him read I looked at him fondly, happy in the easy relationship between us, except when he chose to remind me of his suffering on my account, and if my behaviour was at its most outrageous in his presence, that is often the way between close kin, a brother and sister, cousins. And Pip was more than just my true friend, he was the one man who loved me always, while the lips of Bentley Drummle who wanted me for his wife remained sealed upon that subject. As yet he had not yet uttered one syllable that one might interpret as a declaration of undying love.

I was torn between disappointment and relief, for search my heart as I might, I knew that Miss Havisham's instructions in her letter were wise, for I was not in the least danger of loving Bentley Drummle. I did a simple test. If I never saw him again my pride would be hurt exceedingly, but if I never saw Pip again, the heart I was not supposed to possess would ache – and ache, for ever. (Oh, Estella, there lies your answer).

Bentley put in a brief appearance to announce that our marriage plans and urgent estate matters required his presence in Drummle, Shropshire, the residence of his grandfather. He anticipated a lengthy absence. I was not to concern myself, for I would be ever present in his thoughts. I was somewhat put out, to say the least, at not being invited to be formally introduced to the head of his family as his bride-to-be.

Smiling, he patted my hand, not in the least concerned. 'My dear, I must beg your indulgence and patience. The situation is a difficult one. My grandfather is, not to put too fine a point on it, a little distressed to find his heir intends marriage with a young lady of considerable charm, but lacking a title. I must tell you quite frankly that he finds your orphaned state disquieting, for good breeding is of the utmost importance to the Drummles who received their arms and estate lands of the Abbey from the hands of King Henry the Eighth. However, although I am quite certain that I can persuade the old gentleman to accept my decision, I would not wish to subject you to any unpleasantness. He is apt to be outspoken, a failing of many of his generation, alas.'

Reassured that it was in my best interests to stay away from Drummle Towers until he had smoothed away the thorns that apparently beset the path for my entrance, I also suspected from whence my future husband had inherited his somewhat dour manners.

Very well, I told myself, here was excellent reason for not putting an end to Pip's pleasant visits. Perhaps my lack of comment on Drummle's absence encouraged him in the fond belief that I had sent his rival packing at last. I am ashamed to admit that for my own personal convenience and enjoyment, I was content to let him think so and the name of Bentley Drummle never once threatened the agreeable and happy hours we spent together.

Such was the state of affairs when Pip escorted me to Satis House for the last time and the facts of my impending marriage were revealed to him. I had summoned him by letter to come to Richmond and escort me to Satis House and back again. My guardian was heedful of the dangers lurking for young ladies travelling alone. In normal circumstances Jolly could have accompanied me, but this did not suit Alicia Havisham's sly plans of throwing Pip into my society upon every possible occasion. The excuse for travelling without my maid was: 'A recluse's terror of servants carrying gossip about Satis House.'

That was quite untrue. The Small Person was utterly trustworthy, she would have cheerfully laid down her life for me although I had already decided to discard her, God forgive me. Drummle wished me to have a French maid, so very much the vogue, who would attend to my hair and toilette, à la mode. Jolly was to be abandoned at Richmond along with my outworn clothes and other possessions too shabby for my new life in London.

How eagerly Pip awaited me that day. As always he had some little gift for me. Today he thrust a handsome vellum-bound book of Mr Tennyson's poems into my hand. We were almost gay and light hearted as we discussed the latest party we had attended, reviewing the many acquaintances we shared. So much so that our frequent merriment brought forth fond glances from other passengers in the coach, who took us for lovers on a day's outing or else a devoted brother and sister, although Pip was fair and I was dark. As he tucked his arm into mine, I looked at him and thought: would that he had been my close kin, poor orphaned blacksmith's boy or no, for, with the wedding in mind, I was selfishly concerned that the bride's side of the church would be empty. I had no male relative to give me away and Bentley would not allow Pip's presence, although I knew had I asked, he would have come to please me, despite the agony of seeing me lost forever as another's bride.

Such were my thoughts when we entered Satis House, where my mother-by-adoption awaited us. She clutched me eagerly, hugging and kissing me, and not forgetting to turn to Pip and ask: 'And how does she use you?'

I saw at once the reason for her unholy glee. She was about to torture Pip with the knowledge that he had fulfilled the purpose intended for him all these years of faithful service. Estella had broken his heart. The *coup de grâce*, her marriage to his rival Bentley Drummle. Pip's role in her diabolic drama was at an end, he too could now be discarded.

Poor Pip. It was all so unfair. I knew that he had never entertained a moment's doubt that his benefactor was not Miss Havisham. Indeed, until she had approved Bentley Drummle's proposal, both Pip and I had secretly understood – without saying a single word on the subject – that when he came of age, she would formally reveal her identity to him and that my hand in marriage would be offered: Pip's just reward for enduring my cruelties and torments so nobly over the years. And I had long known that Pip was ready, nay, eager to forget his dependence on her whims and my ill-nature, his constant degradations and humiliations through the years.

Knowing her love of secrets, of intrigue, it was a perfectly logical conclusion. The vital link was Mr Jaggers, her lawyer who had been appointed Pip's guardian. Did it not therefore also follow that although Pip was like the prince in the fairytale who had to suffer many trials and tribulations, he stood to win the sleeping princess at the story's end?

That simile was plainly in his mind as we walked in the garden and he read one of Mr Tennyson's poems:

'More close and close his footsteps wind:
The Magic Music in his heart
Beats quick and quicker, till he find
The quiet chamber far apart.
His spirit flutters like a lark,
He stoops – to kiss her – on his knee.
"Love, if thy tresses be so dark,
How dark those hidden eyes must be." '

But as we re-entered Satis House, I was painfully aware that in those upstairs rooms where nothing changed, today the atmosphere was subtly different. Beyond the candles high in their sconces, seeping through tight-closed shutters, a hundred birds in a hundred trees greeted the still warm autumn sunlight with a song of ecstasy, while inside the candlelight glittered remorselessly upon that ghastly scene of decay and corruption. Grim charade, with corpselike woman whose yellowed unhealthy skin had not felt God's wind or rain or the blessing of sunlight for a quarter-century, wearing her fusty yellowed bridal gown, all withered and rotted like the obscenity of skeletal bridal flowers their petals long returned to dust. And dominating that ghostly wedding banquet, the crumbled tower once a wedding cake now woven through and through with curtains of cobwebs, the crawling spiders and the mice who scampered, squeaking into retreat at our footsteps.

Today my mother-by-adoption could not get close enough to me. Normally less demonstrative, her kisses and hugs and hand holdings were extravagant and I tried in vain to detach myself from the unpleasantness of this smothering affection.

'Are you tired of me?' she demanded.

'Only a little tired of myself.' That was true. I did not exaggerate. I was very tired of myself and at that moment, would gladly have been rid of Satis House for ever. I was also ashamed of the emptiness of the role I had been called upon to play, as if I stepped back and saw my true character reflected in all its disagreeable intensity for the first time.

Angered, she struck her stick on the ground, called me ingrate. 'Cold, cold heart,' she accused.

This was too much. 'You reproach me for being cold. I who am what you have made me. You therefore take all the praise and all the blame. You take all the success and all the failure too.'

With a disagreeable shrug, she turned to Pip who stood by watching us, without uttering a word. God only knew what his thoughts could have been. 'Look at her, so hard and thankless on the hearth where she was raised. Where I took her into this wretched breast when it was first bleeding from its stab and where I have lavished years of tenderness upon her.'

'At least I was no party to the compact,' I reminded her,

'for if I could walk and speak, when it was made, it was as much as I could do. But what would you have? You have been very good to me, and I owe everything to you. What would you have?'

'Love,' said my guardian.

'You have it.'

'I have not.'

'Mother-by-adoption, I have said that I owe everything to you. All I possess is freely yours. All that you have given me, is at your command to have again. Beyond that, I have nothing. And if you ask me to give you what you never gave me, my gratitude and duty cannot do the impossible.'

'Did I never give her love?' she implored Pip. 'Did I never give her a burning love, inseperable from jealousy at all times, and from sharp pain, while she speaks thus to me? Let her call me mad, let her call me mad.'

'Why should I call you mad, I, of all people?' I said. 'Does anyone live who knows what set purposes you have, half as well as I do? Does anyone live, who knows what a steady memory you have, half as well as I do? I who have sat on this same hearth on the little stool that is even now beside you there, learning your lessons and looking up into your face, when your face was strange and frightened me.'

'Soon forgotten,' she said. 'Times soon forgotten.'

'No, not forgotten, but treasured up in my memory. When have you found me false to your teaching? When have you found me unmindful of your lessons? When have you found me giving admission here,' I added touching my heart, 'to anything that you excluded? Be just to me.'

'So proud, so hard,' she moaned.

'Who taught me to be proud and hard?' I asked in exasperation. 'Who praised me when I learnt my lesson? I must be taken as I have been made. The success is not mine, the failure is not mine, but the two together make me.'

My guardian had settled down through this tirade among the faded bridal relics on the floor. The heat of the argument was suddenly over and I looked down at her with only pity, and turning I saw that we were alone.

Pip had departed. Almost immediately her attitude changed, all the histrionics vanished, like a slate wiped clean. As I assisted her to her feet, she was kindly, gentle and talked gaily, excitedly, like every other mother in the world about the plans for her daughter's marriage. And I saw that once again I had been duped. Tricked into taking part in her charade in all its ghastliness, chosen to act out a scene opposite her especially selected for Pip's benefit.

The revelation sickened me, for as if the heated argument had never taken place, she was saying that I was to be married from Mrs Brandley's. She could not, of course, be present, but she wished to know ever detail of my gown, which I was to wear here before the ceremony. When next I came I was to be armed with patterns and materials for her approval. Her sudden relish for weddings was almost horrible considering the funereal surroundings, and caused me to wonder what sick joy the bride of the past and the bride of the present standing side-by-side together in this dead room would bring her.

Pip slept that night in the cottage across the courtyard. In Satis House's more opulent days, the Dower House of a widowed Havisham, grandmother of my mother-by-adoption, was now used to house rare visitors, forced by inclement weather to remain overnight.

I was to see Pip only once again at Satis House before my marriage. He came one day to Richmond unannounced, shocked by his own troubles and in need of my friendship. Astonished to discover that I was not at home, with Jolly evasive about my whereabouts, and Mrs Brandley not at home to him either, he was puzzled, even alarmed.

'Is Miss Estella then at Satis House?'

The Small Person bobbed a curtsey. 'I couldn't rightly say, sir.' But never an accomplished liar, her face gave away the truth of the matter.

'Is she ill?' he demanded white-faced, in a voice of doom.

'No, sir. No.' A cautious pause. 'Not as far as I know, that is, sir.'

Pip was greatly perplexed. Had I then travelled to Satis House alone? Why had Jolly not accompanied me? How long would I be staying? But the maid was struck dumb, her face scarlet, aware that she had said too much already.

'I'm sorry, sir. I couldn't rightly say how long she'll be gone, or how she went neither.' Pip had been kind to her as he was to all servants and she didn't like to see the poor young gentleman so distressed. 'But I dare say Miss Estella'll be coming back. But only for a little while. To collect her things.'

And before Pip could demand further explanation the door was closed sharply. 'A little while – to collect her things?' What could such ominous words mean. For Pip, there was only one way to find out.

The truth was that Bentley had escorted me to Satis House where he had been most cordially received by my guardian before departing for London to visit Mr Jaggers and conclude the marriage settlement which put into his hands my not inconsiderable dowry. Many of the jewels which my mother-by-adoption had lovingly bestowed upon my every visit, were valuable heirlooms dating from that brief but memorable visit of King Charles the Second when the then Mistress Havisham had pleasured the Merry Monarch exceedingly, and had in return received the gems as a more lasting token of His Majesty's gratitude. Such information no doubt had been brought forward to convince Bentley's grandfather of the ultimate worthiness of his heir's orphan bride-to-be.

However, upon that fateful day, Pip was also intent upon Satis House. He could hardly storm the Dower House late at night without previous intimation and his expectations of a fortune had served to make him uncomfortable with Gargery, and the blacksmith with him, feeling that Master Pip was now too grand a young gentleman to sleep in his tiny bedroom at the blacksmith's forge.

Accordingly, Pip took rooms at the Blue Boar, where next morning who should he find standing before the fire there but his old enemy, Bentley Drummle. Both gentlemen pretended hard not to recognize one another, a wry state of affairs which Bentley described with unusual merriment. Had it not been Pip, I should have found his account amusing too: Of how he had impressed upon Pip, through the waiter, that 'the lady would not be riding today' and by many devious ways made absolutely plain, but without spelling out Estella, that Satis House had been the purpose of his visit.

There was no escape from the consequences of this chance encounter.

'Of course, we will receive him. Surely you wish to see your old friend Pip?' demanded Miss Havisham at my cry of alarm. But while I shuddered, dreading the encounter, her gloating expression and heartless laughter made plain her own excitement and satisfaction at the confrontation between the two rivals for my affections.

Not knowing where to look and wishing only to avoid Pip's sad accusing eyes, I picked up my knitting, a refuge too for my trembling hands. After a minimal interchange of polite greetings, Pip came to the point. He had been to Richmond from whence, concerned that my abrupt disappearance might token some misfortune, he had followed me here. There was one other reason for the urgency of his visit which he hastened to explain. The identity of his benefactor had been revealed ...

And it was not Miss Havisham. This had been a great shock to him. As it was to me, for I had never considered her encouragement of Bentley Drummle as evidence that she was not Pip's secret benefactor.

'When you first had me brought here, Miss Havisham, when I belonged to a village over there, that I wish I had never left, I must but suppose I came as any other chance boy, as a kind of servant to gratify a want or a whim and to be paid for it.'

'Aye, Pip, you did.'

'Then I must suppose too, that Mr Jaggers –'

My guardian raised her hand. 'I am in no way to be blamed for the coincidence that Mr Jaggers is also the lawyer of your patron.'

'But when I fell into the mistake, I have so long remained in, at least you led me on, encouraged me.'

My mother-by-adoption nodded. Yes, she had led him on.

'Was that kind?' cried Pip, with a rare rush of anger.

'Who am I, for God's sake, to be kind?' was the reply.

Pip bit his lip and continued to look steadily at her. 'I was liberally paid for my attendance here in being apprenticed and I have asked these questions only for my information.' He pointed an accusing finger at her.

Unrepentant, my guardian merely shrugged. 'You all made your own snares and when you fell into them, I cannot be blamed, for I never made them.'

Pip studied her calmly now. I admired his dignity and self-control, in the face of such disillusion. The collapse of his dream that Alicia Havisham was his benefactress and that I too was included in her plan for his future. Now both had vanished into thin air.

'I have been thrown among one family of your relations in London, who have been as honestly under my delusion as myself. And I should be false and base, if I did not tell you, whether it is acceptable to you or no, and whether you are inclined to give credence to it or no, that you deeply wrong both Mr Matthew Pocket and his son Herbert, if you suppose them to be otherwise than generous, upright, open and incapable of anything designing or mean.'

Again my mother-by-adoption shrugged. 'They are your friends.'

'They have made themselves my friends, when they supposed me to have superseded them, for they too believed that you were my benefactor and had shown me preference over them.'

I was please to hear him speak up for Matthew Pocket and Herbert.

'Well, what do you want for them?'

'If you could spare the money to do Herbert a lasting service in life by continuing an allowance I have given him out of my income – without his knowledge – but can no longer continue to do so. I cannot explain why, only that it concerns the identity of my late benefactor which I am not at liberty to reveal, then you would have my lasting gratitude.'

'I will do as you wish. Is there anything else?'

I had hoped to escape, but conscious of the silence and that both pairs of eyes were concentrated on my downbent head, I knitted on.

'Estella.'

The word came out like a pistol shot and I dreaded raising my eyes to his face.

'Estella, you know that I love you, that I have loved you long and dearly. I should have said this sooner but for my mistake in believing that Miss Havisham intended us for one another. While I thought you could not help yourself and acted in accordance with her wishes, as it were, I remained silent. Now I must say it.'

My fingers continued to move at great speed across the shawl I knitted, as if they were no part of me but enjoyed an independent existence of their own, brisk and dedicated to the matter on hand.

'I know I have no hope that I shall ever call you mine. I am ignorant of what may become of me very soon, how poor I may be, or where I may go. Still, I love you. I have loved you ever since I first saw you in this house. It would have been cruel in Miss Havisham, horribly cruel, to practise on the susceptibility of a poor boy, and to torture me through all these years with a vain hope and an idle pursuit, if she had reflected on the gravity of what she did. But I think she did not. I think that in the endurance of her own trial, she forgot mine.'

'I have tried to warn you,' I began. 'Have I not –'

'I thought and hoped you could not mean it.'

Suffering for his agony, and conscious of Miss Havisham's watchful eyes, I said gently: 'I make a great difference between you and all other people when I say so much, I can do no more.'

There was a pause as if he weighed the sincerity of my words, then he asked: 'Is it not true that Bentley Drummle is in town and pursuing you?'

'It is quite true.'

'That you encourage him and ride out with him and that he dines with you every day?'

'Quite true.'

Another longer pause while he sought for words. 'You cannot love him, Estella. You would never marry him?'

The silence seemed to continue for ever as his words hung in the air. Long afterwards I was to relive that scene and think of how different would have been both our lives, had I said: 'No. But I will go with you, Pip. And I shall not mind our circumstances or how poor we are, as long as you love me.' The force of destiny would have been averted and I might even have met my true father, though that would have given me, I fear, as little pleasure as it did Pip in finding his true benefactor.

Instead, conscious of my guardian's hand strongly on my arm, I said miserably: 'Why not tell you the truth? I am going to be married to him.'

Pip dropped his face into his hands but not before I had glimpsed his expression, like a man condemned to the scaffold. Even my mother-by-adoption was impressed for she stirred uneasily in her chair. But Pip recovered instantly.

'Estella, I beg you not to allow Miss Havisham to lead you into this fatal step. Put me aside for ever,' he cried, 'you have done so, I well know, but bestow yourself on some worthier person than Drummle. Miss Havisham gives you to him as the greatest slight and injury that could be done to many far better men who admire you and to the few who truly love you. Take, for God's sake, one of them, and I can bear it for your sake.'

My compassion for him was quickly usurped by anger at his unjust remarks regarding Bentley. 'Why do you hate him so?' I asked knowing only too well. 'What has he ever done to you, other than offer for my hand?' And when he regarded me tight-lipped, silent. 'Come, you must give me better reason than that.'

'Very well. He is an unmerciful bully to those smaller and less fortunate than himself.' He paused before adding.

66

'And dishonest for I have seen him blatantly cheating at cards.'

I lowered my head, suppressing a smile.

'And why does that amuse you, pray?' he demanded sharply.

'Gentle folk have to keep the lower orders in their place,' I said sternly, for I had been encouraged during my companionship of Miss Havisham to bully tradespeople as well as the unfortunate Jolly. As for cards, in order to win and maintain my superiority over Pip, I had been guilty of cheating ever since our first game in Satis House long ago. Indeed, sometimes I suspected that he was aware of my perfidy and condoned it by allowing me to win.

'Everyone cheats at cards,' I added, unrepentant.

Pip shook his head sternly. 'Not when this involves taking large sums of money from fellow-pupils considerably poorer than himself. Nor does his dishonesty end there.' He paused and then with a shrug continued, 'He broke a window in one of his fiendish rages and indicated to Mr Pocket that I was to blame and that I should accordingly pay for the repair.'

'Which you did, of course, being too much of a gentleman to tell the truth,' I said scornfully.

'Which I did, Estella, to save our tutor from any further distress or embarrassment.'

'The more fool you, then. Such a fuss over a broken window.' I laughed, regarding him triumphantly. 'Did you think that this tale-telling could possibly change my mind? I am going to be married to him. The preparations are being made and I shall be married soon. It is my will. And do not accuse my mother-by-adoption. I am tired of the life I have led, which has very few charms for me and I am willing enough to change it.'

'Such a mean brute, to fling yourself away on – a mean and stupid brute.'

'That he is not,' I said indignantly. 'He is a fine cultured gentleman. His family is noble, well-bred –' I bit back the words that almost slipped out: 'better bred than a black-smith's boy'. Instead I whispered, 'I doubt I shall not be a blessing to him.'

'Oh Estella, Estella,' he wept openly now, 'even if I remain in England and could hold up my head with the rest, how could I see you Drummle's wife?'

'This will all pass in time, Pip. You will forget me. Why, I will be out of your thoughts in a week,' I said lightly, not believing a word of it.

He stared at me for a moment before replying. 'Out of my thoughts?' He shook his head. 'You are part of my existence, part of myself. You have been in every line I have ever read, since I first came here, the rough common boy whose poor heart you wounded even then. You have been in every prospect I have ever seen since – on the river, on the sails of ships, on the marshes, in the clouds, in the light, in the darkness, in the wind, in the woods, in the sea, in the streets. You have been the embodiment of every graceful fancy that my mind has ever become acquainted with. The stones of which the strongest London buildings are made, are not more real or more impossible to be displaced by your hands, than your presence and influence have been to me, there and everywhere, and will be.' He paused for a moment.

'Estella, to the last hour of my life, you cannot choose but remain part of my character, part of the little good in me, part of the evil. But, in this separation I associate you only with the good, and I will faithfully hold you to that always, for you must have done me far more good than harm, let me feel now what sharp distress I may. Oh, God bless you, God forgive you.'

Through this tirade in a voice that wrung my heart, I had bowed my head, unable to face the embodiment of such anguish. When I looked up, the door had closed. He had gone from my life.

My guardian did not bother to gloat either – I could not have borne that. She sat with her hand covering her heart as if it meant to proclaim its existence and deny the falsity of her play-acting.

'What have I done, what have I done?' she whispered at last. 'When he spoke to you, he held up a looking glass and showed me what I once suffered, how I felt. Until that moment, I did not recognize my own folly, how I had wronged him – and you, my dearest child. Can you ever forgive me?'

'Readily, dearest mother, I forgave you long ago.'

'Dearest child, dearest child.'

I held her in my arms and we both wept. At last I gathered up my knitting, kissed her.

'Not you too, Estella, you will not desert me?'

'Not desert, nothing is further from my thoughts. But I think I will retire, for I am very tired. Until tomorrow morning.' At the door I turned. 'Do what Pip asked you about Cousin Herbert.'

'Anything, anything.'

'Anything? Then ask Pip's forgiveness as you have asked mine. Before it is too late.'

I sat by my bedroom window, lonely, desolate and watched over by a pale moon. I felt as if I should never sleep again and in a desperate effort to thrust out Pip's voice I so loved, speaking those terrible words echoing over and over, I took up the book of poems he had given me. At a passage marked and oft-read by him, it fell open:

> 'All precious things, discover'd late,
> To those that seek them issue forth;
> For love in sequel works with fate,
> And draws the veil from hidden worth.
> He travels far from other skies –
> His mantle glitters on the rocks —
> A fairy Prince, with joyful eyes,
> And lighter-footed than the fox.'

And I seemed to hear his whisper: 'You are in every word I read,' as, sick at heart, I longed with all my being to turn back time as readily as had my mother-by-adoption. What did I want with marriage anyway? I did not love Bentley Drummle, except in the mercenary way of what he could provide for me, for I had always promised myself that I would marry a Lord, and an heir to a baronetcy was the next best thing. As for Pip, would I be even contemplating this marriage if his expectations had come home to roost, if he had been rich instead of poor, if I had not felt that allying myself to his poverty would degrade me.

I found myself weeping. Oh, that I could bid carefree yesterday's return, with its picnics and boating and laughter and Assembly Balls at Richmond. A chapter of my girlhood, now ended.

For even as I closed the book, it too was gone for ever, and had taken Pip and a joyous heart with it.

Part Two
Marriage

I was married from Mrs Brandley's villa in Richmond. Drummle would brook no delay. If I had thought passions of desire were responsible for this urgency, I should have been gratified indeed. As for romantic love, this motif was swiftly trampled underfoot by the many tradesmen hastening to the door, alert to vast profits in the marriage business. There were jewellers to consult – not many, as my mother-by-adoption had parted with most of her precious gems, decking me with some new bauble at our every meeting over my years at Satis House. But there were milliners, dressmakers and pastrycooks in plenty to give Mrs Brandley the time of her life.

Her cup overflowed daily with delight at this unique opportunity to shine forth in the role of foster-mother to the bride, especially as my mother-by-adoption had authorized large sums of money to ensure that the future Lady Drummle had everything she could wish in the way of trousseau.

'Everything necessary. Those are her very words,' said Mrs Brandley rapturously, trotting out lists of items whose limited appearances and appeal I would have never dreamed of, left to my own initiative in the matter.

'We are to go to town and take up residence in a good family hotel, so that we can appraise ourselves of the latest fashions in the shops in Regent Street. Richmond is much too countrified, alas, for all the milliners, dressmakers and shoemakers, to say nothing of pastrycooks.'

In London, every shopkeeper's eyes mirrored this well-to-do bride-to-be as a purse of golden guineas to be acquired with as little effort as they could exert. They would have sold me not only the item I required but were prepared to ransack their stores to offer all manner of goods, no matter how absurd or inappropriate, in order to get their hands on a substantial share of money flourished by Mrs Brandley, courtesy of Alicia Havisham.

I must confess that as I smiled and postured from fitting to fitting, and earnestly weighed the merits of this velvet against that satin and lace, my other self occasionally stepped back to wonder cynically what my mother-by-adoption would have made of this beaming, fluttering empty-headed ninny I had become. This other Estella, who was secretly addicted to newspapers and was made uneasy by accounts of the Chartist movement and cholera epidemics caused by appalling conditions of sanitation. An Estella who gave a great deal of thought to the poor sickly seamstresses and milliners but never once looked closely homeward and considered that the slavery of her own faithful Jolly, was little better than that of these poor wretches, with their bad eyes, weak chests, unhealthy pallor, underpaid and underfed, who sat up half the night to finish her extravagant trousseau. Women for whom ten of Mrs Brandley's guineas, could have turned the hell of poverty into a heaven of plenty.

When I drew attention to their plight, Mrs Brandley was quite shocked. 'My dear girl, I beg you, do not concern yourself over such matters. You are a happy bride and how such wretches live is nothing to do with you. You must not sully your innocent mind with thoughts of how others less fortunate than yourself choose to make a living. And,' she added with a disdainful sniff, 'if such ideas are what you learned at Dame Clarissa's Academy, then I am all for a speedy return to governesses for young ladies.'

Mrs Brandley meant well, I am sure, for indeed there was nothing I could do but make myself miserable at nights lying awake in my comfortable warm bed and pondering why the good Lord had not seen fit to allow me to sleep upon a filthy straw pallet in an overcrowded room, shared with a modest seven or eight of a family. Was it to escape such thoughts as these, that I had been bred without a heart and was so eager to embark upon the perils of a loveless marriage?

Expecting catastrophes, national or personal, to delay the wedding, my fears were groundless and as Bentley set the marriage ring upon my finger and I promised to take this solemn stranger for better, for worse until death did us part, I was glad indeed of my guardian's absence. Had she seen me by my bridegroom's side, bursting with pride, she might well have supposed that all her teachings had come to naught and that Estella was the possessor of a heart, its emotions vulgarly on display for all the world to see.

Mrs Brandley's organizing abilities over my trousseau had extended to considerable ingenuity in filling the empty seats in the parish church. As neither bride nor groom had relatives present, our wedding breakfast became a charity benefit for her army of friends and acquaintances, who had been pressed into attendance. I had not even Bessie, who refused to be wheedled out of Satis House and across London. It never so much as entered my head that the Small Person would have liked to have seen her mistress wed.

The speculative glances of the guests were sympathetic. The bride they had been told, was an orphan with a guardian prevented by many years of invalidism from attending the ceremony. How sad!

But what of the bridegroom's family? Rumour had it that he was well-connected with the nobility. Surely some of the Drummles were in attendance? As heads craned and speculation was rife, all were doomed to disappointment.

'A mother you say – the Honourable Mrs Drummle. Surely she would wish to see her only son married.'

'Well, now' (came answer) 'she is in poor health.'

'Then what, pray, of his grandfather, Sir Hammond Drummle, a merchant banker and a name to be reckoned with in the City?'

'Well, now, he is also an invalid, the bridegroom the last of a long line of Drummles. Should he die childless, a second cousin, a mere youth stands to inherit.'

'Then where, pray, is this second cousin?'

'Well, now, unfortunate circumstances, examinations and so forth at Oxford, prevent Wilfred from being present.'

I knew better. Bentley and his cousin loathed each other and I was extremely doubtful that any invitation had been issued. I often wondered if Bentley's contemptuous dismissal of Wilfred was mixed with fear, that if he married and produced a son, and we did not, then Drummle would go to him.

I was well aware that only faintly obscured by warm congratulations and brilliant smiles, we were the object of some strange glances and behind-hand whispers.

'Such a sickly history of melancholy invalids, as you've never heard, my dear,' inevitably led to further gloomy speculation concerning the ability of the happy pair to summon up enough health and strength to beget the necessary heir to the Drummle dynasty.

Beget an heir. The words meant nothing to me and I was to discover too late that serious omission in the education of a would-be breaker of hearts. Neither my mother-by-adoption, a maiden lady who could be forgiven the omission, nor Mrs Brandley, nor anyone else, had taken the trouble to explain to the bride the necessary facts of the wedding night.

We left the house at Richmond and made our way to the Red Dragon, a coaching inn where we were to stay over night en route for Paris, from whence we would return to Bentley's London town house.

At the inn Bentley had procured rooms for us. I

76

remember little about its location except that the window of our bridal chamber gazed over a moonlit sea. And long before the shutters were drawn against the night hiding that moon from view, I wished that my human body could have also drowned beneath its tranquil waters.

Until the instant when servants cleared away the supper, there had been no more than the chastest of kisses exchanged between us. Even those were rare indeed, in view of Dame Clarissa's sole instruction on proper behaviour when confronted with the opposite sex: 'You may not kiss a man on the mouth until you are wed.'

At last we were alone in a room with a closed door for the first time. How my husband's eyes gleamed with pleasure, and taking my hand in his rather sweaty palm, the result I feared of overheating his blood with rich food and an excellent wine, he led me to the adjacent bedroom. 'I will allow you a little time to disrobe,' he said stroking my shoulder. 'I expect you would prefer privacy for your toilette?'

I smiled shyly appreciating his courtesy. Had he posed the words in the form of a question, unsure of what my response should be? 'I would indeed.'

Frowning, he seemed somewhat taken aback. 'As you wish, my dear.' Still he waited. 'However, as you have no maid with you in attendance –' I looked at him in amazement, since it had been his wish that we travel unaccompanied, '– I will be happy to unhook or unlace as required.' Again his hand, rather heavy now, lingered on my shoulder.

'Oh no, not at all, thank you. That will not be necessary. I can manage perfectly,' I said blushing, 'I am quite used to er, disrobing, without assistance.'

He continued to regard me, head on side. 'Very well, Mrs Drummle, I will smoke a final cigar before I return, when I hope to find you ready for me.'

Closing the door, thankful to be alone, I went to the dressing table and before the cheval looking-glass divested myself of the diamond and pearl necklace, earrings and bracelet, my mother-by-adoption had insisted I wear for my wedding. Next I discarded my blue velvet travelling dress, petticoats and chemise, stockings and drawers. As I snatched up my nightgown I caught a rather comical glimpse of a scared looking naked girl, all pink but for a shaming and prominent black triangle that matched the streaming hair now unloosed about her shoulders. Closing my eyes hurriedly I thrust on nightgown and befrilled wrapper and clambered shivering between the chilly sheets.

I discovered lying against the pillows that I was tired after the exciting events of the day. Stifling yawns, I decided it would be ungracious and impolite to fall asleep before my new husband came to bed and gathered me into his arms. I sighed with pleasure, stroking the still cold side of the bed where he would lie.

I wished he would come, come and kiss me goodnight. All night long I would sleep in his arms, with my head on his shoulder, safe and snug in a nest, as so often I had slept with Bessie in the past when the Nightmare troubled me –

Almost asleep, despite my resolution, I was aware that the door had opened and closed again. My husband now looked down upon me. I had never seen him clad other than with the utmost formality, from immaculate neckcloth to shining leather boots. There was something intimate and endearingly boyish in seeing him thus, barefoot in a quilted velvet robe. In one movement, he pulled back the bed covers, but instead of climbing in beside me, he said:

'Madam, is this how you greet your husband?'

'I – I don't know what you mean.'

'I mean, madam, that I find you clad more for a ball than for your bridal bed. Remove them –'

'Re – move them?'

'Yes. Remove them – take them off. All those silly garments – this instant.' He sounded cross. No doubt I had misheard him. No one – no one in my adult life had ever seen me naked. That was a secret I shared, blushing, with my looking-glass alone.

'You cannot be serious, sir.' I said coldly.

'Never more so,' he said cheerfully.

'I will be cold.'

'That you will not. You will be very warm indeed, I assure you.' Still I hesitated. 'Shall I assist you?'

'No, no – I can manage perfectly.' As he remained motionless, regarding me, I said with as much dignity as I could summon: 'Oblige me by blowing out the candle.'

'Blowing out the candle, eh?' Suddenly the room was filled with great whooping shouts of mirth. I could not have been more astounded, or horrified. This man who rarely even smiled, let alone laughed, was roaring with merriment at my discomfiture. It was not a pleasant sound to hear. Abruptly it stopped to be replaced by a look of utmost savagery and derision.

'Come – here." His hands were far from gentle as he dragged the gown from my shoulders, bending his head as he did so and covering my half naked bosom with kisses. Shocked, I tried to cover my breasts with my hands. These were dragged away as he tore off his robe I saw to my horror, felt to my terror, his wholly naked body against my own.

There was nothing of softness and tenderness or warmth of safe little nest here, or a shoulder to rest a head on. There was a mat of thick black hair on his chest, the smell of sweat, no doubt brought about by excitement – I found later that this was an unpleasant side effect of his exertions – and in the place of the figleaf decorously worn by male statues and from which I had blushingly averted my eyes, a monstrous erect member, searching, pressing. I was hurled on to my back, spread-eagled on the bed by his thighs and a moment later my body was forced open and he thrust violently inside me.

'No, no,' I screamed in mingled pain and horror of what was happening to me. 'Please – oh, please – don't' Terror gave me strength and I rolled away from him.

'What the devil do you mean – don't?'

'Please, I beg you. I must think.'

'Think? For God's sake, what do you think wedding nights are about. Has no one told you what to expect?' He swore – I will not repeat his words. 'For God's sake, dry your tears. What did you expect was meant by sleeping with your husband, by love, honour and obey – surely even a close perusal of your Bible should have given you an inkling, madam: "He arose and went in unto her and she conceived –" ' He paused to let the dreadful significance of the words sink in. 'That is what marriage is all about. And this –' he said his hand shielding his manhood, mercifully somewhat deflated and subdued by its frustrations. 'If no one has told you then I will be your tutor, madam, and this your first lesson.'

He began to kiss me. Never had I known such devouring kisses and then without any more preliminaries, growling like an animal, he pressed fiercely into my body. Pain, terror, suffocation. These were the only emotions, they took over my being, my world, this thrusting violence that would go on for ever. Was this what was meant by 'until death do us part?' At last a great convulsion shook him. He seemed to have stopped breathing.

Cautiously I opened my eyes. Was he dead? Dear God, how would I ever face the world again if he died on top of me, and both of us stark naked? And yet, I would not be altogether sorry, except for the embarrassment. What a blessed relief, to say nothing of a lucky escape. For at that moment, I truly hated him. Then suddenly he rolled off me and a moment later, his snores told that he was still alive and breathing, and my married life, which might last for twenty years, had only just begun.

In the darkness I lay dazed and sleepless, my bruised and aching body accompanied by an even more bruised and aching spirit. How could I escape these nightly assaults? Tears rolled down my cheeks, soaking my hair. As well as hating my sleeping bridegroom I was bitterly angry with those who had not chosen to enlighten me but had allowed me to imagine married life as cuddles and kisses in a cosy warm bed.

Could I run away, back to Satis House? And would my mother-by-adoption understand enough to offer me refuge, even if I could overcome natural embarrassment to explain? My experiences would certainly be a revelation, a setback to her shrine of undying love. Would she be pleased to know how exceeding fortunate she had been to live with only the romantic illusion and never have to face the reality of the pain and brutality that the act called 'love' seemed to require, denying the tenderness of what the word implied to the hearts of sentimental and, alas, inexperienced lovers.

At that moment I felt that Miss Havisham had a great deal to answer for in throwing away the precious years of her own life for a dream and knowing so little of practical importance about marriage, thereby permitting me to ruin my own life by wedding Bentley Drummle. And would the lover who had broken Alicia Havisham's heart have behaved any better on their wedding night than other men, who believed that wives existed merely for breeding and as instruments of their lusts.

And during those dark hours, I realized that running away was no answer. I was no more entitled to escape to indulge in 'finer feelings' than any other bride led to the altar in white as a virgin sacrifice on the marriage bed. I had been duped but there were other compensations in marriage, security and a position in society. There was also Property to be considered. For the sickening realization now dawned of what all those pre-marriage documents meant. That this afternoon's ceremony and this night's performance deprived me, as a married woman, of any rights to my own property.

There was another interpretation for the love, honour and obey, tacit in the wedding ceremony. From this day forward everything I owned in this world belonged to my husband. I was truly his, body and soul. Without my husband, I had nothing, I was the veriest pauper and my survival depended upon remaining and enduring, as other women remained and endured.

At last I slept. When I awoke in the morning and the light streaming in through the curtains touched his dark face on the white pillow, I felt more composed. And when he opened his eyes and smiled and took me in his arms, cradling my head on his shoulder, stroking back my hair as if I were a small frightened child, and making no attempt to repeat last night's gross events, I almost forgave him. Love, I could not summon, but I might try not to hate him.

The steam packet carried us across a solidly grey sea under a sky indivisible from it. The docks and customs shed were packed with travellers who speedily separated and vanished along the road to Paris, a road long and dusty. Our conveyance, stifling under the smell of garlic, had four fierce French horses, wide-eyed, stamping and looking exactly as if they had stepped from the walls of one of the Art Galleries, having decanted their famous heroes who had perched in improbable attitudes upon their backs to be painted.

The countryside was heavy with poplar trees and remarkably light on people, who obviously found it more profitable to lurk down the side streets in the centre of Paris. Now there were other conveyances which jostled with ours for supremacy of the road, while our horses snorted and whinnied at their horses, whether in amiable greeting or downright abuse I know not. Halted, we were immediately beseiged by the filthy hands and whining cries of beggars and cripples and sorry-looking women with sorry-looking grey bundles in their arms, bundles that could only be babies. As the coachman flourished his whip, they quickly vanished leaving me to wonder why the French have so long been regarded as our enemies when the poor of Paris have so much in common with the poor of London.

We had engaged an apartment in the Rue de Rivoli, its windows surreptitiously glancing off the main walk of the Tuileries. Laying aside my bonnet, I was all for jaunting down to the shops in the Palais Royale and Rue St Honoré, but Bentley announced himself tired. Later in the day would do very well, after we had rested.

On a dais with steps to climb, beneath a huge canopy which threatened suffocation, a bed of antique and immense proportions awaited to envelop us. Committing ourselves to its depths, we were overcome by a distinct smell of mice and a constant overture of twanging springs. The comforts offered were by no means compatible with a connubial couch but suggested rather Napoleon's lying-in-state. Combined with the weather, it defeated all my attempts to be cheerful and stoical about the future.

The rain that had threatened now chose to burst forth in torrents from the heavy grey skies, masking the famous skyline and, as the French never do things by halves, behaving exactly like someone emptying water butts over our heads. I saw little of Paris beyond the Hotel apart from regular drenchings when we directed our footsteps towards those shops so tempting on my last visit, and unaccountably 'out of bounds'.

My husband could hardly conceal his boredom, except for the hours when I was in his bed, and I witnessed a return of the dour gloomy creature I had first met at Richmond. I told myself it was the weather's fault, he would be merry again – when *had* he ever been merry? – when the honeymoon was over and we returned to our own home.

One evening after he thought I slept, he rose from our bed and stealthily dressed. Sleepily I asked where was he going.

'Out for some air.'

'Shall I come with you?' The sounds of carriages busily rolling past the Hotel suggested that Paris night life was just about to begin and might be well worth dressing for.

'No. Go back to sleep,' he said shortly.

He returned at dawn and I was unpleasantly aware of the stale smell of drink and tobacco about his person. And what alarmed me more, a woman's stale cheap perfume. I cared about that deeply, for in those two weeks of marriage, my husband was proving to be as good a teacher as he had promised. I had learned a great deal to make up for my ignorance. I learned that our bodies' needs are the controlling forces in our lives, for woman as well as man, whatever the genteel ladies' tea-parties might pretend and however we chose to define that need, as the love of a lifetime or the passing lust of a single hour.

Although I did not love my husband in the least, his rough and ready lovemaking no longer filled me with revulsion. Instead it was becoming a necessity, something to be craved and hungered for each day, like food and drink. And deep inside me, something that had long slept now awakened. A shaming urge, like a flower longing to grow, expand its petals, bloom, consume and lose itself for ever in another's being in an explosion of ecstasy.

Our return to London brought my first sight of Bentley's town house in Cadogan Crescent.

'Is it not a trifle unusual, my dear,' whispered Mrs Brandley's friends, 'for the bride not to inspect her home before marriage?' This I could not deny, but it seemed a mere continuance of the unusual circumstances which surrounded a wedding where bride-to-be had not yet had the honour of being presented to her husband's family.

Surprises were by no means at an end. They had just begun. No sooner had we set foot in the modest villa, which could have been folded three times over into Satis House, than the servants rushed forth to inform Bentley that his mother had left the day before to travel in haste to Drummle Towers where his grandfather was taken ill.

'Madam left word that you were to follow immediately,' the tall housekeeper added, while the more timid maids bobbed up and down behind her, curious for a glimpse of the master's bride.

Bentley ushered me into the hall. 'Tomorrow,' he said firmly. 'Now be so good as to fetch us supper.'

The housekeeper held her ground firmly, folding her arms in the manner of one determined to be heard. 'Sir, I was to inform you that you were to go on the instant. Tomorrow, Mrs Drummle informed me most particularly, might be too late to find your grandfather alive.'

'Tomorrow,' repeated Bentley, eyeing her sternly. 'We are weary. We require a fire in the master bedroom and supper served within the hour. See to it.'

I am ashamed to admit that at that moment I sighed with less concern for Sir Hammond Drummle's state of health than for my own state of comfort. I was in that condition delicately referred to among the Richmond females as 'unwell' and too embarrassed to mention this to Bentley. In addition I was travel-stained, bone-weary and grateful indeed for a short respite, even in surroundings less than hospitable. Dingy, drearily decorated with little evidence of the flourish of paintbrush, or indeed, polishing rag during the past decade. How, I wondered did maids and housekeeper fill in their days? This was hardly the prosperous background against which I had envisaged life as Mrs Bentley Drummle.

The supper came at long last. Cold, uninviting and ill-served, while the fire gave little heat, but smoked furiously and made our eyes smart, as if it had taken a spite against us for having to be hastily lit at short notice so late in the day. An hour afterwards I was heartily glad to close my eyes upon that day. There was little sleep in view, for Bentley had given orders that we were to be breakfasted and on the road by six o'clock. The ferocious activity in the house's lower regions suggested that the servants had chosen to stay up all night and had seized this unique opportunity of holding an Assembly Ball on the premises, to which the stamping carriage-horses had been cordially invited.

'What think you of our little home?' asked Bentley as our carriage leaped forward on the journey to Shropshire.

'It will do,' I added a vague smile, not wishing to commit my thoughts upon the subject to discussion.

'Do? Is that all you can say?' Bentley was so plainly put out that I pressed his hand warmly, hoping this gesture might be mistaken for enthusiasm. The truth would scarcely enrapture him and it seemed neither wise or polite, knowing my husband's somewhat querulous temper, to announce in a spirited manner: Not much, but I have every intention of having the deplorable decor of the master bedroom changed immediately. Diplomatically, I said: 'I imagine it is easier to keep warm there than in Drummle Towers.'

'You will admire Drummle, for sure.' And apologetically, 'I wished our town house to be a surprise for you.'

I had been surprised.

'I intended many changes –'

Good, thought I. We are agreed on something at last.

'My dear mother's indifferent health obviously did not allow these to be made while we were abroad. However, I have left further orders –'

Further orders, thought I. So his commands were not obeyed, he was not master under his own roof, which meant that his mother was still in charge, and I fancied, by failing to attend our wedding and ignoring his wishes, intended to remain so.

'The tradesmen are to be notified immediately and you will find it quite transformed on our return.'

'Are we intending a lengthy stay?'

'I should warn you, my dear, this may be the end. The poor old gentleman cannot last for ever, and then Drummle will be ours.'

Perhaps the prospect of such a rare prize justified neglect of the London house, I thought, as the coach delved deeply into the Shropshire country and entered imposing arms-crested gates. Mile after mile of parkland lay ahead, solely inhabited by roe deer grazing at a safe distance, surrounding a great mansion built upon the ruins of the wealthy Abbey confiscated by King Henry the Eighth.

Servants rushed forth, lining the steps to greet us, and I followed my husband through a flurry of bows and curtseys across a marble-pillared hall and into the drawing room occupied by a lady in a lace cap, of considerable age to be Bentley's mother.

Closer scrutiny revealed lines of perpetual discontent and disapproval that had pruned her lips, were answerable for this unhappy first impression. Somewhat reluctantly she greeted me, her action managing to convey that she cared little for Bentley's choice of bride and had, sight unseen, set her face against ever doing so.

Beside her on the sofa, with an air both defensive and protective, a tall thin girl with eyes like a frightened mare and very restless hands, introduced as: 'Bentley's dear cousin Ruth and my dearest ward.'

Even a person of blundering insensitivity could hardly have remained unaware that the two women were united in their condemnation of Bentley's bride. The very atmosphere seemed charged with their whispered speculations, even alarming spiteful echoes from the curled lips of family portraits that looked down upon the scene.

I was hurt, deeply so. However, I told myself it was foolish to be discouraged so early and that many a long and lasting affection has survived a less than agreeable first impression. I was a bride with a loyal husband. Indeed the scene I witnessed suggested that he had fought no easy battle to overcome parental disapproval and take me as his wife and he must have loved me deeply in his own dour fashion. I respected and admired him for that and, as long as our regard for each other was strong, our relationship was indestructible. I resolved immediately to set about winning over Edwina Drummle and her ward.

'Your grandfather is resting now, dearest Bentley. He will see you tomorrow,' and as a frowning afterthought in my direction: 'Mrs Drummle also, I imagine. But he is not to be over-excited, you understand,' she added sternly, as if I had every intention of marching into his presence accompanied by the clash and cymbals of a brass band.

When we were alone in the suite of rooms set aside for our use, I asked: 'Was Cousin Ruth the reason why your mother disapproved of your marriage?'

Bentley looked so unusually uncomfortable, I realized my arrow had fallen little short of truth. 'What makes you think that?' he demanded.

'Because she wanted to marry you herself. And what is more, with your mother's approval. That is as clear as the nose on your face, husband dear.'

Bentley shuddered. 'I do wish you would refrain from using such common language, my dear, pray remember that you are in a baronet's house. They did not consult me about their wishes, or they would soon have learned that I preferred to make my own matrimonial arrangements.'

And smiling now, as he looked at my reflection in the looking-glass. 'They will come round in time, never fear.'

'I intend that they shall.' But they never did. From the very first day they made firm their hostility, their resentment. I was an interloper who had alienated dear Bentley from his loving family and seduced him into marrying very much beneath him. Blushingly, I observed their daily scanning of my figure, as if to confirm their unspoken thoughts that I had seduced him by a servant girl's vulgar pretence of pregnancy. If I had entertained any idea that my virtue was not under discussion and heavily suspect, then my first meeting with Sir Hammond removed any doubt that this thought was prevalent in everyone's mind in Drummle Towers.

'Damned fine filly. In foal too, didn't they tell me?' barked the old gentleman, who was what might be termed a cool customer, ancient in the skeletal, ivoried manner that brings thoughts of melancholy churchyards rather than the benevolence of old age. His eye for the ladies, however, was quite undimmed by time's relentless march, for this death's head on the very brink of the grave was still capable of leering, whispering lewd invitations. And if I ventured too close to the bed, he thought little of stretching out an ancient claw to stroke whatever portion of my anatomy was within his reach.

This state of affairs threw the Atrocious Pair, as I now summarized Edwina Drummle and Ruth, into even greater paroxysms of wrath. Not content with seducing their darling boy, I was now attempting to disturb the peace of Sir Hammond's deathbed, delaying his earthly departure with an unseemly resurgence of carnal desires.

By way of reinforcements against me, Edwina Drummle made constant glowing references to Ruth's virtue and her loyalty to the family, sighing: 'She is, as was her namesake Ruth to Naomi, a daughter to this house.'

Bentley's mother continued to choose the daily menus, and, it seemed, obtained a malicious delight in choosing dishes which I found disagreeable. If I refused a course, it was certain to reappear within the week. And when I complained: 'How tiresome. I had entirely forgotten. Such excellent nourishing food too, that both Ruth and dearest Bentley have enjoyed and thrived upon since childhood. Indeed this dish was ever one of their particular favourites. Now, alas, I suppose we are all to be deprived.'

I suffered many such daily and unjustified meannesses but complaining to Bentley, received the short reply: 'You must be mistaken. As for Ruth, why, she is like a daughter in this house,' was the inevitable response.

'How long do they expect to remain with us when we return to London. Have you thought about where they are to live? Have you any plans in mind?'

He gave me an odd look. 'Plans? What sort of plans?'

'Surely I do not need to remind you, my dear, that as your wife, I expect to run your home.'

His answer was a disagreeable shrug.

'Why does that offend you? It is perfectly reasonable.'

'My mother is well aware of your position,' he said impatiently. 'And once Grandfather, er, passes on, we will inherit Drummle and they will occupy the town house. We will reside there only when occasion takes us to London.'

Sir Hammond had made a miraculous recovery. My presence at Drummle raised in his mind the possibility of imminent offspring, an idea which had such a tonic effect upon him that he showed unmistakeable signs of delaying his departure for the next world. This did not endear me to the Atrocious Pair, who as beneficiaries under his will, laid this shattering of their own expectations at my door.

Bentley, alas, refused to recognize the disharmony in his household. The advisability of ending his wife's discomfort (at being made to feel like a visitor who had somehow contrived to outstay her welcome) by removing his mother and cousin back to the house at Cadogan Crescent, never entered his head. I was soon to discover that this was yet another of my husband's failings. He was seldom troubled by any blinding glimpse of the obvious.

I did not even have a personal maid. The promised French maid failed to materialize since Edwina Drummle objected to foreign girls in the house. Suspicious of their honesty and their morals, she maintained that they were well known to be flighty with the male servants.

She was not prepared to take this desperate risk. 'You may share Perkins, who does very well for dearest Ruth and myself.'

But I had no wish to share even one third of Perkins, a sly-looking individual whose close-set eyes were small and rather red, the result I suspected, from a too frequent application at keyholes. I sympathized with their reason for wishing her to serve me. Such opportunities for spying would be unique and I would gladly deny them that pleasure.

'I shall send for Jolly.' I told Bentley who said brusquely 'Please yourself, madam,' adding, 'you generally do,' with ill-grace.

The letter I sent via Mrs Brandley was returned with the message that Jolly had departed to take care of an ageing aunt. 'She turned very despondent after you went away and was really little use to us. She left no forwarding address.'

I felt a momentary qualm. Poor Jolly who had been my devoted slave. I wished I could see her again, have her comforting loyalty in the face of so much indifference from the Drummle servants. I wished that I could apologize, make amends for my treatment of her through the years, my indifference at Satis House, where her status had been somewhat less than the stray dog. My selfish behaviour in leaving her behind at Richmond now rebounded fully upon me, for Jolly had not only been an efficient servant but also trustworthy. And now I desperately needed such loyalty as all the actions of the Atrocious Pair seemed calculated deliberately to upset me.

Mealtimes I dreaded, as they moved their chairs close and whispered together, while Bentley and I sat in splendid isolation separated by the full length of the long table. Bentley remained oblivious as usual, applying himself so heartily to his food and drink as to be blind and deaf not only to agreeable conversation, had agreeable conversation existed, but also had the roof caved in upon us I doubt whether he would have regarded the event as of enough significance to divert his attention from his plate. Timidly I suggested that sometimes we might dine together.

'Heavens, what a request. Do we not do just that, madam? What ever will you want next? There is no pleasing you.'

'I thought – sometimes – just the two of us, in our sitting-room.' Wistfully, I gave him my most beguiling smile, optimistic that this might bring forth a little attention between courses, instead of the belching and picking of his teeth with which each meal ended. But my suggestion grazed off him in the same disquieting manner as overtures of friendliness were greeted stony-faced by his mother and cousin and the implacable servants. All but the frisky old gentleman upstairs, with his wicked winks and suggestive nods, who seemed to have more life in him than the rest of Drummle Towers put together.

'We must not make Mama and Ruth feel as if they are in our way, that we are driving them away from our hearth.'

Such was Bentley's invariable response. I was astonished to find how ready he was to interpret in them areas of imagined sensitivity and yet remain so indifferent to the feelings of his own wife. My optimism remained, that when Sir Hammond passed on, a subject distressing to myself but discussed with what I considered rather more frequency than delicacy allowed, then maybe Bentley would set his face to firmly establishing them in the London house. I also had hopes that with his own inheritance, he might be a little freer with my dowry, the not inconsiderable fortune I had brought him and over which he and, I suspected, his Mama kept very tight rein indeed.

The weeks became months, and the months stretched into almost a year by which time I had learned that it is as blessed to give insults as to receive them. The Atrocious Pair were not to be won over with charm. I had failed but was no longer daunted. I was not Alicia Havisham's ward for nothing. As Bentley's wife I was undoubted mistress of Drummle Towers, however Edwina Drummle might pretend to the contrary. Very well, she and Ruth should know their place. The long truce at an end, war was declared and they knew the sharpness of my tongue on many occasions.

Such hostilities were mere annoyance, and they soon ceased to disturb the tranquility of each new day at Drummle, which brought to me a sense of wonder and gratitude for the natural beauty of my surroundings. There were paths to walk, horses to ride, acquaintances eager to cultivate Mrs Bentley Drummle. By day, my husband ignored me and by night proved a disappointing lover, speedily seeking satisfaction of his own desires. I doubt he wasted a moment's thought on the possibility that I too had a body which hungered. After all, respectable matrons were required only to submit to their husbands' lusts in order that children should be begotten. Only low-class women, gipsies and prostitutes took pleasure in love-making.

There was one small impediment to my content. I knew how desperately my husband yearned for a son to secure his inheritance, and as our first year together drew to its close, I noticed that upon certain days each month which proved his efforts at paternity had been once again unsuccessful, Bentley was inclined to retire in a state of inebriation. More disquieting, was his participation in cock-fights arranged by our wealthy neighbours in the county. This cruel and illegal sport distressed me considerably. Besides the dangers of prosecution, the wagers ran high and Bentley, a man not usually regarded as open-handed, I knew was losing a great deal of money.

This concerned me only a fraction less than his addiction to strong drink. When joviality overbalanced, he was apt to become excessively amorous, a condition to which no young wife might object in the intimacy of the bedroom. He was also subject to swift and unaccountable changes of mood, from over-affection into what could only be described as, sheer wicked brutality. Fortunately he did not strike me often and was so abjectly miserable and contrite afterwards, even tearful on rare occasions, that while unable to forgive him completely, I soothed my bruises to body and spirit by declaring his doting Mama, Edwina Drummle, responsible for his brutish behaviour, with its echoes of small boy bullying and tantrums which she had overlooked.

At the same time I resolved that when our children arrived, they should be brought up sternly but kindly, picturing our son and heir riding his pony in the parkland, our daughter laughing on the swing beneath the trees. If only it would begin to come true. Surely it must, for I was young and healthy and had every material gift that a bride of one year could desire. My window overlooked a handsome terrace where peacocks strutted in dazzling array, a fountain played and a fine rolling lawn gave way to formal gardens and acres of parkland which continued to delight me in all seasons. Inside the house portraits of past Drummles, heroes of many land and sea victories, looked down from the panelled walls and were a constant reminder of the history of an ancient noble house. Their suits of armour and battle accoutrements hinted at troubled times, while I was comfortably surrounded by modern luxuries in pleasing apartments where Bentley's late grandmother had exercised her exquisite taste, which had also extended to the laying-down of the formal gardens.

I sighed with the pleasurable realization that one day all I surveyed would be mine with servants in plenty, several carriages, as well as horses to ride. Bentley already hinted at visits to German spas and Highland estates where he had many acquaintances. These, for the future. Meantime, he declined to leave Drummle Towers while his grandfather's melancholy health gave cause for concern.

With the present I was content. Our neighbours were agreeable members of our own strata of society, constantly leaving cards and exchanging visits, ready to exchange gossip, drink tea or play a game of croquet.

On one such occasion there occurred an incident, curious and disturbing. A day of outstanding warmth and sunshine had given way to the shadows of evening growing stealthily across the lawn. The air still languid, heavy with the perfume from the rose garden, was made more deliciously fragrant by the absence of the Atrocious Pair, visiting a relative in Brighton.

The croquet mallets had been laid aside as shawls were produced. Tea was over, but no one seemed in any hurry to end the visit and I listened politely to rather violent views being exchanged on the burning issue of Paris fashions for the coming season.

Suddenly our small circle was broken, unpleasantly invaded by the shrill whining tones of a gipsy woman who had appeared out of nowhere, somehow managing to slip through the gates and down the drive unseen. The ladies assembled in their finery of satin and lace and parasol, were struck dumb by the condition of this apparition. Toothless, filthy and ancient, she grinned at us, then glaring rapidly round the group, she nodded eagerly in my direction:

'You – you are the lady of the house. My business is with you.'

'I am indeed the lady of the house, and I must ask you to leave immediately. This is a private estate.'

She cackled with unseemly mirth at the statement as if my reply had been outrageously amusing. Leaning forward, raising claw-like fingers, unspeakably loathsome, she said in a wheedling voice 'I will leave, my lady, that I promise you, but I am sure you would wish to have your fortune told before I go. You and these other fine ladies too. There's lots of things they are dying to know about, things that old Elspeth could answer to their great advantage.'

There was something about her, more than the odour of a seldom washed body, that made my heart beat faster. Something which made my gorge rise with misery and the sense of inescapable doom. As if a black spectre from the past leaned across the lengthening shadows and would have recognition. I felt the familiar twitch of the Nightmare, as it threatened to engulf this peaceful lawn and snatch me up from the midst of those who would be my friends.

'As you may observe, we are somewhat busy at the moment,' I said frostily, fighting to remain calm despite the raging sickness, the foreboding within my breast. 'We have more important matters on hand than listening to our fortunes.'

'Important matters, eh?' The grey eyebrows raised and the eyes were jet pinpoints in her wizened face. Again the filthy hand was raised, the finger pointed. 'T'would do well, my lady, for you to lend your ear very carefully to what fate holds in store for you. Aye, you, madam, and that bairn you carry.'

There was a suppressed exclamation of excitement from the little group around me, as I replied:

'I carry no child.' Was I indeed speaking truth, for I had not yet confided my suspicions to anyone, not even Bentley.

She nodded vigorously, 'Aye, but you do, madam, and what is more, the babe is a lad. You would do well to reflect on what a change this will make to your own life, for nothing will ever be the same for you again. Nothing,' she added fiercely, staring hard into my face. 'Enjoy these lovely days, my lady, you will have cause to remember them by and by. Peace and tranquility, aye, and plenty too. Not the usual kind of life for the likes of yourself.'

Annoyed and embarrassed, but frightened too, I rose rather shakily to my feet. 'I must ask you to leave,' I said again conscious of hands that trembled.

'Leave, is that so?' Insolent now, she looked me up and down. 'You ask old Elspeth to leave – how does that fit into Romany hospitality, ladies?' she asked appealing to the group, her whining voice returned.

'I neither know nor care for your Romany hospitality, old woman –'

The old crone nodded, not in the least put out and again turned to my companions for support. 'That is always the way of it, ladies, for those who come up in the world. Is that not so, ladies?' and addressing me with a sly smile, 'But they can fall as quickly as they rose. Remember that, my lady.'

'I find your tone extremely offensive –' Amazed that I could still sound calm and dignified, I continued, '– and I must ask you to leave before I call the servants and have you put off the premises. I must warn you against returning. You have been fortunate so far since my husband's dogs make short work of any intruders.'

'Dogs, is it now? Well, well.' Just a shadow of fear touched her face although she continued to stare at me boldly enough. 'Turn the dogs on one of your own kind, would you?' she added with a sad shake of her head.

'I am not of your kind – how dare you.' And how shrill my voice sounded now shattering the clear air. I was conscious of the leaden silence, of every bird call suddenly mute, as if they too listened.

'I dare, my cruel pretty lady, because you are gipsy born and Gorgio bred. You are still haunted by the Romany world. Take care, madam, that one day it does not reclaim you entirely, that a day does not come, aye – *will* come, when you will be grateful to lose yourself with your own again –'

I was conscious of the stillness, the astonished expressions of my neighbours. The spell was broken by the sound of a rider and to my delight Bentley approached, his two great mastiffs galloping alongside. The old gipsy's eyes were keen. She needed no further warning. Her rags fluttering about her like bedraggled feathers of some bird of prey, she hopped briskly towards the drive with a speed and agility remarkable for one so ancient.

As Bentley dismounted to acknowledge politely my croquet guests, one excited old lady could contain herself no longer and was already telling him about that horrible gipsy woman.

'You should have heard her, sir, the things she told your dear wife.'

'Such as?' Unperturbed by this storm in his domestic teacup, Bentley saw my white face, and sickly expression. 'Fortune telling is all nonsense; my dear, surely you know that.'

'She made some very personal remarks, sir, she did indeed,' interrupted the senior lady who had appointed herself spokeswoman.

'Is that so? Well, we will have none of her. I will ride down the drive and see her safely off the premises.'

Quickly he rode off towards the drive and I tried to resume normality by suggesting another game of croquet before dark, while hoping and praying that none would accept.

Bentley returned almost immediately. 'The woman has vanished completely.'

'But she couldn't have done so. She must be hiding somewhere,' I said desperately. 'I beg you search again.'

'The drive through the parkland is quite open, concealment would be impossible. Besides the dogs were unleashed. They would soon have sniffed her out, but I assure you they were quite uninterested, even mystified by my command.'

And so was I. Bidding my guests goodnight, eager to speed them on their way, I was terrified that the old woman lurked somewhere inside the house.

As soon as our bedroom door was closed that night, Bentley asked, 'What is this news you have for me, Mrs Drummle?'

'News?'

'News indeed. One of your good old ladies gave me plenty of hints and nods that you had something to tell me, something that I am very eager to hear.'

I smiled. 'Oh that. The gipsy told me that I carry a child.'

He sprang towards me, his brow dark, eager. 'And do you? Do you?'

I backed away from him. 'I know not – for sure.' Dear God, if I should have to disappoint him once again.

'You must know. How late are you, madam?'

'A week – maybe ten days.'

'Maybe ten days,' he mimicked, with a mirthless laugh. How often in those early days had we based hopes on ten days, our dreams to be shattered within the fortnight. 'Did you not think I should be informed.'

'You did not ask.'

'My dear, such matters of the womanly calendar are your business, your husband to be kept informed if the matter is of importance.'

'I wished only to be certain.' I did not dare add: 'this time' for I could not endure his vengeful cruelty upon me should I be wrong once again. Dear God, dear God, help me.

But he was prepared to be kind. 'Then let us hope that the gipsy woman told the truth for once.'

And there he let the matter rest. But counting the days, within the month I was able to confirm the gipsy's prophecy though how she knew before I did continued to chill my blood. We may laugh and make nonsense of prophecies, but the primeval doubt remains, that there walk among us some who have this strange gift.

Doctor Bidwell, almost as ancient as his patient Sir Hammond, had been summoned to treat cousin Ruth for a persistent cough which confined her to the sofa, a pitiful sight more akin to one dying of consumption than the residue of a chill taken in Brighton. While her aunt held her hand, the invalid eyed Bentley tremulously, begging compassion, through a tide of damp lace hankerchiefs. This was her moment of drama and the sighs of both ladies were meant to leave neither Bentley nor myself in any doubt that I was the culprit. His cousin was dying of unrequited love, for I had wantonly stolen her beloved. And by vaunting my cruel triumph had reduced her to this – this wrecked piece of humanity. Each time Edwina Drummle set eyes on me it was to bow her head and sob anew. And now before us the expiring lady heard the verdict. She was told most cheerfully by the doctor: 'A passing malady, nothing more than a severe infection of the throat.' He added that she might have expectations of living to be eighty, or even a hundred, given the good example of her grandfather. He then turned his attention to me.

'And what of yourself, Mrs Drummle? You look a trifle

pale. Does aught ail you?' As he spoke he examined my face closely, my eyes and neck. 'Are you sick?'

I did not feel like vaunting my symptoms before an audience but in truth the room was swirling about me in an alarming way.

'Sick,' said Mama-in-law, 'if that is so then it is your own gluttony, my dear. Have I not warned you?'

The room continued its mad waltz. I heard my name called from far off and floated away into a tranquil sky. When I opened my eyes again it was to the flourish of smelling-salts and two angry female faces staring down at me as I lay on the sofa reluctantly vacated by cousin Ruth.

'Bentley?' I whispered and saw that he stood by the window in earnest consultation with Doctor Bidwell who now walked over and drawing up a chair, sat by my side.

'There is no doubt about it, Mrs Drummle, from what your husband tells me.'

'No doubt? About what?' demanded his mother. 'That his wife continually looks down her nose at good nourishing food, soups and offal that have always been served in this family –'

Doctor Bidwell cut short this tirade and smiled at her. 'You will be delighted to know that digestion is not the cause. Your daughter-in-law is with child, Mrs Drummle, and you may entertain happy expectations of becoming a grandmama.'

'A grandmama,' was the horrified shriek. 'This is monstrous – monstrous, Bentley.'

Bentley had the grace to look extremely diffident as if he shared no part in this miracle. While Edwina Drummle sobbed, Cousin Ruth clutched her bosom and moaned. Poor Doctor Bidwell merely stared bewildered at each of us individually as if hoping someone would enlighten him as to what it was all about.

'I realize this is a little disturbing, even frightening at first. But you will soon get used to the idea. Especially as your daughter-in-law is in excellent health –'

A small scream issued from cousin Ruth's open mouth and was hastily stifled.

'– I see no reason why she should not, in due course, give her husband a dozen healthy sons and daughters.'

As Doctor Bidwell left us Bentley stirred from his reverie. 'A son – I am going to have a son – at last.' And this strong unemotional husband of mine did the strangest thing, quite out of keeping with his often dour character. He knelt by the sofa grasping my hands, his eyes brimming over. 'My dearest, my dearest,' he said kissing me, holding me to his heart. 'At last, at last.' There was a flurry of skirts around us, a sharply banged door and when I emerged from his embrace, we were alone.

During the weeks that followed I continued to be very sick indeed, but once midday was passed I felt restored to excellent health and optimism, daring to hope that a child might also make me love my husband, suddenly so concerned for my welfare. I dared also dream that a son might turn him into a paragon of virtue, end the cockfighting, the convivial evenings which so often had him carried to bed by the servants, and always with a purse growing increasingly empty.

Sir Hammond received this news, with some stiffly roguish repartee, as he pawed at me over the bed covers. Blushingly I smiled and seeing my distress, Bentley interrupted:

'Fillys and stallions, sir. May I respectfully remind you that such talk be kept to the stables. You are embarrassing your grand-daughter-in-law. It is not genteel or even decent of you, sir,' he said sternly.

The Atrocious Pair remained aloof, their manner huffy and inconsolable. I do not think I was greatly wrong in surmising that I had foiled their hopes that should I be barren, Bentley might send me away and take Ruth to wife. I imagined they consoled themselves with anxious daily enquiries about the state of my health, taking every opportunity to gleefully describe how pale and unwell I looked and by assuring me, as if from considerable personal knowledge, that many babies failed to survive birth and infancy. Indeed our dinner table had now one sole topic, beset by doleful tales of frequent childbed deaths in the Drummle family. Under a cool, gently mocking exterior I concealed my fears. Their words could not harm me. I was producing an heir for Drummle, and they had lost. Occasionally I did hope that Bentley in solitary state at his end of the dining-table might feel obliged to cry out against this morbid conversation. But utterly dedicated to his food, he remained unaware of his mother's lack of tact, or his wife's discomfort.

Eagerly, I awaited my mother-by-adoption's response to my news. We had not visited Satis House since our return from Paris and I was disappointed that her letter expressed only conventional sentiments, mild interest and hopes for my continued health. Meanwhile, I longed passionately to see her again, to confront her in the full bloom of pregnancy. How then could the breaker-of-hearts charade be maintained when she observed in this rich fulfilment of my womanhood, the ultimate evidence of complete submission to man's desire?

The months passed, and as I learned from my more experienced croquet-playing friends that women craved exotic foods or even chewed a piece of coal at such times, so did my longing for my childhood home become an obsession, a desperate need to reach out and touch my mother-by-adoption, a yearning to be clasped once more to her bosom. Perhaps I had a premonition that I was never to do so again in this life, for as winter drew its curtains and often isolated us from the world beyond the parkland, Bentley set his face firmly against travel over rough Shropshire roads.

'You must be patient and wait until our son is born. As soon as he is strong enough, I promise we will take him to greet Miss Havisham.'

Then quite without warning as I began to count the weeks in days, I received an unannounced visit from Herbert Pocket. One glance at his blackclad figure, his solemn face, warned me of the news I most dreaded upon this earth, even before he clasped my hands:

101

'Our dearest Aunt Havisham is dead. Dear Estella,' he sobbed, 'dear Estella, how I dreaded bringing you this word.'

'I cannot believe it – she never ailed – oh, oh –' I gasped between bouts of weeping. 'She was so pleased about – about –'

Herbert's glance did not linger on my swollen body. 'She was delighted, Estella, so proud for us all to know that she who had never been a bride was soon to be a grandmother.'

'I had not the least idea she was ill. That is what is so horrible – why, in her last letter there was no mention –'

'Do sit down, Estella.' He took a seat beside me on the sofa and continued to hold my hands. 'You must brace yourself and be very brave.' He paused, not knowing where to begin. 'There was an accident, a most hideous accident. As she dozed in a chair, a spark flew from the fire and settled on the skirt of her bridal gown. So old and dry, it blazed like a tinder box. Had it not been that good old Pip was still on the premises at the time, having just visited her, then the whole of Satis House would have been a blazing inferno. As it was, he attempted to snatch her like a brand from the burning to his own detriment. His arms are severely burned.'

'Oh, poor Pip, my poor dear friend. And Bessie, what of her?'

'Bessie escaped, the only damage was to the upper floor. As for our dear friend Pip,' Herbert sighed. 'Alas, this was not the full extent of his agony, dear Estella. Fortune has indeed turned her face from him, for his benefactor, upon whom he had such noble expectations was naught but a scoundrel, alas, and in trouble with the law.'

'Poor Pip. No wonder the revelation of his true identity was such a shock. He must have felt shamed and betrayed; such an end to all his hopes. We both believed, of course, that Miss Havisham was his secret benefactress. Who was this person?'

Herbert looked uncomfortable. 'No one we know, Estella. Doubtless Mr Jaggers will be in possession of all the facts.' His usually pale countenance was rather red, and I detected an eagerness to change the subject. 'He will, of course, be acting on your behalf regarding Satis House.'

'Oh, dear cousin, I do not want Satis House. I wish it could come to you.'

Bentley arrived at that moment and took the grave news and my tears with considerable equilibrium. Of course, he would leave for Rochester immediately, and attend the funeral. Of course, I could not accompany him. The idea was unthinkable.

'But I must go. I must see her once again,' I sobbed.

Bentley and Herbert exchanged looks and the latter said hurriedly: 'Better to remember her as you knew her. Before the fire, I mean.'

'I am not afraid of what I shall find. And I ought to go. There's Pip too. Poor Pip, so badly burnt in trying to save her, Bentley. I must go to him, thank him for what he tried to do –'

'Be assured that I shall perform whatever duty I think necessary on your behalf when I represent you at the funeral,' interrupted Bentley whose face had taken on a look of thunder at the mention of Pip. When Herbert had gone, I reopened the subject, but Bentley was not to be moved by my pleas. His decision was unshakeable.

'Mr Jaggers, I am sure, will have information to satisfy your curiosity regarding the condition of the blacksmith boy's injuries,' his sneering comment a reminder that his cordial dislike of Pip still existed.

After a tearful and sleepless night, I again pleaded with him. 'The baby is not imminent and, I have on good authority, that first babies seldom arrive punctually.'

Stubbornly he shook his head. 'Our son' (strangely, he never referred to the child as a possible daughter), 'our son will be born early next month. I will not allow you to put him at risk by such folly as travelling to Rochester.'

'But I have never felt fitter in my life,' I protested and that was true. I hated being treated like an invalid, even by this token of husbandly devotion and concern. There were many tears shed in the days that followed. My mind refused to accept bereavement and I seemed to hear my mother-by-adoption's voice by day while I dreamed of her constantly by night. Oh such glad dreams, for she was alive and well, and I was a girl again in Bessie's kingdom of delicious cooking aromas below-stairs at Satis House. All her precious letters I re-read and kissed, before tying them up in a black satin ribbon to be laid carefully away with girlhood's other treasures. Almost all I now retained of those happy days, was the book of Tennyson's poems, Pip's last gift to me.

And so another chapter of my life was sealed into its tomb and gone for ever.

Bentley's account of the funeral was impersonal, a mere chronicle of those present. 'Pip? Oh, the blacksmith's boy. I do not remember seeing him. Perhaps the extent of his injuries prevented his attendance.'

My thoughts on Pip, I only half heard of his visit to Mr Jaggers and the information that I was now a wealthy woman, my fortune thirty thousand pounds. But I would gladly have returned each golden guinea to have my mother-by-adoption alive again, I thought, and anxious for Pip's welfare, I resolved to write to him immediately.

Suddenly aware of my listless response to his enthusiastic plans for investment, Bentley sighed: 'But I weary you, my dear. Mr Jaggers will present all the details so that we can study them at leisure.' He paused, watching me intently.

'Is something wrong?'

He shook his head. 'Nothing. Merely that I find Mr Jaggers a very odd individual.'

'Indeed, I have seen little of him in recent years but remember finding him extremely formidable in my childhood.'

'He appeared quite out-of-sorts when I called upon him at Gerrard Street and kept me waiting longer than was civil. As for his housekeeper – tell me, have you ever seen the creature?'

'I haven't. But I would imagine anyone associated with

Mr Jaggers to have impeccable qualifications of respectability.'

'I don't know about respectability,' he said.

'For goodness sake, pray tell me what kind of a woman is she, for I am intrigued?'

'What kind of woman?' He gave me an odd look. 'Wild and strange indeed. On my rare visits to dinner when I was reading with Herbert Pocket's father, she was mostly relegated to the kitchen except for serving us at dinner. A handsome bold woman. Startop and I used to speculate if housekeeper was all she was to Jaggers, for I suspect now there is something deep, very deep indeed between them.'

His insinuation was plain although it was impossible for me to associate emotions of illicit passion for any woman burning within the stern and intimidating person of Mr Jaggers.

'She's a wild one, right enough. Wild and strange.' He repeated again, smiling at me thoughtfully. 'A common gipsy, by the looks of her.'

'You must be wrong. Mr Jaggers would never give such a low person houseroom, let alone put her in charge of his establishment. He is a gentleman, after all, a man of some consequence in the Law Courts.'

'Gentleman or no, I will swear there is some mystery there. Besides even gentleman have their lapses, my dear, for there is something of the gipsy in you too,' he added lightly.

'What nonsense you do talk, sir,' I said indignantly.

He wagged a finger at me. 'Ah, but there is, there is. And that was what first attracted me to you. That magnificent black hair of yours,' he said taking up a stray curl and kissing it, 'so wild and untamed, your fine dark eyes. So different from the pale Havishams or the lack-lustre Pockets, I'll swear. Even your name – Estella, so foreign and exotic.'

When I protested he held my swollen body close to him. 'Do not take the trouble to deny it, my dear. For that is the woman I desire,' he whispered. 'I want no simpering milk-maid sharing my bed.'

Although the desire I could still arouse in him pleased me with a sense of power, I misliked its source, loathing the very name gipsies, and his words seared me like a disfigurement I could never erase.

After a long absence, the evil Nightmare returned, with more than usual vehemence, as if lying dormant had fortified it with new strength and vigour. And Mr Jaggers had his part to play, washing his hands, smiling in his sinister knowing fashion. Although the frightening details denied my waking hours were revealed fully, it was to awake and find them lost once more. Only a faint disturbing echo, too elusive to grasp, remained to haunt me.

I knew that women suffered in childbirth, for the Bible taught such punishment was proper for the temptation and downfall of Adam. Expecting extreme but bearable discomfort, I was unprepared for the onslaught of such pain that I wept, not wanting to die. But when pain was exchanged for searing agony that tore my body apart, I prayed only that I would die – and quickly. At the end of many hours, at last my son was born.

Exhausted I slept and when I awoke Bentley was at my bedside. Watching him, jubilant with delight, with his son in his arms, I tried not to remember how often during that long and hideous labour when I had called out for help in my agony, his main concern had been with Doctor Bidwell shouting:

'The child, for God's sake, tell me about the child. Surely the child will live. You must save the child.'

Had that been a figment of my suffering, that I had become in his eyes a mere vessel to produce an heir to Drummle. Memory prompted no husbandly comfort or concern for the wife who had almost died giving him a son. All Bentley's attentions were centred upon 'young Hammond' and as the sound of drunken noisy celebrations drifted upstairs from where he caroused with his gambling cronies, I realized that my purpose served, I might no longer have existed at all.

In the next two days I rarely beheld him, except as a hovering shadow in the vicinity of Hammond's cot or as host to a group of grinning companions, staggering in to hiccup their slurred chorus of admiration for his son and heir. I was of little interest, except for those sober enough to remember their manners and enquire how I did. Out of politeness I bore the brief intrusions with passable good humour, for they soon returned to the more interesting matters of claret and cards.

The Atrocious Pair, once curiosity was satisfied, found no reason to sit by my bedside. I was glad to be spared any hypocrisy from that quarter knowing how Ruth must hate me for further destroying all her hopes of Bentley. Indeed, my most constant visitor was Sir Hammond, who displayed utmost concern about my welfare to the extent of leaving his bed each day. Propped up in a chair, carried between two servants, he visited me faithfully. Holding my hand, heaping praises upon this ordinary wifely achievement, he told me over and over how proud I had made him, that I was a grand little filly and scarcely even glanced at his new great-grandson asleep in his befrilled cot.

During that first week my other visitor was Herbert Pocket, to announce his forthcoming marriage. Thanks to Miss Havisham's legacy he and his Clara were departing these shores for Cairo where he was to open the Eastern Branch of Clarriker & Co. To the question predominant in my mind, he smiled sadly: 'Oh yes, Pip is in fairly good health but his spirits are low, deuced low, Estella. We are hoping to persuade him to come to Cairo with us and make a new life there.' I wished I had written that letter after Miss Havisham's funeral as I remembered that Herbert's thanks were also due Pip who, at our last sad meeting, had persuaded her to change her mind about Matthew Pocket.

Bentley had arrived home and hearing of my visitor, came upstairs to greet him. He must stay to dinner. We were not again to be alone, so my further questions about Pip went unasked and the conversation drifted to the fate of Satis House, to be demolished and sold for building materials, of its long romantic history with the Havishams, only the little Dower House would remain.

As Herbert took his departure I asked after Bessie. Herbert looked at me in blank amazement. 'She was well the last time we met, before Satis House went up for sale. She missed you greatly and even talked of paying you a visit. You have not heard from her?'

'Not a word.'

'I imagine her immediate task was to secure another situation. Besides people of her class are indifferent letter-writers,' said Bentley.

I had entrusted Bentley with a letter for her after the funeral, suggesting that if she had no situation then I would find her a place at Drummle Towers. As she had been the nurse of my childhood, I had imagined, wrongly it seemed, that she would be delighted to take charge of my child too.

It was during Herbert's visit that I first felt desperately ill, not in pain but hazy, fevered. By the following morning I was unable to feed Hammond who stubbornly refused nourishment. When evening came, I was in a coma, far from the world, delirious, drifting towards the gates beyond which there was no more pain.

When at last I had regained strength to open my eyes, it was to find Doctor Bidwell and Bentley staring into Hammond's cot.

'The child is dead.'

The child is dead. Those were the words that brought me back to life, to the agony of living after the cool serenity of dying.

'I do not believe you. It is not true – it cannot be true,' Bentley was shouting. 'You insane old devil, it is all your fault. I shall have the law on you for neglect.'

'Control yourself, sir,' said the doctor. 'For such behaviour will do you no good, nor will it bring the poor child back again. I beg you, sir, to find solace in the fact that your wife still lives. You must concentrate all your energies on seeing her restored to health and strength again. Consider yourself extremely fortunate not to have lost them both. It is up to you to give her the will to live.'

'It is her fault my son died. She would not feed him –'

'I advise you to watch your words, Mr Drummle. She could not feed him, and that through no fault of her own making.' I watched him put a steadying hand on Bentley's arm. 'I well understand your grief, sir, but your wife is still gravely ill and the greatest care must be taken if she is to recover.'

'Presuming that she does, how soon will she be fit to bear another child?' Bentley demanded.

Even the doctor was a little taken aback by this heartless cry, while I lay back against the pillows, too far gone even for tears. 'We must see her on her feet again before we consider such matters,' said Doctor Bidwell sternly. 'But console yourself, sir, with the melancholy fact that you are not alone in the role of grieving parent. All too many infants fail to survive their first weeks alas, and that is no fault of their mothers. As for Mrs Drummle, she is young and with care will soon be strong again.' He paused to let the words sink in before adding, 'We must all be patient, sir, and in God's good time, I dare say she will present you with many strong healthy sons and daughters.'

When I was fit enough to leave my bedroom and recline on a chaise longue in the drawing room, I spent many hours staring out of the window, brooding on the babe I had held so briefly and unsuccessfully to my breast. The babe they told me had turned such a strange blue colour before relinquishing the frail thread of life we had shared together. I wiped away tears that flowed, a river of endless grief through those sad, sad days. Had little Hammond been mine for a whole lifetime, had I remained at his side through infancy, boyhood and into man's estate, I could not have loved him more or missed him more passionately, than on the passing acquaintance of a few beguiling smiles that tore my heart.

Upon the heartless behaviour or want of tact expressed by the Atrocious Pair, I shall not dwell but say only that their lack of sympathy was not untinged with secret jubilation at my grievous loss. For I was no longer a

paragon in Bentley's eyes. I had failed him and they were
witnesses of the bitter reproaches he made no attempt to
conceal. My own disquiet was increased by the observation
that, his son's short earthly life ended, dearest Bentley now
applied himself with great diligence to strong drink. He
was frequently inebriated at luncheon, and incapable at
dinner, more often than not falling heavily asleep over the
soup. He rarely finished a meal without some calamity of
broken dish or spilt wine, or shouting drunken fury, calmly
received by his mother with reproachful looks in my
direction.

As the months passed, I reached a stage of being grateful
when the servants put him to bed and I was spared one
other night of his humiliating and futile attempts to father
another son. By the time I was strong enough to endure
such odious attentions by night and my duties as mistress
of Drummle Towers by day, a post which Bentley's mother
relinquished with ill grace, I was forced to admit that the
bridegroom with whom I had entered these portals with
hopes of a happy future, had vanished entirely. As if such
mechanism had been forcefully removed from his still
handsome but increasingly florid exterior, in much the
same way as the broken inside of the once valuable French
clock swept from the drawing-room mantelpiece in one of
his drunken rages. Tenderness had long since flown out of
the window. The word love was a stranger between us and
even trying to understand, I found it hard to forgive his
punishment, his brutality on those melancholy occasions
each month when I was forced to confirm that his attempts
at paternity had again been unsuccessful.

The third year of marriage slid to its close by which time I
despaired of producing another child and grew daily more
aware that my husband's shortcomings included squan-
dering away my fortune in gambling.

Our absences from Drummle had been rare. Short visits
to friendly neighbours, with a ready pack of cards for my
husband, summarized our activities. As for Sir Hammond,

he amazed everyone by exhibiting unmistakeable signs of achieving his century. Clinging relentlessly to life, battered and beseiged by every infirmity, yet determined to see a great-grandchild before he died, he grinned at me, declaring: 'It is all your fault, m'dear, that I'm here today. Before you came my life didn't seem worth the candle, none of Them would have shed a tear had it been snuffed out. But you changed all that. You gave a tired old man something to feast his eyes on – a pretty face does wonders, especially when a smile and a kind heart shines out of it.' Leaning over he took my hand, and I found neither this nor his tendency to lewd conversation vexed me any longer.

Since my baby died a deep affection had grown between us and I had introduced him to my book of Tennyson's poems. He loved to have me read them and with a memory amazing for one so old, was soon quoting several stanzas which he had learned by heart.

When we read in *The Times* of the Prince Consort's exciting plans for the Queen's Great Exhibition, and that our dear Alfred Tennyson had been made Poet Laureate, we were both as jubilant as if this honour had been conferred upon a personal friend. Soon we had added *In Memoriam* to our afternoon readings. There was so much, almost too much, that I found personally poignant and often, too often, I brushed away a tear:

'I hold it true, whate'er befall;
I feel it, when I sorrow must;
'Tis better to have loved and lost
Than never to have loved at all.'

And as if written for me alone, the verse:

'And was the day of my delight
As pure and perfect as I say?
The very source and fount of Day
Is dash'd with wandering isles of night.'

Alas, my own isles of night seemed inescapable. And such

111

was my melancholy state of mind, when to my astonishment I discovered that I was again pregnant.

Only optimism bordering on idiocy might have expected news of my interesting condition to improve my husband's irascible behaviour, his total lack of responsibility and constant insobriety. To have pretended tenderness in the circumstances, would have been a greater hypocrisy than either of us could have managed.

The approaching birth did unite us briefly, and when at last, after considerably less suffering than before, I was able to sit up in bed almost immediately and share my husband's rejoicing over the successful delivery of a son and heir to Drummle.

His delight included everyone, myself too and I regarded him almost wistfully, pleased by this miraculous return to geniality. Perhaps it meant that I was forgiven for keeping him waiting so long for his expectations. Perhaps even, whispered a tiny voice deep in my heart, all was not lost after all, and Bentley might yet learn to be a gentle, kind, loving husband and I, a devoted wife.

Dear God, how I needed such consolation. And so much more. So very much more I thought as I clasped my son to my breast, the bruising marks of birth still upon him, and stroked his downy head, I wondered what pains did these poor wee mites suffer coming into this world? If they could talk, then they might well have a story to equal a mother's birth-pangs. Again and again I kissed him, considered the names that Bentley had suggested: Alexander, James, Hammond – no, not Hammond, please not that ill-fated name again. His forehead was damp and even as I looked on him, his tiny face began to undergo a rapid change, a strange bluish colour tinged his complexion, he seemed to have difficulty in breathing.

I listened unable to believe what was happening. Suddenly I screamed, shook the tiny body as one might a watch that had suddenly stopped ticking. And even as my wails of terror echoed through the house, the tiny heart beat no more and his head lolled, eyes still open, but oh, so still, against my arm.

Any words to describe that bitter grief would be inadequate, any suffering that still lay ahead, immeasurable beside that sense of loss. Bentley perhaps suffered even more than I did for he locked himself in the library and drowned his sorrows in a doleful procession of vintage ports and clarets carried up from the cellars by the servants, seeing no one although I begged to be let in, feeling that if we cried together, we might ease the pain. Eventually he emerged, stony faced and silent as one struck dumb. Again I pleaded with him, weeping, but he pushed me brusquely aside and I bowed my head to the inevitable truth. There existed no hope for our marriage and instead of being united by our grief, little by little, each passing day, he retreated from me, and the chasm widened between us.

One day the doctor's visit to me concluded with a demand to consult my husband. I was not long kept in ignorance of the reason for this request. Indeed the whole of Drummle Towers, alerted by the disturbance, heard every syllable.

The library door flew open and Bentley who had been shaken into sobriety was also seizing this unique opportunity violently to shake the poor doctor.

'What is it you are saying, man? Unlikely – unlikely that Mrs Drummle will ever produce a healthy child.'

The doctor tried to hush him with a frantic indication of my presence. 'Hush, sir, hush. I beg of you – this is very distressing.'

Bentley caught sight of me and scowled. 'Is it to be a secret between us then? She might as well know. Hear this fool of a doctor we have entrusted with your life. Hear what he has to say to me, your husband. That you are unlikely – madam, yes unlikely – ever to produce a living child.' My horrified cry at this dire announcement went unheard as Bentley roared: 'Now hear what I have to say to you, Doctor Bidwell. I have suffered your infernal incompetence long enough and you will never again be admitted to Drummle Towers. And before you go, I will tell you that you are wrong – wrong, do you hear. Look at my wife, you old fool, a young healthy woman. No one in his right mind could believe that a woman so endowed with life and beauty, so robust and vigorous, could be barren –'

I heard no more, the hall swirled dangerously around me and when I next opened my eyes I was on the chaise longue with the doctor applying smelling salts. There was nothing I could say, I could only weep for myself and apologize for my husband's outrageous behaviour.

'Do not take that to heart, my dear,' said Doctor Bidwell with a wan smile. 'Such moments are all part of a doctor's day, and I assure you that yours is not the first distraught husband to become abusive in such sorry circumstances. Poor souls, poor souls. A terrible thing to face such a truth when so many expectations hang upon producing a son.'

'It is true then, doctor?' I whispered.

'I fear so, Mrs Drummle. A common case, which we see often but do not yet understand. Some malformation in the infant's blood circulation is at fault. In many cases, the first child survives but subsequent ones die at birth or soon afterwards.'

Somehow I lived through those terrible days, clinging for my survival to the frail belief that no misfortune awaiting me in the future could ever be worse than the grief I had already suffered. Would that I had lacked a heart to be broken as my mother-by-adoption had intended, now that I had learned that the intimacy of the married state can exist without love and I was not even to have the comfort of a little child to fill the void. I would have had much to tell her about the folly of those precious years wasted by her in requiem for man's fickle love.

> 'The seasons bring the flower again,
> And bring the firstling to the flock;
> And in the dusk of thee, the clock
> Beats out the little lives of men.'

And so less poetically for me, with Tennyson to comfort my spirit and Sir Hammond to comfort 'the slings and arrows' of everyday life at Drummle, I found blessing in my surroundings and took heart from the peaceful gardens outside, the growing library indoors. We were not entirely removed from civilisation, we received *The Times* and the *Illustrated London News*, while *Household Words* and the *Englishwoman's Domestic Magazine*, constantly added to my information and education.

As for Bentley and myself, life was not quite so dismal as I had imagined, once we had learned to accept our childless future. To the society around us, we continued to present a civilized front and I was only depressed when I realized that this was yet another charade in the fabric of my life. But as time went by we were respectful to each other and very occasionally, passionate. The result of these rare bouts of kindness between us resulted in two further pregnancies, neither of which alas, came to term and thereby made the gulf between us even wider and, for a while, more bitter than before.

Occasionally we visited London and as guests of the noble lord who was our nearest neighbour, attended the great tragedian William Charles Macready's farewell performance of 'Macbeth' at the Drury Lane Theatre and also the public dinner afterwards in his honour. There I was enthralled to have a glimpse of my hero Tennyson, as well as two other literary giants of the day. Thackeray, whose novels I greatly admired was one of the speakers, lofty and eloquent, while Dickens, Macready's great friend, laced his talk with delightful shafts of wit.

In October of that year we again accompanied our friends to the Crystal Palace's Great Exhibition which had been open since May. I had read so many glowing accounts of its magnificence that I had to confess myself disappointed in the reality. I had not regained my full strength after my last miscarriage and had little to spare for mingling with large crowds and walking down apparently endless lanes of mighty eminences in steel and metal. Although I appreciated that machines were the new wonder of the civilized world, I failed to find anywhere justification for the words used to describe the Exhibition as: 'magic – Aladdin's cave of delights – the Jin's palace –

this exotic fairyland'. Such descriptions raised in the female mind, wonders of a quite different kind: costly jewels, fashions in lace and satin, millinery and boots and rare ornamental treasures.

The day was unseasonably hot, the sun's rays through massive areas of glass brought about many casualties of fainting in the seething crowd. Exhausted, I was fearful that I should shortly be adding to their number, when above the heat and the din, there were shouts of alarm. A cry that all present heeded:

'The glass. Look at the glass. The glass is breaking. The walls are caving in. Watch out –'

We needed no second bidding. Bentley seized my arm and we joined the mad stampede towards the nearest exit, our rout accompanied by quite dreadful crashing sounds behind us which betokened the upset of a stand of valuable French china. To our horrified ears in that moment of panic, the sound was indistinguishable from shattering glass walls.

Safely outside, expecting the whole structure to collapse like a pack of cards, we discovered the innocent cause of the riot. The Duke of Wellington, now very old and frail was paying his final visit to the Exhibition and had been mobbed and cheered to the echo by well-wishers, their cries misinterpreted as imminent disaster, by those too distant to observe the true cause of the commotion.

And now we were rewarded by the sight of an ancient and very angry man being carried out of the Exhibition protesting violently, but firmly clutched by six sturdy policemen who were his escort.

I was glad to have seen him, but sorry that this undignified scene was how I remembered the noble Duke who died some months later. He represented an extinct world of chivalry and the *Illustrated London News* produced a black-bordered supplement, as if he had been Royalty. He was deeply mourned by everyone including Sir Hammond, who had oft shaken him by the hand:

'When we were both young, m'dear, and shared many a convivial evening. He was a naughty man too where the ladies were concerned. But popular, always popular, despite the occasional scandal. Indeed, the common folk think more of the likes of Dizzy and a real dyed-in-the-wool Englishman like Wellington, than they do of our Queen with her foreign relatives, and her German prince.'

Gladstone was also popular with Sir Hammond, especially when he announced that Income Tax at sevenpence in the pound was to be reduced and finally abolished. Alas, this good intention was defeated by the outbreak of hostilities and by the time troops were embarking for the Crimea, my only true friend at Drummle, Sir Hammond peacefully breathed his last. I missed him dreadfully for over the years a rare companionship had developed between us.

As I held his hand for the last time, he grumbled: 'You're the best of the lot of us, m'dear, and I don't care who knows it. Far too good to be a Drummle, far too good for that lad of mine, he don't appreciate you. Never did like his mother, I can tell you. Always a fool. As for the gel, she should have been sent packing long ago – trouble maker she is, if you ask me.'

Over his grave I read, as he had requested his favourite verses from In Memoriam.

I was now Lady Drummle. I had achieved my ambition to marry a Lord, while my husband celebrated his baronetcy by selling vast areas of the estate to settle his ever increasing gambling debts. His ambition gratified, but without an heir, his part in the dynasty would end with his death and all would go to Wilfred of whom there was disturbing news. Lately in Italy, he had eloped with a rich aristocrat's daughter. That this romance was of the variety classified as 'whirlwind' was further confirmed by their return to England with a child.

'A child,' screamed Bentley's Mama.

'A daughter, Mama,' he said heavily, laying aside the letter. 'Only a son can inherit Drummle.'

It was soon afterwards that my illness began. There had been a mild cholera in the village that long hot summer and my malady was presumed to be the last dregs as other members of the household were unafflicted. It began with sickness, inability to retain the food I ate, a condition aggravated by disillusion, anxiety, unhappiness, those destructors of the spirit far more fatal than the ills of the flesh.

I lay listless on my couch, however, long after I should have been up and about again and was very little interested in what went on around me, day or night. My husband had removed himself to another bedroom at the outset of my illness and showed no anxiety to return to his connubial couch. For this small mercy, I was grateful. I wished for no more sorrowful pregnancies. Soon I would be thirty, middle-aged, my life half over. And what purpose had it served? Even that of being the instrument of an old woman's vengeance, I had failed.

One day, very sick again, I returned to my bed and had almost made up my mind that there I would rise no more, when something happened to change my mind regarding the nature of my illness.

The new young Doctor Fraser had replaced Doctor Bidwell, who had faithfully served three generations as the Drummle physician and had been called to attend me. As he left my room, some curiosity made me follow him, anxious to know what matter my husband wished to discuss with him.

To this day, I can still see the two men in earnest conversation and hear Bentley's voice, which he had never learned to lower, echoing up the staircase: ·

'She talks of doing away with herself, putting an end to her life. We are all greatly distressed and keep a careful watch. But you cannot think what a nightmare it is.'

The doctor laid a hand on his arm. 'Such thoughts frequently attack even healthy young women when their spirits are low. In my experience these threats are rarely carried out.'

She talks of putting an end to her life. As the door closed on the doctor, the words seemed to echo over and over. I clutched the banister. *She talks of doing away with herself.* Never, never had I said such words. I stood trembling, with wild beating heart, watching Bentley as he stared out of the window rubbing his chin and looking oddly thoughtful.

And it was as if I could see clearly into his mind at that moment as I relived the monstrous chronicle of his small cruelties throughout our marriage, and his total indifference to a wife's suffering when our babies had not lived. Unlike Pip who had loved me wildly, blindly for myself alone, Bentley had seen physical beauty, health and vigour only as the potential bearer of his sons. With a hot rush of sickness, I realized the danger in which I stood, that my inability to produce an heir for Drummle Towers had driven my strong, virile husband to the very brink of mental instability.

Suddenly the drawing-room door opened and his mother beckoned him inside, her gesture urgent, furtive and to me, the watcher, significant. For instead of urging restraint, I guessed that she was feeding her son's growing anger and discontent to the very brink of madness.

Later that night, the dogs' barking disturbed me and too anxious and afraid for sleep, I opened my bedroom door and saw from Bentley's room, a figure emerging. It was Ruth and she came out empty-handed, carrying no tray, and looking almost furtively around her. Was Bentley ill? What other cause could have taken her to him at three in the morning? Although I suspected that he might have a mistress among the ranks of our hard-living neighbours, it had never occurred to me that he would entertain thoughts of his cousin in that role. By his own admission, he had never considered her in the least attractive. Had he done so, surely he would never have married me and caused his mother needless anguish.

She talks of putting an end to her life. The sinister implication of such words filled me with a resolve to be especially watchful and exercise extreme caution from that listless daybed where no one took the slightest notice of me. My observations were rewarded by the interception of many fond glances and lingering touches between Bentley and Ruth, far exceeding the normal demonstrations of affection between these cousins sharing a lifetime under the same roof. Besides, I had long since discovered the Drummles to be abnormally lacking in such overtures. I also noticed on Edwina Drummle's face, a wicked flicker of triumph as she also observed the pair with secret gratification.

I could not pretend to feelings of outrage. If Bentley found comfort in his cousin then I had least cause to object since I no longer fulfilled, or wished to fulfil, my role as his wife. Indeed, I soon discovered that I was a beneficiary under this new wave of guilty love. The Atrocious Pair were suddenly solicitous for my well-being, forever tucking rugs about me and bringing cups of herb tea, vile-tasting but with assurances of health-bringing strength.

Bentley's interest extended to a birthday present, an occasion which he had ignored for the past three years.

Kissing my forehead, he said: 'Come, I have something to show you.' Taking my hand he led me out into the garden where the stable boy held the rein of a fine chestnut mare.

'Her name is Star – and she is yours.'

'Mine?' I cried in delight.

'Of course, that is why I named her Star – for Estella.'

'Oh, Bentley, how kind. But surely – surely?' The mare looked valuable but I could hardly reproach him for such extravagance.

He guessed what I was about to say and frowned. 'Nothing is too valuable for my wife.' With an arm around me, his cheek resting tenderly against mine, he said: 'I thought we might resume our old habit of an early morning ride before breakfast. We have spent little time together of late, for which I am sorry. And now that we must reconcile ourselves to being childless –'

'Oh, Bentley –'

'No, no, my dear. You are not to apologize. You have done your best, more than your best. You have suffered greatly in the process, both in mind and body, I fear,' he added with a deep sigh. 'But that is all over. Now we are to be sensible, reconcile ourselves to growing old as good companions, eh Estella?'

'I would like that.'

'I thought you would. And we will begin tomorrow. Fresh air and exercise will soon bring the roses back to your cheeks. You must get well again, soon, my dear, to please your old husband.'

This new smiling Bentley was irresistible. Ashamed, I thought of how I had allowed my own sufferings to malign him, to blind me to manly pride humiliated by our inability to provide an heir. Could past condemnations of his conduct be due indeed to hallucinations wrought by melancholy illness which perhaps extended to imagined wrongs, of a conspiracy in the house to do me harm? Now my husband indicated that he wished only for our happiness. Very well, for my part I was ready to make excuses for everybody, eager to make a fresh start, to live again.

When Star threw me, I was only bruised slightly but my confidence was shaken. She had an uncertain temper and was much harder to handle than my gentle old mare sold during my sad childbearing years when Bentley, supported by Doctor Bidwell, hinted that riding might cause me to miscarry in the early days of pregnancy. I confided my fears to Bentley who insisted that I must persevere since Star came from excellent stables and had been guaranteed as trustworthy.

'She is a little spirited, but that is all to the good. Consider her a challenge, my dear, prove yourself her mistress and she will soon obey you. Come, we will race to the parkland boundary and back.'

The autumn morning was dour, the parkland shrouded in mist which would turn to rain before midday. In the stables I regarded the big mare with some apprehension. She loomed above me, larger than ever and I was far from happy about racing her. But I allowed Bentley to assist me into the saddle, only a little less alarmed at being thrown for I was an experienced horsewoman, than of throwing him into one of his sullen rages which might last for days, and thereby losing the little headway we had made.

'Off you go.' He slapped Star's rump with his riding crop

and as I rode out ahead, I looked back and saw him rein in to speak to the stable boy. As we galloped into the parkland I noticed that I was well in the lead. Was he letting me win, humouring me by holding back his own mount? The movement of glancing over my shoulder made the saddle slide dangerously. The stirrups were loose but Bentley had assured me that he checked them. The next moment I was sliding ...

Falling ... out of control ...

The ground came violently up to meet me and screaming, I was dragged along by the still galloping Star. By a tremendous effort I managed to free my trapped foot. Sobbing, I lay among the trees, bruised and shaken, but otherwise unhurt and grateful for the sound of Bentley's approach.

I sat up, calling to him. I expected concern, not the ferocious expression of anger. In that one sickening moment, I saw that he had no intention of reining in to rescue me. Striking his horse savagely, he was riding me down.

With a scream of terror, in that last instant as the horse towered above me, I rolled aside and instinctively raised the riding crop I still clutched. I struck the stallion in a sensitive area and with a shrill whinny of pain, the beast kicked up its heels and Bentley shot over his head.

He lay still.

For a long time I huddled trembling where I had fallen, terrified to investigate in case he was merely stunned. I was cold, so cold and he so unmoving, I thought he must be dead, as through my sickened mind, raced a procession of his kindnesses lately shown and the true reason for my mysterious nausea. Now I knew what a trusting fool I had been. Bentley, desperate for an heir, intended to be rid of me, to marry his cousin.

Dear God, dear God, that I could have been so simple. And now he lay dead twenty feet away from me. Dead with all my own hopes and dreams. The rain had begun, heavy, drenching. I was chilled to the bone and at last rose painfully to my feet. With one last hesitant look at that still white face, I limped back through the parkland until I found the drive leading to the stables. There I gave the alarm and told the lad to ride fast as he could for Doctor Fraser. Then I walked across the courtyard to the house. Stumbling, sick and faint, I climbed the front steps.

'Bentley has had an accident. I have sent for the doctor,' I gasped to Edwina Drummle and hardly noticed how she screamed or that Ruth sobbing: 'No – no,' slipped to the floor in a dead faint.

I gasped out more directions to the servants and sank down at the foot of the stairs. Climbing them was out of the question. And there I waited until they carried Bentley home and laid him on the sofa in his study. No one came near me. I might have disturbed a gallery of marble statues. It was not merely that I presented the picture of a drowned rat staggering torn and dishevelled into the hall, but that I was not the one they expected to return alone and a part of my mind, still alert, considered their guilty faces. They told me all I wanted to know. That they also were in the plot for my death.

Doctor Fraser arrived. A brief examination revealed that Bentley still lived. 'Alive, but I fear, his injuries are grave. You must be brave, Lady Drummle. We must just wait and pray.'

'If my son dies,' shrieked Edwina Drummle, 'mark my words, doctor, I hold that woman – that woman – responsible. She is his murderess. She wishes to destroy him and leave me, his mother and his poor orphaned cousin, without a roof over our heads.'

The doctor spoke soothingly to her, his embarrassed nods and wan smiles assurance that I was not to take such hysteria seriously and that I was in no danger of anyone accusing me of murder.

As for the orphaned cousin, I heard her screaming in the night. The whole house was alerted to her condition, as she miscarried during the early hours of a male child. Bentley's son.

And as for myself, I was chilled to the bone. I thought I would never be warm again. Shivering I went to my bed and hoped to die and end it all. But as the fever took me, I ran down a long tunnel and Pip was waiting for me in the light. We were in Satis House but I tormented and tortured him no longer, for I loved him and was his.

Later I learned that the doctor had been informed I was not at home when he made his visit to confirm that my husband was both paralysed and speechless. His spine was injured, he was unlikely to walk again.

In my bedroom maids attended sluggishly to my needs, as I weakly summoned them with the bellpull. I grew weaker, steadily drifting into a coma of unconsciousness.

'They are going to let you die.' The words were spoken clearly in my ear, the voice my beloved mother-by-adoption. 'Don't let them, Estella. I didn't rear you for them to destroy. Fight them, fight them, you can win, dearest child.'

I opened my eyes. I had been dreaming. I was alone and the fire long ashes, had not been relit. But the curtains billowed, suggesting that someone had tiptoed in after dark and opened the window, allowing the cold damp air to add to the icy atmosphere.

All seemed lost. Bentley a helpless invalid, the Atrocious Pair plotting my demise, for Ruth might still marry him if he recovered. If only they were rid of me.

In moments of lucidity, I plotted my escape and even dreamed that I got up dressed and slipped out of Drummle Towers, running down the drive with a horseman, Bentley, in relentless pursuit. But even had I the strength in reality, where could I run to? Pip, Herbert Pocket, they were my friends, but both were abroad. Bessie, friend and protector of my childhood had deserted me, ignoring my letters, as if with Miss Havisham's death, I too had ceased to exist.

Satis House could no longer be my refuge and if I escaped to the Dower House, who was to protect me there? Murder would come easily to those whose plans had been thwarted, and two golden guineas in some villainous hand, a break-in during the night ...

I shuddered. Easier by far to be rid of me in Rochester than at Drummle.

My only hope lay with Mr Jaggers. But how was I to reach him?

'Dear God, give me strength,' I cried. And my voice was heard. Strength came from a most unlikely quarter as one afternoon I stirred from my slumbers and saw a smiling angel at my bedside. A guardian angel in the unlikely form of the Small Person, Jolly.

'Drink this, Miss Estella, we'll soon have you on your feet, strong and hearty again.'

No one had addressed me as Miss Estella in years. I was dead and in Paradise, along with those who had loved me long ago. As for Jolly, she was almost as insubstantial as the wraith of my mother-by-adoption who had summoned my feeble being back to life. To life. But what had I to live for?

My shoulder was seized none too gently. 'Wake up, Miss Estella dear. You must take some of this, just a spoonful. It will make you feel ever so much better.' A hand behind my head and the warm liquid in my mouth. 'There now, didn't I tell you? Another sip. There's my good lady. And another. There. You're fair starved, thin as a winter rabbit.'

Truly I now needed no urging and muttered gratefully: 'So good, Jolly. So good. I thank you, for this tastes so different.'

'And so it should. For you must remember this, Miss Estella. It is Bessie's recipe, she showed me how to make it.'

Bessie. How was Bessie? And more important, where was she now when I most needed her? And Pip – Pip? But the words refused to form themselves into coherent speech. No matter, no matter. And for the first time in many weeks, I closed my eyes, tired and content. I was safe. I had been sent a friend.

'Don't go to sleep for a moment yet, Miss Estella. The housekeeper has come back and they will throw me out if you don't speak up for me. You do want me to stay, don't you, Miss Estella?'

The door opened and Mrs Slagsby stormed in. She did not even glance in my direction but demanded of Jolly:

'What is this? How dare you enter this house without permission. Leave this instant, or we will have the law on you.'

'Stop – stop,' I was amazed by the force of my words and so was the housekeeper who stepped back and now stared open-mouthed towards my bed. Her gulping, horrified looks suggested that she too was in the plot and had received instructions to find me dead when she returned.

'Jolly is to remain, as my personal maid –'

'But – but this is unheard of. Who is this creature and where are her references? The mistress will hear about this –'

'Jolly was my maid in my pre-marriage days –'

'Was she now? We'll see what the mistress has to say about that.'

'May I remind you that I am mistress of Drummle Towers and that I could send you packing this instant if I so wished,' I said sternly marvelling at where I got the strength to add: 'Indeed I think it not a bad idea, what say you, Jolly?'

My new maid nodded enthusiastically and Mrs Slagsby snorted angrily. 'Very well, she can remain until his lordship's mother returns.' The door snapped shut while Jolly tucking the blankets round me whispered in a frightened voice:

'What's it all about, Miss Estella? Seems to a body that you are a prisoner in your own house?'

'That's about it. Oh dear –' The sustained effort of talking had wearied me. My eyelids grew heavy and clutching Jolly's hand I whispered: 'Please stay with me. Don't let them send you away. And I beg you, write to Mr Pip – tell him – tell him –'

When I next opened my eyes, it was to find Jolly once again flourishing the soup spoon. I discovered I was hungry and again pleading with her not to leave me, I fell into the first normal sleep since my illness. While I was awake Jolly stayed at my side. Although she frequently applied the bell-pull to summon maid, warming-pan or fresh linen, every bite of food I consumed was prepared by herself.

'What of Mr Pip? Did you write to him?'

She bit her lip, frowning. 'No, Miss Estella. You see, I don't know where to find him.' And she told me how she had left Mrs Brandley soon after my marriage for another position. To take care of an elderly person, great-aunt of the young man who was walking out with her and who lived, by one of God's miracles, in the village not two miles distant from Drummle Towers.

'I was always a great walker, Miss Estella, and it pleased me when my young man came avisiting, to bring him to look through these handsome gates. He does love the story of Satis House and Miss Havisham's strange goings-on. "Go on, you're teasing a chap with your tall stories, Flo," he'd say.'

'Flo? Is that your name?' I had never known her first name.

'Actually it's Flora, Miss.'

'So be it. Go ahead with your story, Flora.'

She smiled at me shyly. 'One day, perhaps you'll meet my Jim and be able to tell him every word about Satis House was gospel truth.'

'I certainly hope I shall. Where is he now?'

She sighed. 'Gone to fight the Ruskies for Her Majesty. He's a soldier in the Scots Fusiliers. But he has it on good authority, that the war will be over soon and then we are to be wed.'

'I am very glad for you,' I said taking her hand. 'But tell me, what news of Bessie? We seem to have lost touch.'

She looked surprised. 'Did you not know, Miss Estella? Bessie's gone back to Derbyshire where she lived as a girl. I thought she would have written to you. I'm right surprised, she thought the world of you, Miss Estella.'

'She used to write to me regularly. And then suddenly all her letters stopped.'

'That they didn't, Miss. Why, she said the same thing to me. Made excuses that you must be too busy but that there would be a letter any day.'

I need look no further for excuses. The Atrocious Pair had seen to it. And that I found almost the worst of their iniquities to forgive. When I asked what miracle had brought her to Drummle Towers so opportunely, Flora Jolly shook her head.

'Jim's great-aunt died a couple of months past, near ninety she was and a right Tartar too. She said Jim and me were to have the cottage on account of taking care of her at the last. But after the funeral we discovered that long before my Jim was born she had left everything to another nephew and hadn't changed the original will. A poor clerk, he is, middle-aged with a wife and eight of a family to support. Well, the cottage was his by right, and 'sides, he needed it more than we did, at present, so I decided to pack my bag and look for another situation until Jim comes back.' She shook her head. 'I don't know where I found the courage to walk down the drive that day, really I don't. Sounds foolish, Miss Estella, but I felt as if – as if Miss Havisham was whispering in my ear –'

I gave her a startled look. Perhaps Miss Havisham was in charge of my guardian angel, and if I were to believe the experiences of Flora Jolly and myself, still powerful beyond the grave. For she who had willed me to live would have found it an easy matter to propel the Small Person down the drive to save my life. For save my life, Flora Jolly undoubtedly had.

An extraordinary woman, Alicia Havisham. I found myself reliving the day she had cried out to Pip: 'If she favours you, love her. If she wounds you, love her. If she tears your heart to pieces, love her. I adopted her to be loved. I bred her and educated her to be loved.'

A tear slid down my cheek. 'Oh dear mother-of-my-adoption, so much for your vengeance. See what bitter harvest your poor Estella has reaped. For every word of your dire prophecy came to pass, except that the heartless cruel lover was Bentley Drummle and I, not Pip, was the helpless victim of your schemes.'

The story I heard from Flora suggested a sinister plot. On the day of her arrival, the Atrocious Pair were absent in London on a visit to dressmakers and milliners since Drummle boasted only a tiny village shop. Bentley had been left in the care of the two nurses paid to watch over him night and day. To very little purpose it seemed, for he remained paralysed and speechless. In their absence, Bentley's sick and ailing wife was left in the care of Mrs Slagsby who promptly decided to visit her relatives some miles away.

It was Flora who whispered: 'I think they were hoping to come back and find you had passed on, Miss Estella, you were that far gone when I found you. And They would have been quite safe, since They could not be blamed, They had not even been in the county, much less the house at the time.'

And every instinct told me she was right.

'They were starving you to death, maybe even poisoning you,' she continued thoughtfully, 'of that I'm certain sure, though we could never prove it. From the moment I saw you lying there in a freezing room, I was never in any doubt about that.'

I looked at her. A small frail pale creature of no significance, Miss Havisham's Small Person had filled out a little with the passing years. But what she still lacked in stature she made up for in strength and determination and her sterling worth had been recognized. Flora Jolly would not go unloved. Her Jim would see to that.

'And what's more, I suspect from things I've heard that your ma-in-law and your husband's cousin had no reason to love you. They wanted rid of you – as for the poor gentleman, what could he do to help you?'

What indeed? Some day I might tell her the truth about that poor gentleman. Meanwhile, as daily I grew stronger, stronger too became my resolve to leave this house for ever. Let the Atrocious Pair have their wish, let Edwina have Drummle Towers and Ruth the poor twilight creature who had once been my husband. His desire for my death had culminated in this sorry state of events, and he had been his own executioner. But should he recover, I would never again rest easily in my bed at night as long as he lived and walked the earth.

Yet under the laws of property relating to Married Women, he still had the power of life and death over me.

Everything I owned was his, including every piece of jewellery I had inherited from Miss Havisham, even down to the clothes on my back. Still the poor wretch had punishment enough, nor did I wish revenge upon the Atrocious Pair for the harm they had done me. I wished only to be free and as far from them as possible. Since the day they returned and found me still alive and Jolly in command, they proclaimed their own guilt in making no move to dismiss her. Had they been innocent, their righteous indignation would have been boundless, for they were never slow at forcing confrontations with me. Instead they had never once tried to gain access to my sickroom.

Flora approved my plan to leave Drummle and observing my confused state of mind, immediately began to direct operations for our stealthy departure.

'We should go direct to Mr Jaggers.' (And he would know where to find Pip, I thought triumphantly.) 'My Jim is kin by marriage to one of his clerks. You can be sure, they will see that no harm befalls you, Miss Estella,' she said proudly and added with a wistful smile. 'There might even be word waiting for me with Jim's cousin at Walworth.'

'That seems a rather inconvenient arrangement. Had you no address he could write to?'

'No, Miss Estella. 'Sides, that would be little use to either of us, since I can't read or write,' she added uncomfortably.

'You mean that you never learned?'

'No, Miss Estella. But Jim's to teach me when we're married.'

Another cloud of guilt descended upon me. Not only had my shameful treatment of the Small Person failed lamentably in ordinary human kindness through the years, to the extent of being ignorant of her first name, it had also failed to bestow upon her one of the greatest gifts to civilized society, the joys of reading. I resolved to begin her education as soon as we reached London and safety.

The carriage was ordered for a shopping expedition. While we waited I wondered whether any curiosity would be expressed, or any pretext made to delay us. All communication between Mrs Drummle and myself was conveyed by maids, and Flora reported that my command had been obeyed and she had secretly deposited our luggage in a disused dovecot along the drive, where it could be uplifted upon our exit. With no intention of returning, I also selected some of my favourite jewels.

Part Three
Flight

Our destination was Mr Jaggers' chambers at Bartholomew Close. It would have needed more presumption than I possessed in my entire nature to call this formidable man my sole remaining friend. But he had known me longer than anyone else save Miss Havisham, since he had arranged my adoption. In the circumstances, I felt it reasonable to suppose that he would also regard it as a matter of honour to see that no harm befell me. With Miss Havisham dead, I hoped he might see fit to confirm the details of my parentage, vouchsafed by Bessie, that Mr Arthur Havisham and his noble wife were my true parents. Mr Jaggers was also the only person competent to advise on what course of action might be taken by an absconding wife, within the limits of the law.

Such were my thoughts on the journey. When we reached London, six o'clock had already chimed and dusk was gathering. In the meaner streets, lurked the torn and ragged shadows of the city's poor, the wretches of the night. My heart failed me at the prospect of proceeding any further, beyond the enveloping gloom into the less salubrious area near Smithfield, and thereby missing Mr Jaggers, his business for the day satisfactorily concluded.

135

To the coachman, I gave revised instructions for Mr Jaggers' residence where Flora stepped out and rapped upon the front door. She had to repeat the action twice before any came to answer her summons, although I had observed by a twitch of the curtains upstairs and the brief appearance of a face hastily withdrawn, that the house was not completely deserted.

At last the door was opened, with reluctance considering the time that elapsed between this action and the rearrangement of the curtains. A lengthy interchange ensued. Should I step out and firmly state my case? Suddenly a head poked out of the door, gazed fixedly towards the carriage. A woman's face, a mane of streaming black hair. I found myself remembering how her appearance had intrigued Bentley as I leaned forward for a closer look.

At the same moment the woman stared hard over Flora's shoulder. Our eyes met and regardless of distance a chill of foreboding seized me. What was it about this woman Bentley had described as 'a wild strange creature' that reached out to touch me? But upon the instant the head was withdrawn, the door closed more sharply in Flora's face than I considered polite.

'I am to tell you that Mr Jaggers is not yet returned. His whereabouts are uncertain but you should wait upon him at his chambers.'

At this hour of the evening? I shuddered. 'I suppose that was his housekeeper.'

'So she said, Miss Estella.'

'An odd sort of person she looked.'

'Aye, odd indeed. Perhaps even a little mad.' And a glimmer of amusement flickered across Flora's face, to be hastily suppressed, as she studied me, frowning in the manner of one who would care to say a lot more on the subject.

'Well, Flora?'

Hastily, she turned away, gazed out of the window. 'Nothing, Miss Estella.' And then somewhat lamely: 'Have you noticed what handsome doors there is hereabouts?

And what a pleasant street Mr Jaggers lives in?'

But as we drove away something made me stare up at his windows. In the dusk, the curtains again twitched nervously. So our curiosity was mutual.

At Little Britain we were ushered into a room which by its sheer bleakness must have struck all hope from those luckless criminals who sought Mr Jaggers' advice. Its shape was uneven, indeed its walls caught together and hung from a skylight, whose many scars and cracks were wretchedly patched with brown paper. This precaution served only to encourage rather than dispel the strong gusts of air descending upon our heads.

A series of cardboard boxes with contents feverishly and inadequately packed plus a few lifeless limp bundles of papers, stranded on shelves here and there, served as furnishings. A desk with horsehair chair of forbidding dimensions whose origins suggested the undertaker's parlour, its padding kept severely in check by large brass screws, arousing melancholy thoughts of coffin lids. This less than happy scene was watched over with a kind of ghastly relish by a series of disembodied heads. My first impression of bygone heroes of Ancient Greece and Rome, was fast dispelled by closer acquaintance with their gruesome countenances. These were death masks. Death masks of hanged men, doubtless Mr Jaggers ever-present reminder of his less successful clients and of life's small but regrettable failures.

Mr Jaggers' clerk, Mr Wemmick, whose top half was visible above the desk, had scarcely more colour in his complexion and only a little more animation than the hanged men. As cold and dry and papery a clerk as any solicitor could wish for, with a mouth like a knife blade, as if the warmth of humanity had long since drained from him, blotted out by the shelves of yellowing papers. When he spoke, to inform me regretfully that Mr Jaggers was still in court, his voice too had the crackly sound of dried leaves.

With the feeling of having endured quite enough for one day, I was eager to depart. However, Flora's hand

restrained me as she enquired after the health of Mrs
Wemmick. My first guess that Mr Wemmick was a
bachelor whose many deceased relatives had overburdened
him with mourning rings and seals which adorned his
person now retreated in the face of the astonishing fact
that his good lady Mrs Wemmick enjoyed excellent health
and had lately presented him with their fifth. At this
information, his papery countenance underwent a transformation and permitted a smile which was in effect, only a
degree less ghastly than those of the plaster casts.

Seizing her advantage, Flora begged Mr Wemmick to
take to his good lady the kindest respects of Mrs
Wemmick's cousin, Jim Skiffins, and his betrothed.

'You are Miss Flora Jolly?'

'I am, sir.'

'Fancy that. Fancy that.' And Mr Wemmick underwent
a further transformation at this piece of news, blossoming
into humanity before our eyes, as if the papery mask had
suddenly been stripped away.

Seized by an uncontrollable outburst of animation, he
dashed around the desk, pumped us both heartily by the
hand and assured us that we were to accompany him to
Walworth, no excuses taken, and there Flora was to be
immediately acquainted with Mrs Wemmick. He would
call a carriage forthwith, the Drummle conveyance having
been dismissed outside Bartholomew Close.

On the journey Mr Wemmick spoke highly of Jim to
Flora's obvious delight: 'A regular fine fellow he is, Lady
Drummle. One we have been proud to entertain at the
Castle.' He pointed ahead and at my mystified expression,
added: 'That's it, m'lady. The true Englishman's home is
his Castle, don't you think?' he said with a dry chuckle
reminiscent of autumn leaves on a conservatory roof.

I could only nod, rendered speechless by the vision we
approached. A small wooden house nestled in a small
garden. There was nothing remarkable about that, except
for its abundance of Gothic windows (some of which were
merely painted on), a nailed Gothic door worthy of a fairy
tale about dragons and a captive princess. This strange

edifice was capped with battlements, a flagstaff and a gun which Mr Wemmick fired every night prompt on the stroke of nine. Solemnly he handed us across a ditch by a drawbridge which he carefully hoisted with no more concern than bolting his ordinary front door for the night.

Harriet Wemmick, plump and cheerful, at first glance an unlikely mate for Mr Wemmick, and custodian of the Castle, greeted Flora with enthusiasm and relief. She immediately produced the letter from Jim which Flora had been so eagerly anticipating.

'It was enclosed with one I received from him at Portsmouth, only last week.'

'Portsmouth? What on earth is he doing there? I thought he'd gone to war.'

'He's been, my dear, and back again.'

'Read it to me please.' As Flora listened, she began to weep, for Jim had been among the first wounded to be sent home. 'Oh my poor Jim, my poor Jim.'

Mrs Wemmick put a motherly arm around her. 'Now, now, my dear, it's not all that serious. He goes on to say: "I'll likely be a bit lame for the rest of my life and there'll be no more soldiering for the Queen. But if you can put up with your wounded warrior, then come to Portsmouth and we'll be married right away." He signs it "Ever your loving Jim" ' As Flora dabbed at her eyes, the Wemmicks sought to comfort her with many a well-worn platitude, suitable to the occasion.

Personally I thought it was a great blessing that the war was over for Flora's young man. I took her hands: 'You must go to him immediately. He will soon recover with you at his side.'

Her face fell and she shook her head, stubbornly. 'No, Miss Estella dear. That's quite out of the question. I must see you settled first, after all you've been through.'

'We will take good care of Lady Drummle, won't we, Harriet,' said Mr Wemmick. 'You can be sure she will be quite safe with us.'

'Oh, I hate leaving you like this.'

'No arguments, if you please. I will find lodgings until

Mr Jaggers can arrange for me to take possession of the Dower House. We will meet again then, Flora.' I felt the future was going to be a little uncertain for them, if Jim was making light of his disablement for Flora's sake. 'Come to me there if you wish to leave Portsmouth.'

'Oh, we will, we will.'

As the talk drifted towards plans for Flora's departure, I was introduced to Mr Wemmick's father, a charming old gentleman who had beamed on everyone throughout. Cheery and rotund as his son was papery and thin, he obviously imagined that some celebration was afoot.

'He gets a little confused, my lady, on account of being so deaf. Thinks he might have missed Christmas or a birthday, don't you, Aged Parent?' Another beaming smile. 'He's taken a regular fancy to you, my lady, I can see that. Take my advice and do not attempt to converse, however willing the spirit seems. Just keep him in the swim of things so to speak. Just tip him a nod now and then. He likes that more than anything, keeps him happy as a lark, it does.'

I did as requested and soon we were engaged in a series of nods which almost threatened the stability of Mr Wemmick's aged parent's head upon his shoulders. Meanwhile, the children having lost their initial thumb-in-the-mouth, hiding-behind-skirts shyness now came forward and assaulted the newcomers on all sides with questions, requests for stories to be told. No amount of hushings or gentle threats would keep at bay their curiosity and wide-eyed stares reserved for strangers.

I looked at Flora with a three-year old charmer in her arms and a two-year old gravely attempting to climb on to her knee. The sight made me smile as I noted how readily children gravitate to those with inborn maternal qualities. As for myself, I regret to say I was treated with distant awe as they eyed my fine cloak and bonnet which bore the affluence of Drummle Towers, the airs of the upper classes which still clung about my person. Even in their short lives they had learned that such people were not as themselves and were to be treated with extreme respect and caution.

Between nods exchanged with the Aged Parent, our tea cups were constantly replenished by Mrs Wemmick whenever the contents threatened to vanish below the brim, while Mr Wemmick abetted the dizzying circulation of a plateful of scones fast diminishing under the sly assault of many childish hands, despite threats which, if they were even heard, were not seriously considered for one moment. At last, the hour of nine having pronounced sentence of bedtime, the children scampered shrieking upstairs, assisted by their mother and Flora.

'I take it that your ladyship does not intend returning to Drummle Towers.'

'That is correct, Mr Wemmick. It is my intention to seek Mr Jaggers' advice before making any further arrangements.'

'Hrmmph. Yes, quite so. Quite so.' Doubtless Flora had whispered her story of my rescue, for there was compassion as well as sternness now. 'Am I correct in assuming that your ladyship would not wish to spend the night in a hostelry?' without waiting for my reply, he hastened on. 'There is nothing suitable of that nature in Walworth, however a widowed neighbour just across the road could be alerted to provide a room, for as long as you like. Nothing stylish like you're used to, my lady, but clean and reliable and comfortable.'

'That will be splendid. One more question, Mr Wemmick. Do you happen to know Mr Pip's present whereabouts?'

'Mr Pip, your ladyship?' He scratched his head. 'Well, it's like this. Mr Jaggers more or less severed all contact with the young gentleman when he ceased to be his guardian. File closed and all that sort of thing. Mr Jaggers is like that, your ladyship. Very tidy in his methods, very businesslike towards his clients.'

Flora and I had a somewhat tearful parting for there was a stagecoach leaving at five the next morning. Mr Wemmick then escorted me to my hired room, which was agreeable enough for a travel-weary soul who had fled from her lawful home and husband. Mrs Moon seized my two shillings gratefully, which was more than I could afford at that moment and I awoke next morning firmly resolved to find a situation as governess, the only way in which I could hope to earn a living.

I did not see Mr Jaggers immediately. A family bereavement had taken him to the north of England. There was an estate to settle, matters which would delay his return to London for a week or more. In the meantime, I discussed my future with the Wemmicks, for I was more often guest at their crowded family table than in the kitchen of my landlady whose name Mrs Moon lacked only the 'a' to turn it into the apt description of the only conversation, dreary and dispirited, to issue from her lips. She did nothing but deplore the present. Its people were vile, their customs vile, with only death and damnation for all eternity.

'When I was young,' she would begin each monologue for an outside opinion was never invited. 'When I was young, you would have found things mightily different. It was a pleasure to be alive then, our lives were so respectable – especially amongst those who are our betters. What joyous virtuous lives –'

I nodded dismally for I could have enlightened that lady exceedingly on what passed for joy and virtue in the deplorable house from which I had made my escape with my life under threat.

Even now I lived with the uncertainty of apprehension, for Mr Wemmick confided to me that Mrs Drummle Senior had been in touch with Mr Jaggers' office concerned at my failure to return with the carriage, and requesting information concerning my present whereabouts.

'She wishes Mr Jaggers to be informed that Lady Drummle removed some valuable jewellery, the property of her son and herself, for which she seeks immediate restitution, or else she will be forced to take recourse to legal action.'

'Those are my jewels,' I cried angrily. 'Here, I am wearing them. The few precious gifts from Miss Havisham, which were all I took with me.'

'I am perfectly aware of that, my lady. But we must not forget, she has the law on her side.'

'And I expect she has also told you – and everyone who would listen to her vile lies, the wicked story of how I had sought to cause my husband's death, when the accident happened as Divine retribution for his attempt to murder me.'

Mr Wemmick's silence confirmed my suspicions, and I added: 'All I took were the jewels I brought with me as a bride and the clothes you see me wearing.'

Mr Wemmick shook his head sympathetically. 'Don't you take it amiss, my lady. I know fine well which one of you is speaking the truth.' He shrugged. 'But then, should Sir Bentley die soon, as would not seem beyond the bounds of possibility, so to speak, the fact that you ran off so precipitously might go against you. It would stand poorly in a court of law, for Mrs Drummle doubtless has the servants on her side.' Rubbing his fingers together he added, 'And an easy matter to make them say what she wishes if a few guineas can change hands.'

'If only I could find a situation as governess.'

'Yes, my lady, and as far from London Town and Shropshire as you can, would be my advice to you.'

Invited to tea on Sunday, I discovered Mr Wemmick hastily clearing the kitchen table of a large pile of yellowing papers and newspaper cuttings.

'Mr Jaggers is contemplating retirement soon,' he explained. 'Before you, behold the product of his lifetime's labours. He wishes as his swan song to bring before the reading public a volume devoted to the Nature of Crime and Criminals, a subject on which no one has greater experience and authority. As I have been privileged to share his confidences through the years, I have been given the monumental task of sorting out suitable material from newspapers and broadsheets. A Herculean labour,' he added gloomily. 'I fear we will never see the end of it.'

'Perhaps I could assist you, Mr Wemmick. I have many idle hours on my hands and I would find it an agreeable and fascinating task.' In truth any opportunity to escape the doleful Mrs Moan for a few hours was worthy of consideration.

Mr Wemmick frowned a moment and came to a lightning decision. 'That would indeed be a great help, my lady. Progress has been very slow, alas, up to now. With our ever-growing family and all, I have little time left. What do you say, Aged P, shall we acquire a lady's assistance?'

With nods and beaming approval all round, on the following morning Mr Wemmick showed me into the parlour where a fire had been lit and the table cleared as my appointed place of work. I was now looking forward to this worthwhile task until Mr Jaggers' return decided my future. I was especially pleased that offering Mr Wemmick a helping hand would allow me to feel less of a beggar at their hospitable table.

Within the hour I was engrossed in 'A for Axe-Murders; B for Baby-Killers; C for Crime Passionel.' What hideous crimes, what fearful drawings had been made during the trials. I tried not to linger upon the horrible subject matter as I sorted through the files. At this stage I wished only to have some idea of the form the book was to take. It would certainly require an index of sorts.

Some of the faces drawn in the dock, stared out at me, depraved and so bestial that, I must confess, by the end of the week I was so engrossed in crime and criminals, my sleep was badly affected. Something very uneasy, nebulous still as a threatening storm, was stirring the depths of my mind with strange phantoms, flickering shadows of terror.

I had reached 'S for Stranglers.'

In a field of crime notable as the province of the male sex, I was surprised to see the face of a solitary woman staring up at me. The artist at the trial had plainly been impressed by this phenomenon, and I found myself examining closely a young woman, almost beautiful for her class, with a profusion of untamed black curls and large tragic eyes. Fascinated I read on: The woman, Provis by name, was a gipsy, the common law wife of a member of the criminal fraternity, a habitual thief since his infancy.

When she found this creature betraying her with another gipsy woman she set upon her rival and strangled her with her own hands. Still not satisfied with her hideous vengeance, this Medea of the gipsies had turned upon her own child in murderous rage.

There seemed some confusion as to whether she had been successful in this second murder. Although she insisted that she had done so, there was no evidence, except for the child's disappearance from the gipsy encampment.

I found myself returning again and again to that face. Why did it haunt me so? It was the first time I had examined this file and yet that face was intensely familiar. But from where? Where indeed could I have encountered such a face before? Certainly not at Drummle Towers. Satis House then? Unlikely. At Mrs Brandley's house in Richmond? No. Paris then? For there was a touch of the exotic about the murderess.

My mind returned again to Drummle and the only gipsy woman I had encountered, who could not by any stretch of imagination be the young face before me. I consulted the date. At the time of the trial I was scarcely three years old.

Harriet Wemmick celebrated her birthday that evening. I had knitted her a pretty lace shawl and baked the cake in Mrs Moan's kitchen. Delight and pleasure were everywhere about me, but I was no longer part of the merry conversation, the cheerful family circle. My thoughts drifted, haunted by 'S for Stranglers', as I longed for morning, when I might return again to the mysterious Provis and her terrible story.

Unable to concentrate on singing and family games, I made my excuses and took my leave of the happy group earlier than was decent, so that Harriet followed me to the door, anxious that I looked tired and pale. Had dear Wemmick been working me too hard on Crime and Criminals?

'Agreed it was to be a pleasant pastime only, my lady. No hard work intended,' said Mr Wemmick sternly.

A pleasant pastime, a pleasant pastime. The words

echoed like waves from an insane sea as I closed my eyes and tried to woo the sleep that would carry me into the bright safe hours of daylight. Suddenly the darkness oppressed me, alive with fears I had not experienced since childhood. All the lurking terrors were there in shrouded furniture, gloating over their chance to seize me.

I pulled the covers over my head. Where – where? Where in the twisted maze of my life had I looked into that sad face, those tragic wild eyes?

When at last I drifted into uneasy sleep, the Nightmare was ready for me. The same Nightmare that had never left me from infancy's first remembrance, through childhood, girlhood, wifehood. Sometimes for many months at a time, I was free of its claws and indeed, forgot all about it. Then suddenly, back it came with its horrors, hovering on the edge of elusive memory.

Again I was the terrified observer of two women fighting, screaming, clawing. One, younger and stronger, with the red murder light in her eyes, at last gaining control. She had her enemy's throat between her hands. I watched as she squeezed, squeezed tighter, ever tighter. At last the threshing limbs were still, the frightful screams trailed off into the silence of death.

But the scene was not yet ended. The victor now dropped her limp quarry and turned, searching the darkness for where I lay hidden. I heard the turf pounding under her bare feet, her hot breath on my face. Streaming hair, likeness in every strand, *was my own*. Strangler's hands, powerful wrists and fingers: They, too, *were my own*.

I awoke screaming, to a further horror. Until now my assailant had been without a face, unrecognizable. No more. Now she looked upon me with the terrifying countenance of the gipsy woman Provis, from Mr Jaggers' 'S for Stranglers'.

Next morning early I had a visitor. Mrs Moan announced Mr Wemmick, with a despairing sigh. 'In my young day, it was never so. Ladies did not receive before lunch time. Such behaviour, so degrading and ill-mannered.'

'I will not delay, my lady, I am on my way to the office, but I received word late last night that Mr Jaggers has returned. He will have many clients to see after his long absence, but I will arrange for him to see you at four this afternoon,' he added, 'I shall, of course, stress the urgency of your case, my lady, and he will doubtless take immediate action to clarify the situation in which you find yourself so unhappily placed.'

I must confess that the forthcoming interview with Mr Jaggers thrust aside my intention of returning to Crime and Criminals and I needed little urging from Harriet Wemmick to sit by her fireside with my knitting for her latest arrival.

All day, the rain was unceasing and high winds battered the windows. In such weather a carriage was a necessary expense. When I reached my destination, however, it was to be told by a junior clerk that both Mr Jaggers and Mr Wemmick had been summoned earlier to Newgate, to visit a dying prisoner. Mr Jaggers was unlikely to return to Little Britain that evening but would doubtless further instruct Mr Wemmick regarding any proposed meeting.

Afterwards I wondered what imp of disaster led me to board a passing omnibus and drive past Mr Jaggers' house in Gerrard Street. Of course he would not be at home and he would be ill-pleased to see anyone, however illustrious the client, without appointment. But even as I sat undecided, and weighed the risk of his displeasure, I beheld him walking up his own front steps.

A stroke of good fortune, indeed. Hastily alighting, I reached his side, as he was about to close the door. A little put out at my sudden appearance, he kept me firmly on the doorstep as I explained to him the urgent purpose of my visit regarding the Dower House. He seemed uncommonly agitated, glancing over his shoulder into the dimly lit hall behind him and then out again at the wind and rain which swept against us, as I apologized for my intrusion on the grounds of extreme urgency.

'Perhaps Mr Wemmick has already told you, sir. That I have reason to believe that I am in some danger.'

That seemed to decide him. 'Yes, yes. Come in, come in.' Taking my cloak, he ushered me swiftly into the study and only with the door closed, did he relax. Warming his back by the fire, he regarded me solemnly. The Dower House had been willed to me, but alas, Mr Wemmick's warnings had been correct. Edwina Drummle intended taking legal action, if she could summon a case against me.

'It would seem in your best advantage, Lady Drummle, to be quit of London for a while. That would be my advice to you until the matter of your unfortunate husband's recovery is resolved one way or another. Perhaps you have discreet friends who would consider sheltering you for a while?'

'Only Mr Pip,' I said hesitantly.

Mr Jaggers surveyed me in darkest disapproval. 'That would be most improper, most improper to involve Mr Pip, in your present state as absconding wife. Even if I knew where he was at present,' he added severely. 'Would you be prepared to consider Derbyshire a suitable refuge?'

'I know of no one there – except –'

'Except Bessie Maydie, your old servant, late of Satis House.' He nodded eagerly. 'Did she not write and tell you? She certainly intended so doing.'

'And I dare say she did, but I have reason to believe that my personal letters were intercepted.'

'No matter, no matter. She left a forwarding address. I have it somewhere.' Opening a drawer in the desk, after great rustlings and rumplings, he triumphantly withdrew a scrap of paper. 'Here it is, Lady Drummle. Now take my advice and bear Derbyshire in mind.' A clock chimed melodiously in the hall and taking out his watch, which he consulted sternly, he snapped it shut in what could only be regarded as an indication of dismissal. Curiously, I was again aware of his unease, as he muttered about an appointment which was to take him across London. In roughly the same direction as Walworth, I might share his carriage.

Still talking he led the way into the hall and as he helped me into my cloak, I glanced in the mirror.

The next moment, it occurred to me that I was suffering from a hallucination. My own face drifted behind me disembodied in the light of a candle flame. But alas, how I had aged in the few minutes I had spent in Mr Jaggers' study. Large eyes and streaming hair were mine, but touched by the frost of age, as if by some trick time had moved on twenty years in as many minutes.

The candle wavered and the face moved. A shocked exclamation, a startled cry, although I had made no sound ...

Mr Jaggers turned about, shouted angrily: 'Get you gone, woman, get to the kitchen. At once. You're not wanted here, Molly. Leave us.'

The woman, tall, slender as myself, obeyed his command. She melted swiftly into the shadows while he faced me, brows down, his look at the same time apologetic and defiant, daring the question I did not need to ask.

For I knew. I now knew everything. For I had looked into the face of the gipsy woman Provis, from 'S for Stranglers'. Aged, it was true, but not too greatly changed to be still recognizable as the face from my Nightmare.

As for Mr Jaggers, plainly embarrassed, he ushered me too briskly for politeness down the front steps, as if I might be ready to change my mind about leaving. Summoning a passing cab, he thrust me inside, clambered aboard and took his seat somewhat breathlessly at my side. He talked volubly about legal processes concerning Miss Havisham's estate, and dwelt, almost poetically for him upon the distant glories of Derbyshire, of which I heard hardly a word. Indeed, I hardly noticed his departure as the coach proceeded to Walworth, or the purse containing twenty guineas which he had thrust into my hand.

I was alone. Alone with the full brunt of my horror. The woman whose face I had mistaken for my own was Molly Provis, Mr Jaggers' housekeeper, the woman from 'S for Stranglers'. She was, without the shadow of a doubt, my own mother, a vile murderess, who had intended me as her second victim. Who then was my father? Surely not the creature who was her common law husband? Did he live still? If so, surely he would have wished to claim his ill-used child?

Content in the belief that I was my mother-by-adoption's niece, or even her own love-child and therefore of noble Havisham birth, I had never given a passing thought to a less salubrious parentage.

Only the Nightmare had been there to relentlessly point the way to the truth. And as if Mr Jaggers himself stood before me and told me in his own words, I could guess how he had saved the wretched Molly from the consequences of her hideous crime and had given her shelter in his home. Perhaps he had taken pity on me, or more likely had seen this perfect answer to Miss Havisham's extraordinary demand for a little girl to adopt. Whatever my subsequent existence, for he must have known that Satis House was no place for the rearing of a normal child, warped and twisted by his client's desire for revenge. But for Molly Provis' hated child, in constant danger of her life, Miss Havisham must indeed have appeared to his conscience as the lesser of two evils.

Even as I recognized the stripping from my soul of any romantic illusions about my nativity, I saw the terrible danger in which I was placed by this revelation, the awful pit that yawned before me, with such a heritage of violence.

I had recognized Molly Provis. The question now was, how many others who were not my friends, knew or guessed about Mr Jaggers' Molly? Possibly Mr Wemmick from his acquaintance with Mr Jaggers' household over many years had good reason when he advised instant flight. There were other sickening memories which fitted the pattern: Drummle's reaction to his meeting with Molly: Flora's suppressed excitement when she had realized the extraordinary resemblance between her mistress and Mr Jaggers' housekeeper. Only the fact that Drummle was chronically unobservant and accepted the story that I was an orphaned Havisham, had saved me. That and his greed,

with such a fortune he could lay hands upon. But should a
discerning eye like Edwina Drummle's chance to fall upon
Molly, one glance and a woman's instinct for such matters
would be enough to reveal the truth.

What if Drummle were already dead and Edwina traced
me to Walworth, and had me arrested for stealing the
jewels that were rightfully mine? When the truth came out
that I was the child of Molly Provis, what chance would I
have in a court of law? Gipsies, vagrants, habitual
criminals were feared and detested with good reason. No
jury of respectable citizens would hesitate to pronounce a
verdict of 'Guilty' on the heartless wretch who had run
away, abandoning her dying husband. The balm of
grieving widowhood would be denied me and few would
believe my word, against Edwina Drummle and her paid
lackeys' evidence, that I had escaped from a monster of
brutality who had tried to murder me. Supposing that I
were acquitted as innocent, what future lay ahead, my
respectability besmirched, my reputation the subject of
behind-hand whispers? I went to bed that night with only
two frivolous thoughts. There would be precious few
friends or neighbours calling to leave cards, that for sure.
And as I heard Mrs Moan moving about in the next room, I
wondered how she would react to the truth of her
illustrious lodger's unspeakable parentage? Here was one
case she would find deuced difficult to dismiss as 'When I
was young there were no gipsy stranglers.'

I saw the dawn break next morning with one desire only.

Escape. Escape to the one person who loved me and into
whose hands I could trust my life, and who might know
where I could find Pip: Bessie Maydie, who believed I had
abandoned her after my mother-by-adoption's death and
who thought, that I had denied her request for a place with
me at Drummle Towers. How that dear kind soul must
have suffered for my apparent ingratitude and lack of all
humanity.

I decided to leave Walworth upon the instant and took
an affectionate leave of Harriet and the children. My
cheerful expression masking the desperate feeling of

approaching danger, I explained my abrupt departure as a visit to my old nurse, in the hope that there might be a governess' situation more readily forthcoming in Derbyshire. Solemnly, she promised to tell no one but Wemmick and Mr Jaggers where I had gone.

Taking my place on the north-bound stagecoach, the future seemed bleak indeed, my destination further afield than the continent of Africa and equally perilous and unknown.

The journey seemed endless for the year was far gone, the days short and the skies already leaden with snow. After an uncomfortable night, cold and sleepless in a dreary hostelry, we drove deeper into the hills where the empty moorland stretched as far as the eye could see.

Alighting at the coaching inn, hardly more hospitable within than the winter landscape without, I watched the stagecoach disappear with utmost misgivings. What a bleak and terrifying place to be lost and alone, I thought, for already great blankets of snow covered the hills, scarcely divisible from the pale sky.

The signpost indicated that Heathyfold lay 5 miles distant and, leaving my box to be collected, I started off, my thick travelling cloak, that memento of more affluent days, well wrapped about me. Walking at a brisk pace to keep warm, I remembered Bessie's advice and breathed deeply. A tranquil pale sun glittered upon undulating hill and shadowy dale. Before me a lane with twittering birds and beyond, a track winding past frosty hedge and overhung by frozen bough.

Take heart, I told myself firmly. Soon you will be safe with Bessie. What a blissful surprise, a joyful reunion in a neat snug cottage somewhere over that furthest hill. And I pictured her sitting by a cheerful fire, quite unaware that I was about to walk in the door.

The brow of the hill reached at last, a distant pall of smoke trailing skyward from the valley, indicated the chimneys of Heathyfold, the sprawling grey building the mill where Bessie had worked as a child. A lofty church spire, and through the black lace of winter trees, a large mansion. Climbing a fence as vantage point, alas, my foot slipped off its icy perch, and hurled me painfully back onto the road. My foot hurt in the prelude of Bentley's attack was still troublesome and I cried out at the agony of putting weight upon it to hobble down the hill.

Troubles as always, never come singly, for now snow began to fall, not in gentle pretty snowflakes but with the ferocity of travelling before a whirling shrieking blizzard, fast consuming the sunny landscape. Blinded by the stinging needles of hail in my face, I hesitated, afraid of losing my way as all signs of the path before me were swiftly obliterated.

At that moment, came the muffled sound of wheels and a brougham swept into view. Hobbling forward, I held up my hand. The driver reined in hesitantly at a command from within, followed by a man's face, peering from the window.

'Is this the right direction for Heathyfold, sir?'

'That is my destination. May I offer you the shelter of our carriage?'

'Indeed, sir, you may. And I would be most obliged to you.' As my rescuer handed me in, he said: 'You are hurt, miss?'

'I slipped on the ice. It is nothing and will soon mend,' I added at the concern on his face, as I observed that my benefactors were a man and woman in early middle-age. The former did the talking, his companion uttered not a syllable, nor did she glance in my direction but continued to gaze out of the window as if she found the prospect of a raging blizzard compelling.

Removing his hat, the man continued to murmur condolences and advice about my injured ankle and I found myself under the relentless scrutiny of eyes, grey and shrewd, under a cap of brown curls, a finely chiselled countenance stern but merry about the mouth. As he conversed in a friendly manner, I decided he was one of the most attractive gentlemen I had met.

'Have you travelled far?'

'From London. I go to visit my old nurse, Bessie Maydie.'

His vague smile filled me with disappointment. Obviously the name meant nothing to him. 'She lives at Meadowbank.'

He nodded. 'Ah, yes, that lies on the far edge of the village.' Turning he smiled deep into my eyes. 'Our paths separate, alas, before that, however, my carriage will see you safely conveyed to your destination.'

'That is very good of you, sir –'

A sudden commotion outside, some cursing from the coachman and swaying of the carriage, jolting to a halt. My rescuer stuck his head out of the window.

' 'Tis nothing to be alarmed about. Only the gipsies,' he said and I caught sight of the painted caravans that had drawn to the side of the lane to let us pass to the accompaniment of curses, mocking laughter and rattling tins.

A man in the prime of life, large and strong-looking, even handsome in a vagabondish way with his curly black hair and bold eyes, a red scarf about his neck and a gold ring in his ear, rode alongside and stared into the carriage with a complete absence of manners. Amused by what he saw there, he gave me a bold salute, a mocking bow. Hastily I looked away, feeling the colour rise to my face. My discomfort as I shrank back against the upholstery was observed by my rescuer who thereupon leaned out and addressed some remarks to the fellow about the 'usual place'. As we drove on, he said to me. 'We allow them to camp on the Common for the winter. They would starve otherwise, these gipsies of ours. They are quite harmless,' he added with a smile.

But as always the mention of gipsies struck terror into my heart. With good reason now, I thought. I still hated them, but knowing my terrible nativity, I also feared them, feared what dregs might lurk in me of their corruption, a destiny I could not escape.

'Blood will out.' Again I saw clearly the old gipsy woman

who had thrown her shadow over the summer lawn at
Drummle Towers and told me not only that I was Romany
bred, but also with child, even before I was sure myself. A
long, bitterly sad, time ago.

The gipsies were far behind now as the carriage rolled
swiftly into the village, past the grey prison-like building,
bleak and unlovely, from where I fancied I could smell the
untreated raw wool. Down a steep street and up again,
where tall church and squat vicarage nestled, onward
through the gates of the mansion house I had glimpsed
from the other side of the vale.

'This is where we leave you,' said my rescuer holding out
his hand. 'Aaron Flint – should you wish to stay and need
advice, do not hesitate to call on us.'

I thanked him kindly and as he obviously awaited an
introduction, gave him my name as 'Miss Havisham'. His
female companion refused to be part of this social
interchange and swept past, nose in the air without even a
nod to acknowledge my existence. Mr Flint turned and still
smiling, watched the carriage depart before also dis-
appearing up the steps and into the house, of relatively
recent construction, despite a penchant for Gothic
windows and battlements.

As for that elegant lady. Who was she? Servant or kin –
surely a wife or sister would have merited introduction. I
must ask Bessie.

'You'll need to get out here, miss,' said the coachman
after a series of twists and turns. 'Carriage can't go no
further. Over there – see, beyond the field. That's
Meadowbank.'

Painfully I limped down the edge of the snow-covered
stubble field to a huddle of sullen cottages. No smoke
issued from their chimneys and my brisk application to the
knocker adorning the first door yielded no reply. Closer
inspection revealed that it was empty, the windows
curtainless.

A new dread consumed me. What if all were empty,
Bessie moved on, and my long journey in vain? At the
second door, a scared young woman answered my

summons by shaking her head vigorously and, before I could utter a syllable, muttered: 'We don't want nothing,' and thereupon firmly slammed the door in my face.

At the next cottage I fared better. An old woman with a high complexion, as if much of her life had been spent over a roaring stove, announced: 'My, but you're early this year. Had a bad summer, did you? Never mind, you'll be glad to settle on the Common, I dare say.'

What on earth could she mean, I wondered. 'I am looking for Bessie Maydie,' I said, rather stiffly.

'Oh, are you?' Looking me up and down, as if to test the truth of my statement, she suddenly chuckled. 'Bless my soul, bless my soul. You must forgive an old woman's mistake. You're a lady, of course, I can see that. At first glance – my eyes are not as good as they were – I mistook you for one of Wolfe Farr's gipsies.' Seeing my indignant expression, she added hastily:

'Next door along, that's Bessie.'

Two minutes later, I was clasped to Bessie's heart. The tears ran down both our cheeks quite unheeded in an excess of sentimentality that would have made my poor mother-by-adoption turn in her grave, realizing that all her work had been in vain and the ice with which she replaced Estella's heart, had melted long ago.

'Oh Miss Estella, Miss Estella. How good it is to see you. I can't believe it, I can't believe it. But what on earth brings you to Heathyfold?' Seating me by the fire, she put on the kettle. I was shocked at the change in her, for gone was my buxom rosy Bessie who had withered into a thin, stoop-shouldered old woman. Her face expressed shocked horror as I told her briefly the story of my marriage to Bentley Drummle and its bitter ending but she listened without interruption, apart from the cough that wracked her slight frame or an occasional exclamation of 'That wicked man, that wicked man'.

When I mentioned Miss Havisham's death, the crisp white cap worn without evidence of red curls, shook violently. I wondered how long ago she had abandoned the elaborate red wig, belief in whose abundant beauty had brightened my childhood.

'It was from then on, Miss Estella, that my letters went unanswered.'

'As did mine to you.'

As Bessie leaned over and taking my hand, held it to her lips, that simple action spoke volumes of how my apparent neglect and indifference had distressed her.

'What word of Mr Pip?'

'He does well. His friend, Mr Startop has an aunt living on the other side of the valley, who is kin to Aaron Flint, cousin I think. Mr Startop visits there from time to time and, bless the lad's dear heart, he always spares the time for a cup of tea and a gossip with old Bessie –'

I had met Startop when he accompanied Pip on several excursions to Richmond. 'Tell me about Pip,' I interrupted impatiently.

'Why, Master Pip has gone to Egypt to join Herbert Pocket in some business over there.' She shook her head. 'I'm not sure what they do, but it's something connected with the folk they worked with in London.'

'That would be Clarriker & Company.'

'Aye, I believe you're right. You knew that Mr Pocket had married.'

'I did. And Pip?' How fast beat my heart, as dreading the answer, I asked: 'Has he taken a wife?'

'Not unless he has fancied one of those foreign dancing ladies we used to see at the fairs. The ones with all those veils, and a lot more covering their faces, it seemed to me, that could have been better used covering their lower limbs with decency.'

Fatima, Queen of the Exotic East was the only connection most of us would ever have with Cairo and the pyramids, those ancient tombs of long-forgotten kings. And my laughter contained much of relief.

As Bessie rose to set the table, her every movement across the broken, uneven flagstones brought a fearful agitation among the cups and saucers on the rickety old dresser. I sat back and took stock of my surroundings. The chair, one of two in the room was wooden backed, a knitted cushion its concession to comfort. As for other furniture, if such sticks as a broken-down dresser and a rough table by the window, could be dignified by the description, the tiny room was dominated by a huge knitting frame.

'Do you still work in the factory?'

'No, lass, I'm not fit for that any more. My first winter here was very bad, with a leaking roof and all. I lay long with a fever and would have died had it not been for Annie Leys, my good neighbour.' Another cough. 'I never got well again, but now I have my frame. You were always a good knitter, do you remember all I taught you?'

'I do indeed. Perhaps I could get work too.'

'Ay, you might, though there's little money in it. Besides its common work for a lady like yourself. I don't like to think of you having to work when there's always a roof for you here, as long as I live. Bessie will never desert you.'

I held her hand. 'That's good of you, but I must pay my way. I have a little to tide me over until I can get a situation of some kind. I was thinking of perhaps a governess or a lady's companion.'

Attending to the teapot she said: 'Folk's poor hereabouts, Miss Estella. Minister's daughter takes care of the village school. As for the Flints,' she pursed her lips and shook her head.

'I've met him.' As I described the man who had brought me in his carriage, Bessie nodded:

'Aye, that's him, that's him.'

'Is he married?'

'Flint? Not him,' she laughed harshly.

'There was a lady with him who said nothing and declined to be introduced.'

'That's Miss Flint as she calls herself.'

'Is there some doubt about it?' I asked amused by Bessie's grim reply.

'Rum goings on up at Big House,' she murmured darkly. 'Abby, my great-niece could tell you plenty, that she could. Best advice I can give you, Miss Estella, is to stay clear of them – Aaron Flint owns the mill and everything around here, everybody too. Now drink your tea, afore it's stone cold.'

It was when she got to her feet holding the table edge and skilfully making her way back to the fire that I realized for the first time what had struck me as strange about her face. Bessie was almost completely blind.

As we talked later this new disability was never mentioned and only very sharp eyes that had known her in earlier days would have noticed, for it did not hamper her skilful manipulation of the knitting frame. The smell of wool, of hot food and a warm fire on my face threatened to overwhelm me. Strange that in this humble cottage with a canary bird chirping in its window, I felt more at home than I had ever done in either Satis House with its melancholy stage set on the upper floor or in the cold grandeur of Drummle Towers.

'I've made up Abby's bed for you, lass.'

I realized I had been asleep, weary through to my bones and I let her lead me to the attic bedroom and help me into bed without a murmur. Tomorrow I would begin asking questions. Tomorrow I would consider my future.

I slept soundly, dreamlessly, for the first time free from nightmare or terror. Secure and serene I felt the whisper of renewed faith in a brighter future in the shimmer of pale winter sunshine. Downstairs there was fresh baked bread and butter and jam for breakfast and as I refused a fourth slice, Bessie asked if Satis House had a new owner.

'Alas, no one wanted to live there. The fire made part of it unsafe,' I leaned over and took her hand. 'It was pulled down, Bessie, and the stones sold for building materials.' She gave a little cry of dismay as I added: 'The land is to be disposed of to build new villas. Only the Dower House remains, and that is mine.'

Bessie wiped away a tear. 'Poor dear old house, and such a romantic history. A body would have thought someone would have wanted to keep it.' She sighed. 'I wish you could have seen it in the days when your dear Mama and I were young. Mr Havisham was one of a large family and the house always filled with visiting Pocket cousins. People soon forget and houses are like dogs. Give them a bad name and that's what folk remember. For it wasn't until after your dear Mama's misfortune that people began to take to the other side of the road, saying the place was haunted. Such nonsense. Why the only ghost in that house, was your poor dear Mama's youth.'

Pausing to stir the fire's glowing embers, she added: 'If only Master Pip had got to her in time. It was a mercy he was still on the premises or the whole place would have burned down. But still, I keep thinking – if only.' Again she sighed: 'How different – how very different – why, my dear lady might have still been with us today.'

And had I listened to my heart instead of my empty ambitions, I might have been happy as Pip's wife, I thought sadly as she continued. 'Poor Master Pip, I hope the lad does well. He deserves to succeed after that terrible bitter disappointment, over his expectations.'

'He always thought that Miss Havisham was his benefactress, too.' I looked at her. 'Did you, Bessie?'

'Aye, I did. And I must admit that I might have even encouraged him to think so. You see, Miss Estella, your dear Mama loved to be secretive. It was part of her nature. She was like a greedy child about personal things, loved hugging secrets to herself. Why, even though I had been with her so many years, through thick and thin, girl to woman, and I was probably closer to her than anyone, she still kept me, well, at a distance. Of course, I was just her servant and she never forgot that for a moment, nor did she fail to remind me if I stepped out of line, that she was mistress and I was just her maid. I knew I had to keep my place or there was no dealing with her.' She shook her head. 'There's a whole lot of things I was kept in the dark about.'

'Such as who were my real parents?' Bessie had the grace to look uncomfortable, to sigh deeply and I put my hand on her arm. 'I know they were not Arthur Havisham and his wife,' I said gently.

'I only did it for the best, for your happiness and well-being, Miss Estella.'

'I know. I know that and I am certainly not blaming you.'

'I shouldn't have let you grow up believing a lie, though. It was different when you were a little lass, all I wanted was to make it easier for you at Dame Clarissa's, so as the other young ladies would look up to you. What seemed more important than the truth then was that an orphan adopted by Miss Havisham should have a romantic and tragic background, like the heroine in a novelette.'

She studied me thoughtfully for a moment, her wan smile begging pardon, before she continued: 'To tell the honest truth on the subject, I was no wiser than you. I never knew who they were. But I expect Mr Jaggers was in the secret. I remember fine the day he brought you to Satis House. No more than three years old you were, we did not even know exactly when your birthday was, but made it the very day you came to us.' Another apologetic smile. 'June the Fifteenth, the same way we would have with a puppy dog or a kitten.'

June the Fifteenth. If I had needed confirmation that I was the daughter of Molly Provis, here it was. The date of the newspaper report of her trial stayed sharp in my memory as early June.

'I can see you clear as if it was yesterday. Not a picking on your bones, thin and starved-looking, all hair and eyes, you seemed to be. Scared-looking, too,' she added grimly, 'poor bairn, poor bairn. I couldn't make head nor tail of what you were doing at Satis House, as I bathed you before taking you upstairs to present to my mistress. What a picture you were after a bit of soap and water, a wonderful difference to the bedraggled object who first set foot in my kitchen, once you were dressed in the pretty clothes Mr Jaggers had brought from somewhere. What was it all about, I wondered to myself, what did she want with little lass, her as never had any liking for bairns at the best of times. I can tell you now, lass, that having children and dying in childbirth was her greatest fear of marriage. Not that I could give her much advice or guidance in that direction.

'I can still see her sitting by the fire and you going to her side and staring up into her face, trembling but trying not to show it, not uttering a word. "Come, child." You let her put an arm around you, without flinching, just gazing over at me beseeching-like with those great tragic eyes. Suddenly she laughed. "Well, Bessie. And what do you think of my little daughter?"

'I thought she was having one of her little games with me, I couldn't believe my ears, but there she was telling me she intended to adopt you legally, to share that life of utmost gloom and melancholy. I was against the idea from the start I can tell you. Poor little lass.

' "Poor child, indeed. What about me? What about my life? Think of me and my sufferings for a change, if you please."

' "Begging your pardon, Miss Alicia, I am thinking of you both and that such a course as you have in mind will bring happiness to neither of you."

' "Happiness, Bessie, what does that word mean? And even if I understood what you are talking about, I might then ask: What is happiness to me now? Be good enough not to mention such a word in my presence again." And she looked down at you, so still at her side. Then she smiled, that greedy look on her face I knew so well. "Plans are what I have now. Such plans as you could never guess. This little child you see before you, Bessie Maydie, is to have a great destiny. She is to grow up strong and beautiful but with one difference to other girls. She will have no heart to be broken as I had. I shall make certain of that. This little child you see before you, Bessie, is to be the instrument of my revenge upon all men."

'I begged her not to do this, to change her mind, for pity's sake. Over and over, I tried to tell her this was wrong, wrong, and that she should send you back to Mr Jaggers to have you adopted by loving foster-parents. How coldly she looked at me. "Oh, I shall love her, have no doubts about that. I shall love her." And so she did, Miss Estella, as much as she was capable of, poor lady, which wasn't a great deal. And so I tried to do the best I could, protect you and where she fell short as a mother, which wasn't her fault for such feelings just weren't born in her, I tried to make amends.'

'And that you did, dearest Bessie, you were the comfort and joy of my whole existence.' As we began to reminisce about those early days at Satis House, Bessie wiped away a tear.

'What do you think the truth is?' I asked, driving her back with difficulty, to the subject of my true parents.

She smiled, stroking my gloved hand. 'You were such a little beauty, Miss Estella, I always thought you had a look of breeding about you. Well, well, I presumed it was the usual story of a servant lass and her well-to-do employer. Why don't you ask Mr Jaggers? He could tell you about your real parents, I'm sure.'

'Perhaps I will do just that,' I lied for I was not yet strong enough to tell Bessie who thought herself so much my inferior that compared to her I licked the foulest dust in the land. No. I remembered childhood and sought refuge there again: If I pretended the truth did not exist, that Mr Jaggers' Molly did not exist, she might then vanish from memory. And after all there had to be a father and Bessie could well be right. By pretending that my father was not the habitual criminal who betrayed her, but a man of property, who had fallen victim to a gipsy girl's charms. If so, where was he now?

'Do you still have the Nightmare?' Bessie asked one day.

'No. Never.' That was true. Since the day I discovered that Molly Provis was my mother, the Nightmare no longer awaited the hours of darkness but roamed inescapable, haunting all my days.

In those first days as Bessie reopened the doors of memory for me, a kind of timelessness descended upon us as if I had indeed returned to the lost world of childhood. The passing hours were balm to heal my wounds, passed pleasantly and productively as I learned the intricacies of the knitting frame, or else often watched her hands gnarled and rheumatic but still deft despite her failing eyesight. Often I sat beside her my hands never empty either, as I knitted a shawl or put the final touches on the stockings she wove. Sometimes when her fingers were stiff and obviously painful I took over the frame.

Indeed, I learned a great deal about conditions in the hosiery manufacture in the mill owned by Aaron Flint and for which Bessie served as one of many 'outworkers'.

'Before I went to Miss Havisham, it was just stockings that his father manufactured, now there's gloves and braces and cravats, even shirts. I earn eight shillings a week and it is all my own, for Mr Flint still owns the frames in the district, he hasn't sold out to middlemen like, I hear tell, is the way with some owners. Then the poor stockingers, the outworkers, are lucky to make a living. Ninepence or a shilling for renting the frame and whether for a week's work or only half-a-week, the full frame rent has to be paid. And my grand-niece Abby who thought she would be better off in Leicester, tells me these frame renters are cruel taskmasters, forever finding reasons, faults in the work as an excuse to dock the wages, leaving hardly enough for a crust of bread to feed a family on.'

Bessie considered Flint a benevolent employer by comparison, but I found the work wearisome with eight shillings a week deplorable wages, although Bessie insisted that she could get me a frame of my own as Aaron Flint was always on the lookout for good workers.

'That is, if you decide to stay for a while.'

Where else could I go? Where else would Lady Drummle be safer than hiding away in a humble cottage at Meadowbank?

Only one thing destroyed my inner peace. The presence of the gipsies on the Common, the same group who had passed us with their painted caravans. As winter hardened they were driven closer to habitation like wild woodland beasts, prowling the narrow street, their women whining at our doors, beggars among country folk with little more than themselves.

The insolent ruffian who was their leader, I could not always avoid, on the short cut across to the village street. He would bow extravagantly and address me in his vile Romany tongue. One day he had the temerity to stretch out his hand and touch my arm. My sense of outrage at such familiarity was out of all proportion to his act, but it had the required effect and drove me to break the lofty silence which I had hitherto maintained.

'How dare you – how dare you accost me in this manner. Mr Flint shall be told of this.'

He looked at me calmly, still smiling and the question he had asked was repeated again.

Exasperated now, but fearful too, I replied: 'I have not the least idea what you are talking about. And I shall be greatly obliged if you will refrain from addressing me in your heathenish language.'

His eyes bold and sparkling now widened with delight. He spoke again in Romany and when I began to walk on, very briskly, his loud laughter followed me. Swiftly reaching my side, he paced with me. A very tall man, he had no difficulty in looking down into my face and putting me at considerable disadvantage.

'Lady, I do believe you are honest.' When I gave an angry exclamation, he held up his hand. 'But then you are one of us, are you not? Although you have inherited the grand manners of the Gorgios from somewhere and learned to speak their tongue tolerably well.'

'I am not one of you.' I stopped walking and stamped my foot angrily, wishing that strong handsome neck lay under it. 'And I have never spoken any other tongue but the English one to which I was born.' I felt my face blazing with fury. Suddenly I wanted to leap at him tear off that smiling mocking mask. 'How dare you – how dare you presume to address me thus. I warn you I will tolerate no more of your impertinence. If you ever accost me again with your insolent speech, I will complain to Mr Flint and he will have you evicted.'

My threat had the required effect and I left him frowning, still studying me, but cautiously. As I continued on my way, I hoped my words had given him something to think about, but I was nevertheless considerably shaken by the encounter. Perhaps the creature was honest in his mistake, I thought with dread, remembering how Bessie's neighbours had mistaken me for one of his begging women.

Bessie smiled and shook her head. 'He's a bold one, that Wolfe Farr. Hear tell he has an eye for the Romany lasses, and is considered a great catch.'

'I expect he has his share of them.'

Again she nodded. 'Like as not. They keep to themselves, the Romanies. Don't talk much to folks like us. But I have heard that he was only once married, and that long ago, when he was but a lad. His wife died and left him a little daughter –'

Hastily I changed the subject. Compassion for the Romany leader was an emotion I had no wish to feel. I realized that I wanted to hate him to vent my spleen upon him because of Molly Provis. And whatever Bessie had to say, I intended to do just that, to the very best of my ability. I was resolved that if he ever as much as nodded in my direction again, I would go to Aaron Flint and complain.

For the time being, I decided to avoid any encounter by taking the longer way through the wood, which was little used when winter turned it into a muddy track. As I walked, I heard the approach of a rider galloping fast, a sound that always brought back the sick horror of Bentley Drummle's murderous attack.

On that narrow path, panic again seized me, my first thought that the rider was Wolfe Farr who had followed me for some evil purpose. With nowhere to hide, I cringed back against the hedge, closed my eyes tightly as if this action would help to make me invisible, and prayed.

'Ah, Miss Havisham is it not? Goodday to you.'

I opened my eyes. The rider was Aaron Flint. He dismounted and asked how I did, how I liked living in Heathyfold.

'Well enough, sir, but I wish to seek a situation,' I said boldly. 'You may appreciate that there is little enough to live on for Bessie and myself.'

'Is that so?' he demanded sharply. 'Have any of my tenants complained to you?' When I said of course they had not, he nodded. 'That is good. I'm a soft employer, compared to my father, Miss Havisham, so the older folks tell me. He ruled them with a rod of iron and, by comparison, they have an easy life with me. House free, the young and able women work in my mill and the men attend the machinery. There is always work on the estate for them too and for old women, like Bessie, there is frame work.' He shook his head. 'I have never put any to the door, without excellent reason. The roof over their heads is theirs for life, or until they are too old to manage alone. Then there is the workhouse, which I also own, so there is food and drink for them there too.'

The retort was on my lips: that his idea of a crust of bread, a bowl of thin gruel and a glass of poor ale each day was hardly a good life, but a bitter existence without hope of escape except by death. As for the women mill-workers, I remembered Bessie's tales of sickness brought on by privation and her own terrible maimings, through an accident with the machines. Such maimings were by no means infrequent and Bessie had been luckier than most. She survived.

He studied me thoughtfully, perhaps reading the words into my silence. Suddenly he slapped his riding crop against those elegant polished boots. 'We always have need of servants up at the Hall, we need a powerful number to keep the house in order.'

When I didn't answer immediately, for I realized I would be little better off than as a frame knitter, he added: 'But I do believe Miss Flint has need of a lady's maid. Fifteen pounds a year with all found.' Remounting his horse, he smiled down at me. 'Think it over, Miss Havisham and if you are interested, come up to the hall tomorrow.'

Fifteen pounds a year and a pleasant place to live, I thought next day as I walked up the drive. Time off to see Bessie and in my spare time I could make a little extra from my knitting. Perhaps the Flints had friends who would buy my goods. The idea gave me hope, hope of a future.

The exterior of the hall was handsome in the prevalent modern taste of battlements and turrets, while stone arched windows overlooked a terrace (in place of a moat), where only strident peacocks strutted for supremacy. The exterior appearance of a medieval castle fighting the nineteenth century was continued indoors with an abundance of panelling, coats of arms, suits of armour, rugs and tapestries, small tables overburdened with china and a profusion of plants must have made the application of a feather duster, an adventure of the utmost hazard.

As for Miss Flint herself, she sat by the drawing-room fire and hardly seemed aware of my presence as her brother ushered me towards her. Indeed her eyes as they met mine with reluctance, even distaste, seemed slightly out of focus and her gaze returned immediately to the flames leaping up the chimney as if they presented a scene which filled her with deep sighs of melancholy.

For the first time I felt uneasy, that she had been bullied into considering this appointment of a lady's maid, for she showed no more sign of interest or animation, than if her brother offered a load of logs for the fire. She sat aloof, detached and even his forcedly cheerful manner and sunny smiles were considerably dampened at the end of it. In the sudden painful silence that ensued, I said: 'I presume you will wish to have references regarding my character,' I had already decided to offer Mr Jaggers' name, certain that I could rely on his discretion about revealing my present whereabouts.

A single frowning enquiry in the direction of his sister's still bent head and Mr Flint swept the suggestion aside. 'That is usual, but not in your case Miss Havisham. Without knowing any of your history, everything about you tells us all we need to know.' He studied me intently. 'Your cultured voice, your elegant bearing betray you. They tell us your story, my dear Miss Havisham, that you are a lady who finds herself in temporarily reduced circumstances.'

Bowing my head in assent as was decently expected of me, I hid an inward smile. Had Aaron Flint an inkling of those dire circumstances, I would not last an afternoon in his home. Even the silent Miss Flint would be animated by shrieks of horror.

He looked deep into my eyes and I fear, would have taken my hand had we been alone, as he murmured softly: 'I am discreet, Miss Flint is discreet. Indeed we are the very souls of that admirable quality in this house. You can rely upon that, Miss Havisham for we can tell a lady born whenever we meet one. Is that not so, my dear?'

This address to Miss Flint went unanswered. Having satisfied herself that the flames held no further gems of inspiration, she was now devoted to a careful scrutiny of the window curtains.

Aaron Flint sighed, unhappily, I fear: 'You will get along splendidly, I am sure and you will be very happy with us, once you get used to it' (with another imploring look at Miss Flint's back turned upon us). 'Just take us as we are, we will all get to know each other and be the greatest of friends in due course.'

I had my doubts about such sentiments as I hurried to inform Bessie of my success. She was delighted that I would be able to come 'home' for so I now regarded Meadowbank, on Sundays and accompany her to the parish church.

My first weeks passed without incident. What the modern building of Flintwood Hall lacked in tradition, it made up for in pretension. Everything was new and fashionable and managed to shout out how expensive it had been, with little evidence of good taste in a positive shriek of colours from every inch of space on wall and table, every corner with its tumble of potted plants.

A tiny room, little better than a closet opposite Miss Flint's bedroom had been set aside for my occupation. Severely plain, empty, it came almost as a relief from the claustrophobic clutter of my employer's rooms and as a monkish cell, would have served as a pious sermon on self-denial. I was surprised to find there were no male indoor servants; no footman or butler, the table waited upon by the servant girls who shared one huge attic room where rows of beds hugged the walls, with an altogether depressing workhouse appearance.

Perhaps the favour of a room to myself caused offence, for I was soon aware of being shunned by my fellow servants who communicated with me as little as I did with their mistress. Among themselves they were most agreeable, but all laughter would cease when I set foot in the kitchen. Strange, for they were young and pretty, almost as if they had been specially chosen for their looks, indeed the uneven standard of housekeeping in Flintwood Hall made me suspect this was so.

There was a newcomer to their midst, a gipsy girl whose looks I had grudgingly to admit were quite outstanding. She had arrived at the same time as myself and as, on our rare encounters in corridor or kitchen, she was in tears, I began to suspect that she was having some rough handling by the other servants: the pecking order of hens had been disturbed and here was an alien in their midst.

Once to my horror, I came upon a scuffle. In a dark corner near the linen cupboard, a girl was being held helpless, while two other servants pummelled and kicked her. Such violence, with its return to my Nightmare, sickened me and without a thought to my own safety, I rushed to her rescue. Why I knew not, except that instinct to protect the abused, although having extracted her from the melee and her assailants flown, I saw to my disgust that this was the gipsy girl. I decided I had been mad to interfere that, like all her kind, she would be well able to take care of herself.

I took her into my room, bade her sit down and poured her a glass of water. She drank it, and still sobbing gasped out: 'Orlenda thanks you, kind Miss Havisham.'

'Are you recovered now.' A nod.

'Do you hurt badly?'

'No, miss. Thanks to you, or they would have half-killed me, that for sure.'

'What had you done to offend them?'

She stared at me through a tangle of hair. 'Nothing, miss, nothing. They have been against me since I set foot in the kitchen.'

'People are not attacked by their colleagues without

some reason.' The reason was not hard to guess, that the servants liked the gipsies as little as I did and doubtless with better reason.

'Oh is that so, miss?' she demanded and as if she read my thoughts: 'Just because I'm a gipsy and the Maister has taken a fancy to me, is that it? I know all about him – and the Mistress too.'

Such audacity, I thought, hardening my heart and suddenly regretting my impulsive action, which could only destroy my own image in the eyes of the servants. How typical of the conceit of her kind.

As if Aaron Flint would look twice at a gipsy, especially one who was little more than a child.

She watched my face and said: 'Well, why don't you take their side against me? Tell the Maister. Go on. I don't care.'

'I have no intention of taking their side or informing Mr Flint. How old are you?'

She sniffed. 'Fourteen – or so.'

A child. 'If they are cruel to you, you must complain – er, to the mistress.'

'To her?'

'That would be appropriate.'

She laughed, throwing back her head in sudden mirth and eyed me pityingly. 'Well, now, I'd have to get to her very early in the day, wouldn't I? I doubt whether she'd understand one word, or could even see straight after she's had her dose of lady medicine for the day. Medicine, they call it. We've got a better name.'

I bit back angry words at this disrespect. 'Complain to the Master then.'

'And what could he do? Why those girls can twist him round their little fingers.'

Miss Flint's bell summoned me. The conversation was left unfinished but Orlenda showed signs of being my friend for life. Flowers appeared in a cracked and dusty vase in my room, a herb-scented pillow and then a pair of opal earrings, which I suspected might be valuable. The other gifts I had accepted with a gracious thanks, I could

171

hardly throw them back in her face, or stamp them into the floor in front of her as a mark that I found her attention tiresome in the extreme. Perhaps she had reason to regard me as her saviour for there were no more beatings.

'Did you do as I told you?'

A nod and a sly look. 'Maister has been very good to me.'

I had no wish to feel obligated to the creature and the opal earrings aroused a dire suspicion in my mind, that she might also be a thief and should she be found out then I would be regarded as her accomplice.

She had a habit of following me at a little distance and although I confess that all that did for me was to quicken my footsteps, today I lingered. Taking the earrings out of my pocket, I pressed them into her hand. Thanking her, the words choking me, I said: 'I cannot accept such a gift. You must know these are valuable.'

Orlenda grinned delightedly. 'I know, miss, Maister gave them to me.'

'Gave them? Are you sure?'

'Course I am, miss.'

I looked at her sternly. 'Then if the Maister gave them to you, why do you not wear them yourself?'

'Darsen't, miss. Other lasses would do me a mischief, they're that jealous. And Wolfe would skin me alive if he caught me with Gorgio trinkets.'

'Tell him the truth. That they were a present.' I thought Wolfe Farr would find her story even harder to believe than I did.

She shivered. 'No, miss, never. Wolfe is my father, see.' She seized my arm. 'Promise you won't say a word, not a word, miss.'

'I promise. But there must be no more gifts. Do you understand, I appreciate your kindness, but please, no more.'

Her face fell, as if I had deprived her of a great treat, but there were no more offerings in my barren cell and soon I had more important matters on my mind than a gipsy girl's honesty. If she were a thief, then someone would soon find out. Until then it was not my business to stir up a hornet's nest in my peaceful existence.

I did not encounter my employer a great deal, but was strangely conscious of his presence. The possessor of very remarkable eyes, I was aware of their brooding gaze from doorway or window. I must confess that the attraction was mutual for I realized that physically, in height and colouring, he reminded me strangely of Pip, a mature and successful Pip with his great expectations fulfilled, whose eyes, when our glances lingered, held a smiling question that made my heart beat faster.

More comfortable with Aaron Flint than any man since Pip, I realized the folly of idle day dreams about a man I was unlikely ever to meet again and considered instead the advantages of an attraction which might lead to a more lasting engagement than lady's maid. I thereupon decided that I would not be ill-pleased to be mistress of Flintwood – had I not the existing impediment of a husband. As for Aaron, was he truly free, and what was the mysterious bond between himself and his sister whose consumption of 'Lady Medicine' grew alarmingly? I counted several empty bottles each week which seemed to do little for whatever mysterious ailment she suffered from. Once I succeeded in arousing her animation by suggesting that if she continued to feel poorly, then a doctor should be consulted.

'Do not dare, do not dare to presume to tell me what is good and bad for me, miss. If you continue to spy on me for my brother, for I am fully aware of your role in this house –'

'Madam, that is not true. I am here as your maid.'

'My maid, eh. By no wish of mine. You are here at my brother's desire.'

'And what is my desire?' asked Aaron smoothly as he entered the room, as usual without a warning tap on the door. This habit was disconcerting, especially as it often appeared that he might have been outside for sometime, listening.

'You know that best, brother.'

He put an arm about her shoulders, led her to a chair. 'Do not upset yourself, my dear. Miss Havisham is only trying to help you,' – and with a brilliant smile to me – 'to help all of us by her presence,' he added softly.

As she burrowed her head in his chest, I withdrew. Strange man, stranger woman, I wished uneasily that he played less upon my own emotions, that I could harden my heart to his kind looks and words.

Soon I would have completed my first quarter at Flintwood. Spring was already throwing a soft green mantle over trees and lawns where birds now sang ecstatically to greet the world's rebirth. It was a warm afternoon and sunshine poured into Miss Flint's sitting room which overlooked the terrace. I poured out the third dose of her medicine that day and she watched me eagerly, her expression like a cat awaiting a tasty dish of cream. Since my vain remonstration with her, I had remained silent and exchanges between us were more minimal than ever, extending only to yes or no on her behalf, with an occasional more explicit, do this or do that. But such commands seemed to exhaust her.

As I returned to my seat by the window, repairing a torn frill on her petticoats, Aaron who had taken tea with us as was his now established habit, whispered something to her in passing, and coming to my side, stared down at me. 'Do you read, Miss Havisham?'

'I do, sir.'

'And what do you read?' he asked.

'Poetry, an occasional story.'

'Novels, perhaps.'

'Indeed.'

Aaron Flint nodded and taking a book from the drawer in his sister's writing desk, drew up a chair to my side. 'Mrs Gaskell perhaps is one of your favourites. This, I believe, is yours.'

'It is. Where did you find it, sir?' I asked sharply.

'One of the maids discovered it in the conservatory and returned it to your mistress.'

That is not so. It disappeared from my room, stolen no doubt by one of Miss Flint's servants set to spy upon me. I bit back the words.

'*Mary Barton*,' Aaron Flint continued. 'An unusual

choice. May I ask where you came by this copy?'

'I purchased it from a second-hand stall in Derby market for one penny,' I said.

He nodded frowning. 'That is a relief, then you were not responsible for the scurrilous review which is pasted into the back cover.'

'Of course not. I must confess, I have not even read it.'

'Then allow me to do so: "If the rich men, the people on Turkey carpets with their three meals a day, wish to know why poor men turn Chartists and Communists and learn to hate law and order, Queens, Lords and Commons, if they wish to know what can madden brave, industrious North country hearts into self-imposed suicidal strikes, into conspiracy, vitriol-throwing and midnight-burning, then let them read Mary Barton." ' Handing it to me he continued, 'Here is your book, Miss Havisham. Had you been an employee in my father's time, you would have received instant dismissal, as indeed happened to a member of our staff found reading this somewhat inflamatory text, when it was first published in '48. I have read it myself, so I am quite aware of the sentiments it expresses.' He paused, smiling.

'Be so good, Miss Havisham, as to open the book, anywhere will do, and read a passage to us. From the top of a page, anywhere,' he repeated.

I did as requested, thinking as I read out loud that I too would be shown the door. ' "As they passed, women from their doors tossed household slops of every description into the gutter; they ran into the next pool, which overflowed and stagnated. They picked their way till they got to some steps leading down into a small area, where a person standing would have his head about one foot below the level of the street and might at the same time, without the least motion of his body, touch the window of the cellar and the damp muddy wall right opposite. You went down one step even from the foul area into the cellar in which a family of human beings lived. It was very dark inside. The window-panes were many of them broken and stuffed with rags, which was reason enough for the dusky light that pervaded the place even at midday. After the account I have given of the state of the street, no one can be surprised on going into the cellar inhabited by Davenport, the smell was so foetid as almost to knock the two men down. Quickly recovering themselves, as those inured to such things do, they began to penetrate the thick darkness of the place and to see three or four little children rolling on the damp, nay wet, brick floor, through which the stagnant filthy moisture of the street oozed up; the fireplace was empty and black; the wife sat on her husband's chair, and cried in the dank loneliness ..." '

'I thank you, Miss Havisham, thank you.'

I closed the book and looked him straight in the eye.

'Well, Miss Havisham?'

'Well, sir?'

'Have you any observations to make?'

'None in particular, sir, but I expect it is true of many places in Britain.'

He leaned forward. 'But not of Heathyfold.'

'No, sir.'

He seemed satisfied and said: 'You do not sound very emphatic, Miss Havisham, but that I will forgive, for you have been genteel all your life. You have no great experience of the working classes. You will not find such conditions here at Heathyfold among my workers.'

'Heathyfold, sir, is still primarily a rural area. Mrs Gaskell's novel is concerned with the town of Manchester, and I can vouch from my short acquaintance with London, that such conditions, I fear, also prevail there among the poor.

'The poor, the poor. Most of them deserve to be so.' He wagged a finger at me. 'You may ask anyone at Heathyfold and they will tell you that Aaron Flint is a kind man, aye, compassionate too. You may further ask any of them old enough to tell you tales of my late father; a hard man, unflinching. I saw enough in my childhood, Miss Havisham, to determine that I would treat no man or woman harshly, that before the business of profit and loss to my mill, I would consider their rights as human beings first and foremost.'

Turning to the silent woman by the fire, he asked: 'Is that

not so, my dear? Am I not right?'

I doubted whether she had heard a word as she remained, leaning back in her chair, eyes closed. But as if she had been paying us her undivided attention he continued: 'You would enjoy listening to Miss Havisham read to us of an evening, of course you would.' And without interval for denial: 'Miss Havisham has a remarkably pleasant voice. We would therefore be delighted if she would read to us in the evenings. And of course,' he added, ignoring his sister's turned head now alert in our direction, the sudden imploring look which suggested some protest might be forthcoming, 'she will join us at the dinner-table, in future. We are sorely in need of a little diversion. We grow stale in the Hall, my dear.'

The words were addressed to the middle distance and included both Miss Flint and myself. He left us abruptly and I glanced at my employer nervously, wondering how this special treat which was no desire of hers might affect my relationship with the other servants, who seemed to have been chosen for the same monosyllabic qualities enjoyed by their mistress. For servants the world over enjoy a snobbish hierarchy of their own, that I knew from Orlenda's bullying and haranging and, indeed, remember-ed from my lofty station at Drummle. However, my fears were unnecessary and I encountered no hostility.

Bessie chuckled and said: 'You hardly need to feel surprised by the way they treat you – like a lady, in fact. After all, it's only the Flint's money makes the difference, since your voice is considerably more cultured than his. He has a very strong local accent. In their eyes you're a gentlewoman who has fallen on bad times. Mind you, had it been one of their own class so uplifted, then it would have been a very different story. They would not have taken that kindly at all.'

From the very first evening I dined at the handsome Sheraton table, the oak panelling glowing under a many branched candelabra, I was aware of Aaron Flint's appraisal and knew that not only had I been elevated, but why. The mill-owner was paying me very particular

177

attention. When the dishes were cleared away, he asked:

'And what else have you to offer for our entertainment, Miss Havisham, besides Mrs Gaskell?'

'Some poetry, sir, you like?'

He held out his hand for the little book Pip had given me long ago. 'Ah, I see you are also a devotee of our excellent poet, Alfred Lord Tennyson. We find his works most agreeable, is that not so, my dear?' he asked his sister remote from us at the other end of the table. As usual, she was not expected to give any reply. 'Let us have "The Day Dream", if you please.'

> ' "To pass with all our social ties,
> To silence from the paths of men;
> And every hundred years to rise
> And learn the world, and sleep again,
> To sleep thro' terms of mighty wars,
> And wake on science grown to more,
> On secrets of the brain, the stars,
> As wild as aught of fairy-lore;
> And all that else the years will show,
> The Poet-forms of stronger hours,
> The vast Republics that may grow,
> The Federations and the Powers,
> Titanic forces taking birth
> In divers seasons, divers climes;
> For we are Ancients of the earth,
> And in the morning of the times ..." '

He listened, hand cupping his chin, sometimes interrupting to ask what I believed the poet intended by such words. My answers seemed to satisfy him, for he would nod: 'Proceed, if you please.' But mostly he was silent, his gaze fixed and intense as I wondered what were his thoughts as he continued to feast his eyes upon me. I should have been flattered, indeed was flattered, but a little afraid too. Afraid because I too was attracted and when the day came for him to make up his mind, to change my fantasies into reality, what then? If I allowed myself to indulge my senses, to dream of more than an employer's brooding gaze, but of warm lips and strong arms and words of love I longed to hear, what then? When it came to the truth, how would I be able to tell him?

It best served my interests to delay that evil hour and I am ashamed to say that I encouraged his attentions. When we met as if by chance in the garden, I had seen him at a window and had connived at his appearance by lingering outside, knowing that he would find me. For a short while we would talk about flowers and plants and how he encouraged his tenants to grow food in their tiny gardens as well as the frivolity of flowers, all seeds generously provided by himself free of charge, he added proudly. One day seeming preoccupied when we met, he asked almost brusquely: 'And how is Bessie?'

I told him she was well enough most days but suffered from a troublesome cough which kept her awake at nights. I did not add my misgivings about her rheumatism or failing sight, since a crippled sightless frame knitter would be of little use to the mill-owner.

'You have known her many years?'

'Indeed, from my earliest days.'

'She was maid to your mother, was she not?' I nodded agreement. We had reached the arbor whose ghostly white statues gave an appearance of listening, attentive and menacing, in the sudden gloom when he halted: 'Your late husband, Miss Havisham?' he demanded sharply, 'when did he die?'

I turned, faced him. He was not a great deal taller than myself, his eyes disconcertingly level with my own. 'May one presume, since you are no longer in mourning and have reverted to your maiden name, that this melancholy event took place some time ago?'

Taking my guilty look for some other emotion, he stretched out and laughing, took my left hand. 'I am no clairvoyant, Miss Havisham, I merely use my eyes and they tell me that a wedding ring worn for some years leaves its mark upon the third finger.'

I should have told him the truth then, that I was no

widow, but to my astonishment, I heard the lie rattling out, my voice harsh, emotionless. 'He died as the result of an unfortunate riding accident.' Remembrance of my attempted murder by Bentley Drummle brought a fiercer return to the past than I had expected. My distress, my sudden rush of tears were genuine enough.

'Forgive me, my dear Miss Havisham, for intruding upon your grief in so tactless a manner. Perhaps you prefer not to talk about it –?' Taking my silence for assent his murmured, 'Quite so, quite so,' sounded disappointed too. He sighed. 'Truly, I have no wish to pry, only to assure you that my interest arises out of a very sincere regard for you.' His added whisper 'Dear lady,' his pressure on my hand, left little further doubt in my mind regarding Aaron Flint's intentions.

We returned to the Hall, both silent but thoughtful. My employer was a very handsome agreeable man. I had good reason to suspect that he was about to propose to me. How then should I answer? Again I knew that sensible action demanded that I ascertain whether Bentley Drummle still lived. If so, then I must nip my employer's attentions in the bud, before he declared himself and matters between us progressed on to a more intimate level than fond glances exchanged. If I were free, then I might be very happy to be the mistress of Flintwood Hall.

Might? Surely the word was ill-chosen, implying doubts, hesitation, some question not yet resolved in my own mind.

How Aaron Flint made his fortune was not my concern. Despite his self-righteous beliefs his tenants and workers were exploited as were those on the Drummle estate. But I had not given them a second thought or lost any sleep over the fact that luxuries and comforts I had enjoyed, expected as my right, had been bought at the cost of the misery and grinding poverty of those who served us. And I could still blush at how I had treated my poor Flora Jolly with only the ignorance of selfish youth to hide behind. According to the more inflammatory press many landowners' tenants and millworkers fared worse than the African slaves owned by Americans in the Southern States, despite the writings of

Harriet Beecher Stowe in *Uncle Tom's Cabin*. The truth of the matter was that I had not experienced poverty until recently and had learned that one's attitude to, and awareness of, the poor is greatly influenced by the side of the barrier from which the viewpoint is obtained. Had I not lived under Bessie's humble roof, then I doubt whether I would have acquired such sensitivity to the hopeless despair of the English peasants. Now I had witnessed at first hand the deplorable conditions in which many of his tenants lived, and of which Aaron Flint was so proud, but would have found intolerable after one day deprived of the luxuries he took for granted.

Later that same week, I encountered in the Hall a face from the past. Coming downstairs to dinner I found an extra place laid, the unexpected guest Will Startop, on his way to visit his aunt. He had not yet seen Bessie but meeting Aaron Flint at the village inn had accompanied him back to the Hall directly.

Now he bowed before me asking polite but evasive questions, while a smiling but curious Aaron listened closely and I trembled for the revelations that this visitor from my past might bring forth.

Dinner at an end, he turned to Will Startop. 'I'm sure you would enjoy walking Miss Havisham around the garden. Old friends have many things to talk about.' It was indeed a relief that he should show so much understanding and tact.

As we walked through the formal garden with its statues, Startop said: 'I must confess I almost fainted away when he told me of a Miss Havisham now residing at Flintwood. I had visions of your guardian in her ghastly bridal array arisen from the tomb and descending the stairs to greet me.'

I saw no reason to be devious with Will Startop. Once he had been my husband's boon companion. They had quarreled according to Drummle and although the cause had not been revealed to me, I did not doubt that the reason had been my husband's boorish ill-nature and Startop had subsequently become the ally of Pip and Herbert Pocket.

'What of Pip?' I asked eagerly.

'He and Herbert are in business partnership in Cairo. It is several years since I last saw them. An unhappy occasion indeed.'

'You must have been sad to lose them?'

'Sad?' he commented bitterly. 'You cannot imagine, my dear Estella, the events that took place.' When I looked puzzled, he said: 'You know, of course, that his great expectations came to naught? Poor fellow, his benefactor turned out to be nothing more than a wretched criminal, a convict he had befriended as a child –'

'Surely not the one he tried to help escape, who terrified his wits out of him long ago?'

'The very same. So you know the story?'

'Only what Pip told me. But he had not the least idea that dreadful man was his benefactor. We both firmly believed that my mother-by-adoption had chosen to play this mysterious role.'

'A natural assumption and one shared by everyone acquainted with the facts. As for Pip's convict, he had gone to Van Diemen's Land and when he made his fortune, determined that he would raise the blacksmith's boy as his very own young gentleman, but without revealing his true identity. Of course, he realized that returning to England meant certain death if he was apprehended, but I suppose curiosity overwhelmed him. You can imagine Pip's horror when he returned to his lodgings one night and found his old tormentor lurking in wait. Especially when he thereupon revealed the fact that he was none other than the mysterious benefactor.'

'Poor Pip.' I remembered his fear and loathing of the convict. 'He must have been horrified.'

'Indeed he was, but there was worse to come. Magwitch was already a hunted man and once again Pip would help him escape. With the assistance of Herbert and myself, he devised an elaborate scheme for getting him out of the

country, but alas, an old enemy, a fellow-convict, informed
on him and although Magwitch drowned him, in the scuffle
with the law, he was wounded and died in prison.'

'Which he no doubt richly deserved for his past crimes.
But I am sorry he didn't escape after all.'

'I told you there was more to follow, a piece of
information that will astound you. This old enemy of
Magwitch, Compeyson, had been in his youth the close
friend of Arthur Havisham.' He paused and regarded me
triumphantly. 'He was none other than Miss Havisham's
absconding bridegroom. A quite extraordinary coincidence
that Pip's benefactor, should also be the instrument of
your guardian's vengeance.

'While he was in hiding, he became very confidential
with us, to the extent of revealing the sordid details of his
early life. He had loved a gipsy girl and gone through a
form of marriage with her – over the broomstick, they call
it. As well as having dubious qualities of honesty, it seemed
that our Magwitch also had a roving eye. Once it roved too
readily and in a fit of rage, his gipsy wife strangled his new
mistress and then murdered their own child as a terrible
revenge.'

As I listened horrified, I begged and prayed to shut out
the truth of the terrible picture that Startop presented, for
there was no longer a missing father with property, a good
name and some standing in the world, constantly
searching for the daughter lost long ago. So much for idle
dreams, I thought, as they crumbled into ruins about the
twisted quiet paths of the gardens of Flintwood Hall.

'How – how did his wife murder her rival?'

'By strangulation. Unusual for a woman to use such a
method, but she had uncommonly strong hands.'

Yes, I knew those hands, their bloodied nails stretching
out towards me as I cowered in the darkness.

'And the woman's unfortunate child, was she murdered
also?'

He shrugged. 'One presumes so.'

'Magwitch – a strange name.' Even now I hoped that a
miracle might prove the hand of coincidence at work.

'One of many. He was also known to the police as Provis.'

Provis. Ah, that was the final seal of my doom. And as he talked I realized that I could have filled in the details very well indeed. The child his gipsy-wife, Molly Provis, threatened to murder was a girl. Myself. By some last minute intervention or change of heart, my wretched life had been spared, but the scars of those dreadful hours were marked upon my soul for life.

As I walked through the gardens at Startop's side, I thought of the picture I must present. Calm, polite, every inch a gentlewoman in reduced circumstances, while under my skin every nerve in my body screamed out loud, railing against this new horror that I must bear. Not only was my mother a murderess but my father a habitual criminal, for ever in and out of jail and finally expatriated for the rest of his life, his only decent feelings directed not towards his own little daughter, but to a stranger, Pip, the lad who had taken pity upon him.

And because of that one act of kindness, Pip's entire life had been changed. Certain that Miss Havisham was his benefactor, small wonder that Pip had been brought low, disgusted and betrayed by Magwitch's reappearance. But his agony was nothing compared to my discovery that Pip's convict was my own father, that I was that wretched man's flesh and blood.

Retracing our steps towards the house, I wanted to fall on the ground, weep, tear my hair in Biblical fury. Instead I heard my voice ask calmly: 'Do you hear aught of Bentley Drummle?'

'Only that he is a helpless cripple.' He paused. 'The result of an unfortunate riding accident, was it not?' Another pause before he added delicately: 'I gather that you are separated from him.'

'Yes and for ever. I shall never return to him. His treatment of me was vile. He desired my death –'

Startop mistook the rising hysteria in my voice. 'Come, Estella, dry your tears.' Imagining my distress to concern Bentley, he paused while I fought to compose myself before we reached the house. 'I can well imagine the kind of husband Drummle turned out to be. I trusted him for he was my friend before Pip, but he betrayed that friendship in every possible way. I only wish we had been better acquainted at that time, for I could have advised you very strongly against marrying such a brute.'

If only an unhappy marriage was the full extent of my troubles, but in the light of Startop's dire revelations, oh, how I rued the day that we had met again at Flintwood Hall. Trying desperately to keep my mind on what he was saying, I answered dully: 'Pip tried to warn me and failed. I would listen to no one. And I imagine that knowing something of my character from him, you decided that Bentley Drummle richly deserved such a wife as I would make. A cruel heartless female guaranteed to bring him no happiness.'

Startop had the grace to look uncomfortable and taking his arm I said: 'None of you really knew me very well. I was not the girl I appeared to be but like an actress on a stage, my lines written at the dictates of my mother-by-adoption. Once on my own, alas, all those theories of hers flew out of the window and I had to learn the harsh realities of living with a man like Drummle, in a very bitter school.'

Startop nodded to where Aaron Flint was approaching us across the terrace. 'I must leave tomorrow morning early, Estella,' he whispered urgently, 'perhaps you know already that Flint is considerably taken by you. You would do well to consider carefully before making a second marriage. You take my meaning? Good. And before you accept him, I should advise you to question him closely about his sister.'

There was no chance of further private conversation between us. The two old friends talked and drank in the library far into the night and by the time I breakfasted, Startop had gone.

In the days that followed I lived with my Nightmare by day and by night, inescapable as part of my very soul. Concentration I found impossible, my mind like a rat trapped in a cage forever running round in circles, frantically seeking an escape and knowing that none existed. For me there could be no miracle of mistaken identity, no second coincidence to cancel Startop's revelations. I could find no mitigating circumstances: my parents were both murderers and I should carry that stigma until my dying day.

Once I dropped a china ornament and Aaron hearing the crash came in to discover me in floods of tears.

'My dear Miss Havisham, it is nothing. It cost a few pounds but it is easily replaced. Dear lady, dear lady, do not distress yourself.' And so he took me in his arms to comfort me, and inevitably his lips sought mine. It seemed natural for him to do so, natural for me to cling to him and returning that kiss I wondered why it had taken so long for us to make this new discovery about each other.

Releasing me reluctantly, he whispered: 'There now, that is better. Now you are smiling again.'

We sprang apart as approaching footsteps heralded Bertha Flint. Aaron held up the broken ornament as evidence. 'I am sorry about your shepherdess, my dear, I trust it was not one of your treasures.' As anger darkened her brow and she glared in my direction, perhaps observing my flushed countenance, Aaron shook his head. 'I am afraid the fault is mine, I knocked it over with my elbow. Careless of me,' he lied cheerfully taking the blame.

And he walked across to her with the pieces in his hand, giving me a chance to make my escape and restore my tear-stained countenance. Oh how the memory of his kindness, the sweetness of that first kiss stayed with me during those dark and fearful days.

Bessie and I had established an arrangement of meeting at church, since we approached it from opposite directions. When she did not put in an appearance, feeling anxious, I hurried quickly to Meadowbank, afraid to find her ill and wondering how much I should reveal to her of Startop's visit.

She came to the garden gate to meet me and one glance told me thankfully that she was in good health and spirits, her first words that Startop had looked in to see her knowing she was an early riser. 'A few minutes only but as always a parting gift, dear kind young man.' With a chuckle, she added: 'He was very surprised to see you at Flintwood Hall and that you didn't know about Pip.'

'Did you know about his convict?'

'Goodness yes, Mr Startop told me that story long ago. Somehow I thought you knew. But this is my reason for staying at home,' and leading me into the kitchen, she pointed to the chair by the fire where a tiny child swathed in blankets lay asleep.

'That's my Abby's bairn,' she whispered wiping away a tear. 'Oh Miss Estella, I told you how she went off to work three years ago up North. She was ambitious, my Abby, always wanting to better herself, marry well. Here you see the result of her desire for betterment. An unwanted bairn. Some man, her wealthy employer like as not, for she was a right bonny lass, had his way with her and having got her with child, sent her packing. The poor lass – the poor lass. She died a month back of a fever and left instructions with the couple who had befriended her that the baby – Angela she's called – was to come to me.'

'Why did she not come home to you right away? Surely you would never have sent her away, or blamed her because of the baby.'

'Not I, lass, but Mr Flint would have taken that babe from her before he'd give her a job. Aye, send the babe to the workhouse, for that's his stern rule for bastards born at Heathyfold: find decent honest parents where their shame and sin can be forgotten.'

As most unfortunate girls would be grateful to be rid of this reminder of their indiscretions, Aaron Flint's solution seemed both worthy and humane. But Bessie shook her head. 'There's them that says Flint makes quite a profit out of baby-farming on the side.'

'Baby-farming?'

'Aye, lass, selling the little lasses to those who can't have bairns of their own. I dare say for the mothers who want rid of them, that is a blessed relief. But there's another side to it, I've heard tell. The little lads are kept till they are five and then sold like slaves, as chimney sweeps or to work down the mines.

'My poor Abby,' she wept, 'little more than a bairn herself, and I was all the kin she knew, her mother, my only niece, died bringing her into the world.' As I comforted her, she sobbed: 'She was dearer to my heart than any in the world but you and your dear Mama, Miss Estella. And now she's gone too. I don't know what I'm to do. Dear God, how am I an old woman, to care for a babe with my hands as they are –' she held up the gnarled twisted fingers –'and my eyes nearly blind. Yes, you knew that, didn't you, my dear lass, but you never showed it and I thank you for that. Old Bessie never wanted pity. But now, what's to become of my Abby's bairn. I can't let her go to Flint's babyfarm.'

Roused by our voices, the child woke and gurgling with delight, shook pearly fists in the air. 'Angela's her name. A fine fancy name, you'll be thinking, for a servant girl's bastard. But those bonny curls, her eyes are the image of my Abby's,' she added with a sob. 'Just like an angel from a storybook.'

As I approached the chair, she looked up, smiled and held out her small hands in welcome: 'Ma-ma.' Had she mistaken me for her own mother in the gloom? I gathered her into my arms and with a contented sigh, she burrowed her head against my shoulder, arms tight about my neck.

Cradling her thus, I forgot all about Startop and Mr Jaggers' Molly and the convict Magwitch. A plan was forming in my mind. As I fed her and bathed her that night and hushed her to sleep, I felt like one returning home expecting bitter sadness to discover instead that a miracle was awaiting on the doorstep.

My miracle – a child to love, to be mine at last.

I had been sent this blessing when my life was in ruins, when every hope and dream lay shattered, this child had been sent to soothe my mortal agony, for as I clasped her to my heart, she became the embodiment of all those sons and daughters I had lost, born dead to my marriage. Considering my heritage and Bentley Drummle's murderous impulses, only God's divine will had prevented us inflicting some monster of depravity upon the world.

But this sweet motherless child, untainted by blood, I

could have for my own. Not to be raised as the whim of a
vain woman's sick desire for vengeance, but to happiness
and fulfilment. And I closed my eyes and prayed that no
one, no one would ever be allowed to take her from me.
Strange, for as though our hearts were united in spiritual
recognition, she clung to my neck, lisping 'Ma-ma.'

Bessie smiled. 'Why, that blessed bairn seems to know
you already. She has never once cried for her mama until
you came.'

'Did your Abby resemble me?'

'Only in height and general colouring. Though she
wasn't as dark haired as yourself and her eyes were blue,
like Angela's.' She put a worn hand over mine. 'If – if
anything happens to me, Miss Estella,' she whispered:
'promise you'll take care of her.'

'I promise, Bessie. I will never be parted from her, never.
You have my word.' Holding the child to my heart as she
slept, I could hardly bear to go back to the Hall.

Perhaps Bessie had some premonition of what lay in
store. The cough that had niggled constantly worsened into
a fever. Each week I found her a little more frail, a little
more vague and preoccupied, as if she had drawn away
from us in the manner of one about to embark on a long
and fearful journey.

'She eats nothing and is more often in her bed than at
her knitting-frame,' whispered her neighbour Annie Leys,
who for a few shillings a week, took good care of Angela and
saw that Bessie had soup and bread twice a day, and meat
when there was any available, more often than not, rabbit
or hare. Old Annie was reliable. She never failed to remind
me, and to apologize, with many gap-toothed hearty
chuckles, for having first taken me for one of Wolfe Farr's
gipsies when I knocked upon her door.

Meanwhile my lady's maid activities continued as I
looked after Bertha Flint's extensive wardrobe, no longer
expecting thanks of even recognition by her. Without
Angela and Bessie, I do not think I could have stayed, not
even for Aaron. Now from the Hall's upper windows
Meadowbank was no longer visible, obscured by trees

heavy with summer leaves, the great moors hazy under a blue sky and shimmering with lark song from dawn to day's end. I was much given to day-dreams as I pictured my Angel waiting for me in Bessie's cottage, and deploring the times I must be parted from her as I counted the days that separated one Sunday from the next.

Aaron Flint continued to pay me great attention but the expectations of a proposal did not materialize. Angela was a further complication although he had been told that her mother was dead and Bessie caring for her until her soldier father returned to claim her when the war was over.

I continued to permit myself the luxury of allowing Aaron to hold my hand a fraction too long, or of gazing deep into my eyes and thereby losing the thread of an interesting conversation. And when on two occasions he kissed me a lingering goodnight at the foot of the staircase I went to bed with a heart beating fast enough to make its own declaration of my feelings. I was eager to fall in love with Aaron, allured by the prospect of being mistress of Flintwood Hall. Especially as I saw myself living very comfortably in this fine house with my Angel, secure in that land of happy-ever-after brutally denied my first marriage. Perhaps then I could also persuade Aaron to be less accommodating to Wolfe Farr and his gipsies whose winter encampment had long since overflowed into summer. The sight of those painted caravans on the common were an offence to my happiness, for they filled me with disgust and a foreboding I could never quite escape.

Sometimes in the long watches of the night I wondered whether I loved Aaron as much as I was willing to pretend. Surely my experiences at Drummle Towers should have made clear the dangers of selling myself yet again. Did I not sometimes see a fleeting resemblance between Bentley Drummle and Aaron Flint? Although the two men were a complete contrast physically and emotionally, there existed an intangible link between them, something I could neither grasp nor define. And even if Aaron did ask me to be his wife, what then? As far as I knew I had a husband who still lived. That was the first just cause and impediment to our union. Next, my unfortunate history suggested prudence in matters of childbearing and older now, even willing, I might not be able to readily provide Flintwood Hall with an heir, while Aaron might be justified in a certain reluctance to see my foster-daughter in such a role. A childless state might affect a second marriage as disastrously as the first. Had an heir survived, perhaps Bentley might never have known the desperation and bitter resentment that had festered into loathing and the impulse to murder.

I must not make the same mistake about Aaron Flint. Here was no lovesick green lad. Single at forty, he must have had excellent reasons for remaining unmarried, reasons about which I knew nothing. But I would do well to bear in mind that when middle-aged bachelors of property considered marriage, their primary concern was for the continuation of their line. Often their sole reason for choosing some plain and tedious girl was that her wealth and breeding possibilities were excellent.

I had very little to offer in such respects. Thirty was fast approaching and even my looks, I feared, would soon fade. I would do well not to have Aaron Flint believe that I had deliberately encouraged him to make a fool of himself. Having witnessed the sharpness of his anger directed against others who offended him, I had no reason to believe that I would be privileged.

Another impediment existed, which continued to disturb me. His sister Bertha. Remote and aloof, I suspected that I was tolerated only for my usefulness and to please Aaron. As I grew fonder of the brother I found myself remembering Startop's parting words: 'Look to the sister.'

All my timid overtures of friendship had been rejected by this sorry creature who rarely roused from the deepest melancholy, induced, I learned, by taking as 'medicine' vast quantities of laudanum. It was Aaron himself who confided in me his sister's condition. Originally prescribed as a cure for some 'woman's disorder' she had become

hopelessly addicted. On occasions when he had felt
impelled to remove the Lady's Medicine, she had turned
violent and threatened to take her own life.

The story Annie Leys told me gave further reason for
caution. Annie had served in the Hall when Amos Flint
was alive. His twin son and daughter were devoted to each
other, clinging for comfort in a tyrannical household with
an invalid mother, and an overbearing, harsh father who
had never supped the milk of human kindness in his whole
life. Bertha grew up a beautiful, headstrong girl and was
offered many suitors. All were declined. She remained
devoted to her handsome brother, neither with the least
inclination for marriage. Amos Flint took their mother to
Italy for her health one summer and both drowned in a
sailing accident. Under Aaron's management, the mill
ceased to prosper and he was faced with the necessity of
marriage to a rich woman, whose fortune might save
Flintwood, and also provide an heir. He chose a girl
wealthy but alas, not healthy. She died a few weeks after
the marriage and Bertha who had gone into deepest
mourning and refused to leave her room from the day the
betrothal was announced, now rejoiced.

What happened next was anyone's guess, according to
Annie Leys. Aaron's wife's fortune saved the mill and he
and Bertha became more inseparable than ever, until the
day when a wealthy American mill-owner came to visit
Flintwood. He succeeded with Bertha where all previous
suitors had failed, but Aaron opposed the marriage.
Defying him, the couple eloped.

What a blow to Aaron's pride. In hot pursuit he caught
up with them at Derby. In the ensuing scuffle in an
upstairs room at the coaching inn, the American was
killed. The servants who had accompanied Aaron swore
that it was an accident, that Bertha's suitor had been
drunk and fell out of the window, breaking his neck.

'Mr Flint? Why the master was not even in the room.
And Miss Flint would vouch for that.' Which she did,
returning home meekly enough with her brother. Once
again the curtains of life at the Hall were closed to all but a

few devoted servants, while in public the couple seemed happy and content and more inseparable than ever.

Occasional ugly rumours from servants who had left the Hall in some disgrace, hinted that Bertha was more to Aaron than a sister should be to her brother and that she'd had a bairn that died, also that she was insanely jealous of any girl he looked upon with marriage in mind. She did, however, allow him one small concession. The servant lasses were his to command to his bed.

'Now, Miss Havisham, you must promise you won't breathe a word of what I've told you,' said Annie solemnly.

I promised without difficulty, for her story was quite incredible.

Absurd to imagine the rather chilly Aaron and the aloof other-worldly Bertha in an incestuous relationship. I dismissed this domestic melodrama as exaggeration of a kind delighted in by malicious servants with a grievance against their late employer.

Annie and Bessie regarded me sadly. 'Aye, but there must be a grain of truth somewhere, lass, for such a rumour.'

I little guessed as I kissed Angela and returned to the Hall that Sunday night, that within a few days my own fool's paradise was to collapse about my ears.

One evening after dinner was cleared, and my reading to them at an end, Aaron dismissed his sister. 'I wish to speak to Miss Havisham alone. And you, my dear, are looking particularly tired tonight. I fear you have been overdoing things again.'

She gave him a look of reproach and annoyance, followed by a look of blackest hatred in my direction.

'Go, Bertha,' he said sternly. 'Take your medicine and go to bed. At once.'

The door was banged none too gently leaving me with little doubt what was to follow. The inescapable hour had struck. Aaron Flint was about to propose. I listened to him as he sat opposite me toying with the stem of an empty wine glass.

'... my deepest regard. You must have long been aware

that my feelings for you are far greater than those of
employer for servant ...' And so on. I kept my eyes
modestly on my plate in the manner expected of me. At the
end of it all I raised my head sharply.

The words I had heard were not 'honour of asking you to
be my wife.' Had I misheard him? No, he was repeating the
question: 'Taking you as my mistress.'

'Your mistress, sir.'

'That is correct.'

I stood up sharply and he laughed. 'Insulted are you?'

'I am indeed insulted, sir.'

'Before you leave, consider the circumstances. I am
being honest with you, which, I regret to say, is more than
you have been with me. How could you accept me as your
husband, Miss Havisham – or is it Lady Drummle, when
you have a husband still alive.'

I sat down. So he knew.

'Will Startop has always had a poorer head than mine for
strong drink. He is loyal to you, but a chance remark when
he was not quite sober, about the Drummle family, led me
to conduct an investigation. I learned that far from being
dead your husband is very much alive, although a helpless
invalid. I must admit however, that had your circumstances been different, had you in truth been a widow – but
I have no desire for either of us to contract a bigamous
marriage –'

'Had you made me such a proposal, then I should
certainly have felt obliged to inform you of my husband's
existence, and save you the trouble of an enquiry,' I
interrupted indignantly.

He smiled, not one whit put out. 'Indeed yes, my dear,
but such enquiries are not unlike those I should have set in
motion concerning any employee who was to be considered
for a place of trust and responsibility in my household. And
what greater place of trust and responsibility could exist,
do you think, than as my wife and the mistress of
Flintwood?'

As I continued to regard him coldly, he smiled. 'I see you
consider that my actions were not those of a gentleman.'

'I would have thought it more gallant, had you raised the matter with me first.'

'My dear Estella, I cannot afford to be gentlemanly. I have too much at stake. However, you are clever and decorative, and I suspect a passionate woman too. I find you extremely attractive and in all truth, I am growing a little weary of tumbles with serving girls, a rather undignified pursuit for a man of forty. I need a more permanent relationship and whereas my sister's melancholic condition would only be further exaggerated by the presence of a wife, her objections to a mistress might be overcome. However, who knows what the future may have in store for us. Some day I may be inclined to offer you a permanent place in my life, should those charms so agreeably anticipated prove their worth and provided of course, you no longer have a legal husband.'

As he spoke he gazed at me in a brooding sensual manner, from head to foot and back again – 'and missing nothing in between', as old Bessie would have said. 'There is, of course, still the question of an heir, a matter I gather at which you were singularly unsuccessful with your first husband.' He held up his hand. 'No matter, no matter. For the present, both my sister and myself find the prospect of babies most odious. Besides we decided long ago when we ourselves inherited, not to include provision for offspring, but to enjoy all the benefits in our own lifetime ...'

This discourse was interrupted by agitated voices. The door was flung open to admit the Romany, Wolfe Farr, firmly grasping Orlenda. Shrieking protests, she tried to escape his relentless grip as he propelled her forward.

'What does this mean? How dare you enter this house without permission?' said Aaron. 'Leave immediately and take that creature with you or else –'

Wolfe Farr regarded him steadily. 'Or else you will have me thrown out, is that it? Then I would advise you to take on men servants instead of defenceless maids, for I did not come alone. And when I have done with you, Mr Flint, I will go gladly and peacefully. But first, I intend to see justice done and my daughter as your wife.'

Aaron laughed. 'You must be mad, Farr. I marry that vile blubbering wretch. Leave while you can, I warn you.' And when Farr took a step forward, he gasped: 'You are insane.'

'Not as insane as yourself, Mr Flint, if you think the Romanies will allow you to get a daughter of theirs with child and not seek the justice of marriage.'

'I have not the slightest idea of what you are talking about.'

But I had. Remembering those earrings I had been offered by the simple Orlenda and how the other maids had viciously attacked her. So her story had been true and I had Aaron's own words about 'tumbles with the maids'. If further evidence was sought, he presented a study in guilt. His countenance turned first red and then livid with fear as the tall Romany towered over him.

Now Wolfe Farr turned to Orlenda and asked in English that we might all understand: 'Daughter, is this man truly the father of your child? Speak up and do not be afraid.'

'Yes – yes,' she whispered, with fearful glances at Aaron.

'Has any other man lain with you?'

'Never, father, truly. Never.'

'And did this man promise you marriage?'

'He did indeed, when I told him about – about the babe. He said he would make it all right by me,' she added doubtfully.

'Very well, your babe shall have a father.' He called out a command and from the doorway four of his stalwart young gipsies entered and rushing forward, seized Aaron's arms. Slightly built, he was no match for them and he was now visibly shaking as Farr took out a knife, which he flicked lightly across Aaron's face. It drew forth a thin trail of blood and a scream of terror.

'Now listen to me, Mr Flint. This is what you are going to do. You are going to marry my daughter, here and now. If you refuse then I promise you will never father another bastard.' There was no mistaking the grimness of their threat and Flint looked ready to faint as they pushed Orlenda against his side. Swiftly the couple's right wrists were bound together, their thumbs seized, touched with the knife blade and pressed together. Wolfe Farr mouthed a Romany ritual, while bread was produced, broken and drops of blood were allowed to fall upon it, the pieces held up to the couple.

'Eat – eat,' said Wolfe Farr.

Aaron trembling, looked as if he was having considerable difficulty in swallowing the bread. No one spoke to me. I might well have been invisible where I had retreated to a small side table near the window. At last with a benediction pronounced solemnly in their heathenish tongue, Farr declared the couple man and wife.

Orlenda was a tearful unprepossessing bride, but quickly recovered sufficiently to give her reluctant bridegroom a look of triumph. As for Flint, he shook visibly and his wrist freed from his bride, he retreated quickly behind the table, his eyes never leaving Wolfe Farr and his gipsies as they prepared to leave.

Ashen-faced, shaking, at last he spoke. 'A moment, one moment before you go. I have something to give you. A parting wedding present.' And opening the drawer in the table, he swung round, a brace of pistols in his hands.

Smiling, he aimed them. 'These are for you. One for your daughter and this for yourself, Wolfe Farr.' By the door, the Romanies halted uncertain. 'Oh yes, they are loaded. I learned long ago that one must be prepared for intruders, vagrants – who repay my kindness by breaking into my home.' His voice was shrill and as he walked forward, the gipsies exchanged alarmed looks with their leader. An armed Flint had not been bargained for.

Until that moment I believed he could prove that Orlenda had lied. But with a sinking heart I realized that Aaron Flint who would have the past of the woman he supposedly loved investigated like a common criminal, was no better than Bentley Drummle. In that instant, I discovered what had eluded me. Both were ruthless men who would cheerfully commit murder, if it suited their grim purpose and if they believed they could escape detection.

As I watched horrified, I knew how the law would react. Who would take a thieving gipsy's words that he had come demanding justice? Everyone knew that Romany girls were loose-living, immoral creatures. Orlenda had committed the crime of admitting the Romanies for some felonous purpose, fortunately Aaron had awakened and apprehended them. They had been shot trying to escape ... The law would see that Aaron Flint went free, his character unblemished.

'I think my bride should be the first to leave this sorry world.' He was smiling now. 'Tragically, I shall be a widower before I am even a bridegroom. How ironic.' His intentions were no longer in doubt. He meant their deaths. I looked at the group at the door, scared and frozen into immobility. They were only gipsies whom I had no reason to love, but the scales removed from my eyes, I saw no reason to love this new Aaron Flint. Even as Orlenda screamed and he levelled the pistol, my hand touched a glass paperweight. I seized it, hurled it across the room. My aim was better than I had intended, the pistols clattered harmlessly to the ground and he stumbled, fell, striking his head against the marble fireplace. I ran over and he lay like one dead, blood streaming from the side of his head.

Suddenly the room exploded into action. Wolfe Farr leaped forward, knelt by Aaron, raised his head and sprang to his feet. He seized my arm. 'I think he is dead. There is not a moment to be lost. Come, we must be away from here.' He called a command and the room emptied instantly. I was too shocked to move.

'You too, Miss Havisham,' he said gently. 'You had better come with us.'

'No, I cannot. I must stay. Get help for him.'

'I have no time to argue with you. But take heed. It will take them some time to raise a doctor at this hour and to summon a constable – if he is dead. Go while you can, Miss Havisham. For after all it was your blow that felled him.'

The thought that I had killed Aaron Flint filled me with horror. I felt rooted to the spot. I did not want to leave, I was determined to brave it out, to explain to the law that it was an accident that I had only wished to protect the gipsy girl, Orlenda.

I would stay my ground. I would not yield to panic. But as I made my decision, I found myself remembering my heritage of violence, parents who had both committed murder. Bentley Drummle whom I had helped to a possibly early grave and now my kindly employer, Aaron Flint. Who would believe my version any more than they would the gipsies' when the full terrible story came out in court? Who then would believe that I had not been in league with them once my sorry history was revealed?

'You must come with us, it is your only chance,' said Wolfe Farr. 'His sister – where is she?'

'Asleep long since. She takes a sleeping draught.'

He nodded. 'That is well. The maids are all in bed by nine o'clock and Orlenda crept down, unlocked the door for us. So with good fortune on our side, none will be astir until six in the morning. By which time we will have melted into thin air. Come.'

'I must get some of my things.'

'No. Orlenda will bring your cloak. Go, girl.'

'And my jewel box, Orlenda,' I called after her.

'No,' said Farr. 'Only those you are wearing now. When I began to protest he said: 'You are behaving like a foolish woman, for if Flint lives, then better he should believe that we abducted Miss Havisham by force. In that way you will be safe. Otherwise –' he paused. The threat to my own safety was obvious. And that decided me. Flint would have no mercy. Prison, transportation, such would be my sentence. 'Come, we are grateful to you. You saved our lives, we are used to calumny, but there is no need for you to be further involved.'

Orlenda returned, threw the cloak about my shoulders, and thrust a little velvet jewel bag into my hand, with a whispered: 'This was all I could see, Miss.' In answer to her father's question she shook her head. 'All is silent, the maids sleep and the door to Miss Flint's bedroom locked.'

We ran lightly across the terrace, down the drive and

through the darkness toward the Common. Our way passed near to Bessie's cottage. I stopped. 'I cannot go without telling her.'

'Ten minutes, then. We cannot wait for you.'

In the cottage, I found Annie Leys weeping by the bedside. One look at Bessie told me what I had feared most. She was dying.

'She's sinking fast, poor soul,' sobbed Annie. 'I doubt she'll not see another morning …'

'Why on earth did you not send for me?'

'The dear Lord sent you, that's what. The little lass has been awfully sick all day. I was waiting until morning to get someone to look after her, while I came to the Hall …'

'Oh, Bessie, Bessie.'

'She's been very low in her spirits all this past week.'

What was I to do now? Stay with Bessie or desert her in her last hours. As if she was aware of my presence, her eyes opened.

'Bessie, can you hear me?' She nodded. 'Aye, lass and I'm right glad to see you.'

'Bessie, there has been an accident at the Hall. The gipsies and Aaron Flint – He's been injured. I tried to save Orlenda. It was my fault, I might be blamed too.'

In a voice suddenly strong she said: 'Then run, my precious, run as quick as you can. For if Flint recovers, he will destroy all of you. Take the bairn with you, for God's sake, take her. If you don't when I am gone, he will have her put in the workhouse.'

'Right enough, right enough,' murmured Annie Leys. 'Don't worry, lass, I will say that her soldier father came for her.'

Snatching Angela from her warm bed, I wrapped her in a blanket. She sighed and snuggled contentedly into my arms. Leaning over I kissed Bessie. 'I will come back someday.'

She took my hand. 'No, lass, don't you ever come back, for you will only find old Bessie's grave. We will meet one day, but not in this world. Goodbye, my darling lass. God go with you both.'

An hour after Aaron Flint's strange marriage, his gipsy bride who might well already be a widow, and myself clutching my foster child were aboard one of the waggons, racing through the still quiet sleeping dales, along roads and lanes whose very existence was known only to the travelling folk. The night wind rushed past, the swaying trees whispered: 'Bessie, Bessie,' and as the tears streamed down my face, I felt as if my heart would break.

When daylight came, I was surprised by these tiny homes with more room inside than was obvious from their exteriors. Everything was compact and neatly bestowed behind wooden slats, shelves which lined the walls to keep china and other delicate possessions safe while the waggons moved over uncertain roads. There were even rugs on floors and a stove in one corner with its chimney to carry away the smoke. As well as a bed curtained for extra privacy.

I learned in the few days I was with them, if not to love them or their way of life, at least to respect Wolfe Farr who was no wayside beggar or vagrant but as much a man of property in his own society as Flint and Drummle were in theirs.

The plan was that once we were well south of Derbyshire, the Farrs would split up, melt into thin air by losing themselves among other gipsy tribes until nothing was left for the Gorgios to find of Wolfe Farr and his daughter Orlenda.

By the third day we had hit torrential rain and the waggons could no longer proceed fast down the muddied lanes.

'We will have to take to the roads. The waggons will be recognized and we must not be found with them,' said Farr. 'I will take Orlenda and a fast horse. We will ride like the wind.'

'What is to happen to me?' I asked desperately.

'You cannot come with us.'

'So I have served my purpose.'

Farr ignored that. 'Your presence and that of the child would slow us down, as well as making us conspicuous ...' He pointed to the signpost. 'There lies your direction. At

201

Farley, four miles distant, there is a coaching post for
London.'

'London?'

'Aye, Miss Havisham. 'Tis safer for you to lose yourself
in London. Surely you have many friends there.'

'But I have no money for a stage-coach ticket.'

'There I cannot help you.'

'What am I to do?'

'You must earn some money. Learn to steal if you cannot
come by it honestly. But refrain from trying to sell any of
your jewels if you do not wish to attract attention. A gipsy
woman with expensive trinkets will be presumed to have
come by them dishonestly. Here,' and he thrust a basket of
clothes pegs on my arm and a rabbit pie to eat along the
way. 'Off you go.'

'But – but –'

He looked at me, grinning as if he read my thoughts.
'You will survive, for you are one of us.' I felt like protesting
that even gipsy born I had Gorgio ways. 'Your actions
proved it beyond all possible doubt when you struck Flint
down. We will never forget that you saved our lives. Maybe
some day we will meet again, when all these troubles are
forgotten. If you ever need us, tell any traveller of the road
that Miss Havisham has need of Wolfe Farr. If I live I will
find you and yours.'

Dismayed I watched them ride off in the pouring rain.
Whatever my parentage, I had been gently reared, my
constitution could never deal with the hardships of
weather, or life in the open. And what of Angela? Clutching
her to my breast I wanted to cry, not with the grief of
parting from the Romanies, for I had none, but with
distinct feeling of having been very ill-used by them. I did
not want to go on alone. I was afraid. As for Wolfe Farr, and
his grand words, I felt I would never need his moral support
and physical presence more than I did at that very
moment.

I must have presented a sorry sight, a bedraggled
drenched creature trudging along the hedgerows, with my
bundle, my basket of clothes pegs to sell and the child

wrapped tightly in my shawl. I was not brave, I often stopped and wept bitterly for Bessie who I would never see again. Alone, friendless, my spirits were so low, had Death come at that hour I would have welcomed it. Except for Angela, whose life I had promised Bessie to cherish as my own. If aught befell me, if I died like a wayside gipsy, then there would be only the workhouse for her and some terrible future I dared not think about.

I sold few clothes pegs. The drives to the houses on the approach to Farley were long indeed and Angela when she wished to toddle, soon tired and had to be carried most of the way. We were both cold, wet and utterly wretched, no match for servant girls who closed the door in our faces with the words: 'We want no gipsies here, get you gone before we set the dogs on you.'

Only one old serving woman took pity on us. The rain came down in sheets and the sight we presented must have moved her heart.

'We want no pegs, lass, but it is late for you and the bairn to be abroad. You may sleep in the barn, it is warm there and there is naught you can steal. But begone by daylight, or I'll have the mistress to answer to and this will cost me my job, like as not.'

As we settled gratefully amongst the straw and the old woman cautiously slipped out with milk for Angela and a crust of bread, the irony of the situation suddenly struck me. I need no longer fear apprehension. I was quite safe – if I lived. With my unwashed face, my tattered clothes and wild hair, I was a gipsy to the life, who would ever believe that I was or had once been, Lady Drummle?

Next day, the sun shone and by the number of poor folk, I knew I was in farming land. It was harvest time and they sought employment. Quickly I offered my services which were accepted without comment. I looked strong and healthy enough, no different to other poor ragged mothers with babes in arms, handed over to the care of an older child in the confines of a convenient sheep pen nearby. Angela looked with surprise on those who screamed for their mamas. To her this was yet another exciting game.

Loading hay, alas, looked easy enough at first, among folk to whom such toil was second nature, so skilfully did they work. To me, it was soon agonizing, back-breaking work. I had never done a day's manual labour before in my life and I soon fell far behind the others, dazed and weary. The sun blazed overhead, my arms ached, my head spun dizzily with the effort of thrusting hay up on to the cart. A warning yell and a curse, and then the darkness flooded over me.

When I opened my eyes, I was indoors. A young woman bent over me while Angela sobbed at my side. 'You are in the farmhouse, my dear. You have a fever and you must rest now. Yes, my pet, your mama is awake, see?'

I rallied quickly on soup and bread. 'Thank you for taking care of my little girl,' I said touching Angela's clean new gown, her bright shining curls.

Rose Harne was my rescuer's name, her father had owned the farm but since his death she had found it a hopeless struggle to keep it going. 'I was never reared to be farmer or farmer's wife, my father hoped I would marry well, but alas, I did not.' Sighing left the reason unsaid, for she was but five and twenty, already grown stout and her plain looks belied her name.

I was well enough to continue on my road. When I said so, she looked sad. 'Why don't you stay at Harne for a while?'

'Can you give me work?' I asked eagerly.

'The farm's new owner takes over this week. I am moving to Hopely into my aunt's old house. I shall need a maid.'

'Your offer seems like a gift from heaven and I am glad to accept it. Thank you. Thank you.'

I had only one problem. I lived in mortal terror from every stranger who approached. Every footfall, every knock upon the door threatened denouncement, that Flint was dead and I under arrest.

One day seeing my agitation after a harmless visit from the farm's new owner, Rose whispered: 'What is wrong, Estella?' When I shook my head but continued to tremble, she said: 'You are no gipsy, I realize that. Your voice and manner give you away.'

At my look of alarm, she held up her hand. 'Please, my

dear, I have no wish to pry into anyone's life. We are all entitled to our secrets.' And quickly changing the subject, she picked up Angela, by whom she seemed captivated. 'Such a beauty, your little girl, I keep thinking that if I ever had a child, I'd want one exactly like your Angel, for she is well named. Such a sweet disposition.'

'There is no reason why you shouldn't marry and have babies of your own some day, for you're still young.'

She shrugged. 'I will never marry or be a mother. I'm quite certain of that.'

'No one can be certain, Rose.'

'I am. Every arrangement my father tried to make came to naught. The men he chose did not like me or some misfortune happened to them. It was really rather frightening, as if I brought ill-luck.'

'Rose, Rose, what nonsense you talk. Think of the good fortune you brought me. It was the luckiest day of my life when I came to your farm.'

'Oh Estella,' she hugged me, her eyes tear-bright. 'I am so glad you came that day. Promise that wherever you go we will never lose one another, but will be friends for ever. I want to see little Angel grow up into a beautiful young lady.'

'And that you shall.' I paused uncertain and then said: 'She never had a godmother, you know. But now she shall have you.'

'You really do mean it? Why, that is the nicest gift anyone has ever given me, the next best thing to being a real mother.'

So Angel's godmother Rose was also my first woman friend. If men did not like her, then women certainly did not like me. I remembered right back to those days at Dame Clarissa's and how I had strived for popularity. At Mrs Brandley's and during my marriage, I had only acquaintances, no friend who touched my heart. Perhaps I had been too selfish in the past, now all would be different as I warmed to Rose's good humour, her kindness. A dear friendship which I greatly needed, swiftly blossomed and I told her the truth of my adoption by Miss Havisham and

my own disastrous marriage, the babies I had lost. Ending
with the sorry events that led me to Bessie and how Angela
had arrived on the doorstep, so to speak.

'So she is not your own child. Poor Estella, is it not
strange that she came at such a dark hour of your life?
Surely you were meant for each other and she was sent to
be a blessing to you and make up for all those unhappy
years.' She looked at me and smiled. 'I firmly believe that
we have spiritual parents and children as well as those of
the flesh. Just as I was never intended for marriage,
perhaps your Angel is to be my child of the spirit too. But
what brought you to Harne?'

And I told her of how I had intervened so disastrously
between Aaron Flint and the gipsies. 'Now that you see
the fix I am in, I have no right to stay and implicate you. If
it worries you, I will move on tomorrow.'

'That you will not, Estella. You see,' she added
triumphantly, 'I can find out for you if Aaron Flint still
lives.'

'How so?'

'Because,' she said smiling, 'my cousin Justin takes his
son to boarding-school not five miles distant from
Heathyfold this very week. And what is more, our old nurse
is married to the manager of Flint's mill. I don't doubt
what you say, for there are very strange tales about
Flintwood Hall, that the master keeps a harem and a mad
sister too. Tell me about them, is it all true?', she asked
eagerly as we put on our shawls and walked to the old
house which had been empty for some years. Large and
rambling, there was much to be done to make it habitable
again, and putting it to rights seemed a formidable task.
But Rose was undismayed.

'The stables, an excellent barn. Means I can keep my
two horses, and Daisy my dairy cow. Besides the hens, and
the eggs we can sell.' The following morning, she showed
me the letter she had written to her cousin. 'I have kept it
mysterious, without mentioning you, of course, my dear.
Justin likes a touch of mystery and intrigue.'

And so, it was through Rose Harne that Doctor Justin Faverley became part of my life.

Part Four

Homecoming

Intrigued by his cousin's mysterious letter, Justin Faverley
had visited their old nurse. He brought the news I most
longed to hear, the words that set me free from all guilt.

Aaron Flint was fit and well. His broken head allegedly
the result of an accident with his carriage.

'No mention of a gipsy wedding or of a missing lady's
maid.'

'Now what is this all about, Rose?'

'Miss Havisham will tell you.' As I did so, I think I was
aware within that first hour that the doctor was attracted
to me and for my part, I found him most agreeable and
pleasant. Like his cousin he had little to offer in the way of
looks, his face too craggy, his sandy hair sparse, but there
was strength, sincerity and reliability.

A widower since his wife's death five years earlier,
besides the son Henry, there were three little girls from six
to thirteen, under the care of a nurse in his London home.
In the course of conversation over dinner, I learned that a
governess was urgently required.

I think my eager expression told him that his search for
such a person was ended. He was delighted and so was
Rose, poor lonely Rose. Between them they tried to

persuade me that for the time being Angela should remain here at Hopely and Justin scrupulously pointed out the many advantages to such an arrangement. For a governess, taking care of a baby would be disruptive to her teaching duties. Besides the child would thrive better with Rose in good country air.

I was not easily swayed. The only decision possible for me to make was what was best for my Angel.

Rose hugged me tearfully. 'Dearest Estella, it will be heaven for me to take care of her for you, but I shall never allow a single day to end without reminding her of her dearest Mama. That I promise faithfully. And you have a home here with us, whenever you wish for one.' Shyly she looked out of the window where he walked in the garden. 'But I have an odd feeling ever since Justin arrived that you are going to remain with us. Perhaps, if God wills, we will be more than friends. Some day we may be cousins too. Can you not see all of us united in one loving family?'

I could not. I was not the least in love or even attracted to Doctor Faverley, but I hoped that the warm undemanding companionship of this truly good man might unfreeze in time, the cold chill around my heart, when I remembered the fear and distrust bred by men like Bentley Drummle and Aaron Flint.

As we spent more time together, I became aware of a strange phenomenon. As once Aaron Flint's physical appearance had reminded me of Pip, so too did Justin's forthright honesty, his kindliness. Even his gestures and smile most markedly took on the ghost of Pip. I sighed. Had Pip chosen to haunt me thus with fragments of himself, and I wondered how many more men must I meet before that vision was complete, before I would be free of the cold echoes of those saddest of all words: 'What-might-have-been?'

The doctor's house on the outskirts of London was a handsome villa newly built in Islington. With airy big windows and fine high-ceilinged rooms as was the modern fashion, it was an agreeable residence and I was soon absorbed with three very agreeable girls, thirteen-year old

Judith, Jane who was eleven and Jessie the 'baby' aged six.

The weeks of peace that followed my arrival were a blessed oasis for my troubled soul. Almost every post brought reassuring letters from Rose that Angela was happy and well, and every day's end Justin sought my society. As the weeks passed, my position in the house seemed far more mistress than governess and without a word being said between us, or any declaration made, we allowed ourselves to drift into an affectionate relationship, where it seemed perfectly natural that we should kiss goodnight, and that he should escort me to concerts, to the theatre and the music hall, to which he was addicted.

The London of that early part of 1857 was very different from the one I had left with the war in the Crimea at its height. Now on everyone's lips and in every newspaper, were three great black words: Delhi, Cawnpore and Lucknow, as familiar to the Englishman in the street as Derby, Coventry and London. The horrors and needless slaughter of the Indian Mutiny made sickening reading and under siege, only the faith of their fathers had upheld the poor unfortunate women and their families. And I fancied rather cynically, the certainty of the British that the worst could never happen to them for God was on their side and would never countenance such an outrage. Alas, they were proved all too terribly wrong in such an assumption.

By June we attended a service of thanksgiving in St Paul's Cathedral for our gallant soldiers and their families who had perished. But the war was over, and a speedy return to the gallant and romantic as a theme in literature and art, personified by Alfred Lord Tennyson's *'Idylls'* and executed in colours and on canvases larger than life by the pre-Raphaelite brotherhood, led by the eccentric painter Dante Gabriel Rossetti.

There was also a sensational murder trial in the newspapers, the details of which I found very disturbing. Madeleine Smith, a Glasgow woman had poisoned her lover with arsenic. Justin as a doctor, was greatly intrigued by her motives. Here was a woman who openly admitted the sin and shame of enjoying low emotions and what was regarded by respectable women as the unwholesome experience of sex, rendered necessary only for the bearing of children.

Later that year I wore my first crinoline, a new diversion from France where the Empress Eugenie had created the fashion to encourage trade in expensive materials by using many yards on each gown. Personally, I had never been addicted to the vagaries of fashion unless they happened to be pretty and practical too. I found the huge steel framework in which I walked rather trying and exhausting. It certainly looked dramatic enough and my ball gown of primrose satin with its flounces and frills of lace was an object of admiration to the bystander. However, I was a woman who had never taken mincing steps in her life before, but enjoyed the freedom of walking briskly and uncluttered. Now I found restraint and considerable inaction in the gliding steps which threatened ruin to every small table and delicate piece of furniture with which every drawing-room was fashionably cluttered, and where a simple walk across the floor became a negotiation to be conducted with utmost skill.

Time passed quickly, with joyous visits to Rose and Angel, soon I would be celebrating the anniversary of my arrival in Justin's household. Although I guessed that he regarded me affectionately as I did him, I also knew he was a shy man, reserved and proud, in no hurry to remarry. Besides if I did not respond to his advances with enthusiasm, such would be his embarrassment that he must lose both admirable governess and agreeable companion. As for myself, my late experience with Aaron Flint suggested extreme caution in my relationships with employers. I had allowed attraction, loneliness, perhaps even despair to masquerade as love. I was not foolish enough to pretend any such feeling for Justin. Had I thoughts that he was about to propose then I should never have continued to let him believe that I was a widow, the story he had heard and accepted from Rose and which I had never troubled to deny; that I had been cruelly treated by my first husband, now dead. Before I went to Islington, I felt that Justin knew as much of the truth as was good for either of us. I still had reservations about revealing to anyone, even Rose, the shameful truth about my parentage.

Justin's illustrious patients had for the past two years included a member of the Royal Family and his treatment had so impressed Her Majesty that there were hints of a knighthood forthcoming.

'I am invited to join Her Majesty at Balmoral Castle this summer,' he told me over dinner one evening. When I congratulated him upon such an honour, he smiled and studying the contents of his wine-glass intently, whispered: 'Perhaps you would care to see it, Estella. According to Her Majesty, the Scottish Highlands are very romantic and might even be ideally suited to a couple on honeymoon.'

'Have you someone in mind, Justin?' I asked teasingly.

'Need you ask that question, my dear, you who know the answer so well.' Leaning across the table he took my hands and held them in a strong fist that nevertheless trembled. 'Surely you know, dearest Estella, that each day I long for you to be my wife. We get along splendidly in every way. Sometimes it seems as if we are married already as we sit here, side by side of an evening.' When I said nothing, he asked anxiously: 'Well, what is your answer to be? Do you need time to think?'

At the disappointment in that question, I shook my head. 'I have had time to think, Justin dear, and I am very flattered by your proposal.'

'But you do not love me?'

'I am not sure how I should answer that question. I agree with you that no two people could get along better than we do. But – oh dear – I am afraid I have not been completely honest with you. The truth is –'

He laughed, patting my hand. 'Dearest Estella, I can guess the truth. Indeed, I think I have known it for some time. Your hesitation, a certain reluctance in your manner when discussing your husband, leave me to wonder if he is still alive. What other reason do you imagine has held me back all this time?'

'You do not mind?'

'Not in the least, except for the delays it must cause in our marriage.'

And so I told him about Bentley. He listened, occasionally clenching his fists and saying 'Blackguard. Damned scoundrel.'

At the end of my story he took me into his arms. 'No more secrets, Estella, now I know everything and love you all the more. We must find out tactfully as possible, whether the wretch is still alive. But by God, if he is, then I shall feel like going and killing him personally, for making you suffer so.'

That night a step further in our relationship seemed inevitable and not in the least indiscreet, a step down from his table and up into his bed. Long starved of a man's love I responded with passion to his kind and considerate behaviour. Next morning I had no qualms, no guilt or regret. Justin assured me that we would marry eventually and I was content. Many respectable widowed or unmarried doctors had housekeepers who were more than that. As long as the relationship remained discreet and did not reach the ears of their virtuous lady patients, all was well.

In this testing time for two lonely people, both needing each other, I discovered that the joys of physical union brought added harmony and well-being to a deeply satisfying relationship with a man I respected, admired and who might one day be all-in-all to me.

Happy to let past mistakes be forgotten and to allow the future to remain hidden, the present was all I needed. For the first time in many years I felt safe, protected, from the dangers inherent in my own nature, and also from my violent heritage. I still regarded my parentage with loathing but was confident that when the opportunity came and Justin must be told, then as a doctor experienced in so many aspects of life and how mortals functioned, he was the one person who would understand and love me all the more for the early tragedy in which I was but a helpless victim.

Until then, I was happy to delay the evil hour of revealing all and exist from day to day with no greater ambition than to rest upon this peaceful plateau I had found at last. But Justin would have none of it. Marriage was what he wanted, and that soon.

'What is wrong, my dear? Have you changed your mind?'

'Of course not. It is just – just that we are so happy together. We have all we need, without marriage.'

'Surely marriage will not make us less happy?'

'No, but perhaps we should not tempt fate by asking for more when we have so much.'

Justin laughed. 'That is nonsense, my dear, we will only be happier, that I promise you. Besides I want the whole world to know that you are mine. Think of Balmoral Castle this summer and later this year when my knighthood comes, then I want to show off to everyone at Court my lovely Lady Faverley. Besides the children adore you.'

That was true. The girls excitedly looked forward to being 'bridesmaids' to their new Mama and suitable gowns for the occasion became the foremost lesson each day. As for Henry, his father assured me that he had become my devoted slave after his first vacation.

Justin had questioned me tactfully about the infant mortalities and stillbirths of my marriage. I realized that I was in little danger of becoming pregnant again, and could rely upon him, for he practised the birth control that he privately urged upon his patients with large families.

'It will not distress you that we may not have children of our own?' I asked.

He smiled, stroking my hair. 'Not in the least, my dearest, for I feel that four of a family is enough. Too many of my patients have bred first wives into the grave and repeated the procedure with a second and third. It shows abominable lack of thought and self control in a fellow to treat his wife like breeding cattle. And whatever the example of our dear Queen, I do not approve of indiscriminately large families especially where the wife's health is endangered, for so to my shame, my poor wife's fatal illness was brought about as a result of her last pregnancy. I have never forgiven myself for her death.'

We little knew then but our 'family' of children was to be tragically increased within the next month when news came, the most unexpected in the world, that Rose had died in an accident at Hopely.

In a sudden unexpected thunderstorm of considerable intensity, concerned for the cow newly calved and her horses, she had taken an oil lamp to inspect them. Awakened terrified by the storm, Angela had heard her go out and followed her, falling in the darkness. Her cries sent Rose rushing to carry her back into the house. The lamp, temporarily forgotten, was kicked over by one of the frightened animals. A raging inferno resulted and Rose without a thought for her own safety rushed in to rescue the terrified beasts. They were saved but a blazing beam fell ...

We were both in tears at this cruel blow of fate which had deprived me of a dear friend and Justin of his beloved cousin, close as a sister through the years. Weeping, I remembered the promises we had made for a future never to be as I found Angela changed already, babyhood departed in the lengthening limbs, the sweet and winsome manners of a three-year old. Mercifully she was still too young to understand what it meant by the Faverley girls telling her how Aunt Rose had 'gone to heaven'.

She soon settled into the household, and Justin watching us together, whispered:

'What a perfect mother you are. I was wrong, I should never have let you part with her. Had I not given in to Rose, this tragedy need never have happened.'

'My dear, the thunderstorm and Rose's concern for her animals, that would have happened whether Angela was with her or not.'

But gloomily he shook his head. 'I feel responsible.'

He was now firmly against any further delays to our marriage. I was to communicate with Mr Jaggers immediately to discover whether or not Bentley Drummle still lived.

I was strangely apprehensive awaiting his reply and as the girls finished their lessons and we sallied forth into the park, I looked proudly at my laughing chattering girls bearing Angela in their midst. Soon I was to be a wife, mother of these four lovely girls. If only Rose had not died my happiness would have been complete. I kept remembering how certain she had been that she would not marry or have children and how she thought of herself as the bearer of ill-luck. I was glad indeed that she had known Angela, even though I was convinced that she had paid for that brief foster-mothering with her life.

Next morning I received word from Mr Jaggers that Drummle had died some months ago in dire circumstances of penury, the land at Drummle Towers sold off to pay his debts, inherited by cousin Wilfred with no male heir but a tribe of daughters for whom to find dowries. Thanks to Wilfred's charity, Edwina Drummle and Ruth had been installed in a small house in the village. For them, I felt no pity but remembered my dear friend and father-in-law Sir Hammond with compassion. What tears he must have shed in paradise over the ancient proud home of his ancestors, sacrificed at the gaming tables by his grandson.

'Mr Jaggers congratulates us upon our betrothal and asks that we call upon him at his home, where he is indisposed with gout, so that certain legal documents concerning Satis House might be attended to'.

We set forth jubilantly and I laid aside my gloomy forebodings. I told myself I was to be married to a man I loved, not with rapture but with deep affection, tried and trusted by more than a year of living under the same roof. As well as virtues, we were also aware of each other's shortcomings and not unduly perturbed by the minor disturbances with which the happiest of domestic lives are troubled. I firmly believed that by living as Justin's mistress, I stood to gain more happiness than in that disastrous first marriage to a man about whom I was ignorant of everything except attraction to his looks.

Such was the flimsy basis on which most marriages were built, when I recalled Dame Clarissa's oft-quoted: 'No respectable girl kisses any man on the lips until the day she is married.' What arrogant nonsense on which to build a marriage.

In London we paused only in Regent Street where Justin bought me as a betrothal present a diamond and sapphire necklace with matching bracelet and earrings. He laughed away my protests that it was far too expensive, a simple diamond ring would have pleased me as well. 'You are to have my mother's betrothal ring that has been in the Faverley family for three generations. But the necklace is what you will wear when you are presented at Court as Lady Faverley. Only the brightest and best in the world is good enough to adorn you when you are received by Her Majesty. You will like Prince Albert, I am sure, I know he is not greatly admired by the masses but I have the greatest respect for our industrious conscientious prince.'

The door at Gerrard Street was opened by my mother. I had not forgotten that she might be there, but was confident that I could deal with the situation. I had still to tell Justin but first, I told myself, he should meet her. Would he see the strong resemblance in fact, or did it exist only in my imagination? He knew only that I had been adopted by the wealthy eccentric Alicia Havisham but expressed little interest in my origins halting my stammering attempts at explanation with: 'Many children are adopted. You are one of thousands who know little of their background.'

I was soon to be his wife. Happy and secure in his love, what harm could this unfortunate woman do me? A woman for whom, alas, I felt nothing, except perhaps a tinge of pity. A woman to whom I was nothing, bound to her only by the accident of birth.

As I treated her with a polite disinterest of visitor for servant, her face expressed no emotion at seeing me again. However, as she removed my cape, her reflection in the looking-glass made me realize that we were more alike than ever as the passing years closed the gap between girl and middle-aged woman. She was still slender while I had put on a little weight in the well-being of my happiness with Justin.

Mr Jaggers, unable to rise from his chair greeted us cordially. To say that he was warm in his reception would be the greatest of compliments, as Justin offered professional advice about the treatment of his gout. A remark about Her Majesty's household pleased the old lawyer exceedingly. He even went so far as to repeat it to our fellow guests: two elderly brothers, who were retired judge and lawyer, on holiday from Wales, had arrived unexpectedly that afternoon and had been prevailed upon to remain to dine with us.

Mr Jaggers was in excellent spirits allowing Justin to assist him to the dining table and see him comfortably bestowed.

'Plain fare you'll get here, gentlemen, plain but good. My housekeeper has learned through the many years she has served me,' he said as Molly put the dishes before us, 'that I am a man of plain facts and plain fare.'

'Excellent advice. Take people and the food the good Lord sends us for what they are,' said the old judge.

'Quite right, sir, quite right. I am sure the good doctor here could confirm that you have hit it excellently. No room for the fanciful when you are in the business of dealing out life and death. I remember the case of –'

As he talked warming to his subject, with Justin's interest and theories regarding the nature of crime and criminals as a proper stimulant, I took the opportunity to study Molly who remained in the background, a statue with a serving cloth, ready to dart forward and removing plates, serve the next course. How many times had she remained thus at how many dinners?

'What think you of this Madeleine Smith case, doctor?'

'Guilty, wicked, but with an insatiable passion for life …'

I looked at Molly. Did she listen to the conversation? And I was longing to ask her what she thought of the Madeleine Smith case, she who had vastly more experience

221

of the 'crime passionel' than any of the gentlemen dining around the table. Did she have a fellow feeling for the murderess, that: 'there-but-for-the-grace-of-God,-go-I?' What would have been the outcome of that agreeable evening, I thought, regarding my fellow-diners, absorbed, lofty and pompous (and it was not beyond dear Justin to be pompous sometimes), had I interrupted their loudly proclaimed theories to reveal Molly's past and her true identity?

Her face told me nothing nor did she respond to my polite smile as she removed my plate. Had she ever thought that one day she might be serving her own child at Mr Jaggers' table? Was she proud of the woman her child had become, with a place in the world beyond her own wildest dreams, the future Lady Faverley?

Mr Jaggers continued to expound with sweeping gestures and a burning enthusiasm which signalled that he did not entertain too many guests at his table. But with the awareness between couples who are close, I saw that he no longer had Justin's full attention. For Justin too was intent upon Molly, his responses to his host's remarks abstracted by a frown of concentration as his puzzled gaze flitted to me and to Molly and back again. In that instant I could read his thoughts. Since the moment he set eyes on her, she had reminded him of someone. And now he realized with considerable astonishment, her likeness to his wife-to-be.

Dinner over, while the gentlemen consumed their port, Mr Jaggers was assisted to his study, where he invited me to accompany him and sign various legal documents.

'There is little left I am afraid. The Dower House which remains empty, awaiting your instructions, plus a small legacy that your mother-by-adoption set aside for your thirtieth birthday, and which I am happy to say now yields the handsome sum of two hundred and fifty pounds a year.'

I sighed. 'That would have seemed like a fortune in the days before I met Doctor Faverley.'

'Soon to be Lord Faverley, if rumour is correct,' said Mr Jaggers, studying me as he nipped his lip between forefinger and thumb in a manner I remembered from the past. 'You think a great deal of the good doctor, do you not?'

'So much must be obvious if I am to marry him, sir.'

'Not so, alas, not so. One would wish it to be true, but it scarcely ever is so.' He wagged a finger at me in his courtroom manner. 'Take a point that marriages are contracted between very improbable and often very unhappy people. Take a point that these contracts are entirely at the behest and for the well-being of the parents concerned, where the wishes of the heart come a poor second to the financial rewards expected.'

He regarded me solemnly. 'I realize that you have no such motives, it is obvious to all that you wish the good doctor's welfare, that you have his best interests at heart?' Again he frowned at me, brows down, fingertips touching. Suddenly he demanded very sharply: 'Tell me, Estella, if I may so call you, what think you of my Molly? Do you remember her from your last visit?'

'I do indeed.' I could feel the colour suffusing my face.

'Has she changed greatly?'

'No – no, I do not think so, hardly at all.'

'You do not think so? Ah! Your manner tells me that you are aware of Molly's true identity. That you know who my Molly is?' he added triumphantly: 'Exactly so, exactly so.' And now adopting his best legal manner, he continued, an admonishing finger poised in my direction:

'Put the case in which your mother was involved as bad indeed, I felt at the time that it was unlikely I would secure her release. Put the case that I knew of your existence, knew that my client's inclination for motherhood was nothing short of disastrous. Put the case that I also knew of a rich woman who wished to adopt a female child. Again, put the case that in the evil atmosphere of Newgate all I ever saw of children was an unwanted spawn heading for destruction. Put the case that I have seen them tried at a criminal bar, where they were held up to be seen; that I knew of such infants being imprisoned, whipped, transported, neglected, cast out, qualified in all ways for the hangman, and indeed growing up merely to be hanged.

Put the case, dear lady, that nearly all the children I saw were spawn likely to develop into fish for my net in later life, to be prosecuted, forsworn, defended, made orphans and generally bedevilled.

'And now I put the case that here was one pretty little child out of the heap that could be saved; whom the father believed dead and would make no stir about. To the mother all I need say was: part with the child whom you do not love unless it is necessary to produce her to clear you, then produced she shall be. Give the child into my hands and I will do my best to bring you off. If you are saved, your child will be saved too; if you are lost, your child is still saved.'

The picture he presented was terrible indeed.

'You look apprehensive, dear lady, but I assure you, there is no need for you to fear my Molly. She is a gentle creature now, I believe I put the fear of death into her long ago, and certainly there is no more violence in her. She seems only vaguely aware of the past, for she has buried it very deeply.' Pausing a moment to let this small consolation sink in, he continued gently: 'It remains only for me to inflict further pain on you by revealing the identity of your real father.'

'I know the identity of my true father. Thanks to the indiscretions of Will Startop.'

'Is that so? Ah, yes, an unfortunate failing of that young man, who is also a client of mine. Among his many excellent virtues, he retains alas, the student's poor head for imbibings. Discretion goes to the winds and his tongue loosens in a very indiscreet way. No one should ever trust secrets to Mr Startop's care, alas, unless they want them to be spread all over London Town when he is in a convivial mood. Pray continue –'

'From his account of the convict Magwitch, I was able to piece together what I did not know for sure already,' I said bitterly, 'that Magwitch, or Provis, who was Pip's benefactor was also my father. And, I might add, brought no great joy to the expectations of either of us.'

The admonishing finger was again raised. 'You know

then of the other link? That Magwitch was once the confidant of your foster-mother's lover, Compeyson and that he eventually destroyed him. It was Magwitch who by his own death, avenged your mother-by-adoption.'

His tone suggested that I should make allowances for this sacrifice. I shook my head. 'He was a murderer, Mr Jaggers. And so was my mother.'

In the small silence that followed, the urgent question unasked, hung upon the air. 'Is the good doctor then in possession of these somewhat lamentable and unpleasant facts about your parentage?'

I shook my head. 'No. I have not told him yet.'

'Then you must do so,' he said sternly.

'Why should I? What difference will that make?'

'It might make a great deal of difference to the prospects of his knighthood.'

'That is ridiculous. How could my parentage possibly affect the reward due to his good services?'

'As the governess of his children, perhaps little. But as his wife, your parentage will come under Royal scrutiny. And not to put too fine a point on it, as is well known Her Majesty is a stickler for decorum and respectability. Just a hint regarding your parentage and we have no idea how many people have received such a hint from our rather inebriated friend Mr Startop.' He leaned forward. 'Just one hint,' he emphasized, 'needs only confirmation of the Criminal Courts' proceedings and a few old newspapers. I fear that the highest in the land might consider such information as quite detrimental to any expectations of a knighthood.'

'I think you are wrong, if I may say so, Mr Jaggers. But I will certainly put Doctor Faverley in full possession of the facts before our marriage.'

'Do so, Estella, do so.' And so saying he tucked my hand into my arm as if he was pleased with me and as we returned, said: 'Mr Wemmick sends the compliments of Jim and Flora Skiffins who sailed for America last year.'

Dear Flora, I was so glad for her, I thought, as the carriage returned us to Islington and I pretended to sleep with my head on Justin's shoulder, for I had much scheming to keep my mind occupied. Why should I tell him all and destroy his happiness as well as my own? Molly belonged to the past, fast approaching thirty years. Besides her crime was no fault of mine. Was it not completely unjust that I should have to further suffer for my wretched parents' sins?

I resolved to forget Mr Jaggers' advice, and as I sat before the dressing table mirror, removing my necklace and earrings, Justin came and stood behind me, his hands on my bare shoulders.

Looking at my reflection, he smiled wryly. 'You know it's even stronger in the mirror.'

'What is?' I asked and knowing perfectly well, as I placed my betrothal gift in its velvet box.

'Your astonishing resemblance to Mr Jaggers' housekeeper – Molly is she called? It has intrigued me all evening.'

I continued to look at him, unsure of my ground or of what to say. He mistook my manner for outrage at such a suggestion, and sitting down beside me, he smiled. 'My dear, it was just a thought and a very romantic one. It did occur to me when I saw you together and so alike, for the woman is still very handsome and youthful in appearance despite her greying hair. I suddenly had this extraordinary idea, knowing you were adopted and that Mr Jaggers had been your guardian's lawyer. Could it possibly be that you were his housekeeper's illegitimate child?'

'How clever of you to guess.'

'You mean that it is true,' he beamed, excited and pleased by his discovery. 'Well, what a romantic story, my dear. But why didn't you warn me? Ah – I know. You wanted to see if I noticed the resemblance for myself. Tell me about it, while I brush your hair.' Normally I found this nightly ritual soothing. 'There now. Were you a love child?'

'No. As a matter of fact I was not.'

He paused and laughed at my reflection. 'Good Lord. Don't tell me the good Mr Jaggers is not your father?'

'Alas, would that he was. And I was not illegitimate

either. At least, if a gipsy wedding can be considered legal.'

'A gipsy wedding, eh.' The brush strokes paused for a moment. 'Come along, my darling, I must hear all this marvellous story. What an intriguing woman you are, always full of surprises,' he laughed and bending over kissed my bare neck. 'I think I know all about you and suddenly you reveal the fascinating story of your romantic birth.'

'I don't know whether you will feel it is all that romantic, Justin, when you hear it,' I said and taking the brush from him laid it aside while as we sat there together before the dressing-table mirror, I told him all. Everything. Beginning with the Nightmare and how I had discovered the drawing of Molly among Mr Wemmick's papers and had pieced together the rest of the story when Will Startop told me about Pip and Herbert Pocket and the convict Magwitch.

As I talked I was aware that he no longer laughed but was all of a sudden solemn, biting his lip, shaking his head. At the end of the story, I waited to be gathered into his arms, as I whispered: 'And now, dearest Justin, there are no more secrets between us.'

He sighed, shook his head again. 'My dear, my dear Estella. The story you have revealed is indeed terrible – terrible.' He was silent again. 'I can hardly believe it.' Springing to his feet, he paced the floor, occasionally pausing to stare at my reflection. 'Criminals – murderers – my poor darling girl.'

'Not a very romantic story, is it?'

Ignoring the hand I stretched out to him he shook his head: 'My dear Estella, to have such parentage, a woman of your sensitivity and beauty, it is almost more than one can bear. And I wish, oh how I wish for your sake, that not one word of it was true.' Again that forlorn shake of his head and as I looked at him I felt for all his hand clasped mine that a huge gulf now yawned between us.

'You wished to know, Justin. And I have told you the truth. I cannot change the facts of my birth.'

'Would that you could, and more important, would that

we could conceal it somehow. I would give the world, Estella, at this moment to have had you some serving girl's daughter born on either side of the blanket, humbly born –'

'Is not a gipsy's brat humble enough for you?' I demanded impatiently.

'You do not understand, do you? How are we to keep this story quiet? Already if Startop's indiscretion is to be relied on, then there will be whispers, whispers which – which in time – will inevitably reach Her Majesty's ears. There are always malicious people eager and ready to carry such stories and Her Majesty's statesmen would feel honour bound to investigate.' He sighed. 'It will be goodbye, alas, to my hopes of a knighthood, or even to further serving Her Majesty's family, if we are married.'

'What absolute nonsense, Justin. I fail to see how your competence as a physician can be in the least affected by my parentage.'

'Then you don't understand Royal circles. Illegitimacy is frowned upon by the strict moral principles of Her Majesty. Even to be divorced is to be sullied and removed from Royal favour. Perhaps we could still get away with the information I intended to put forward, that you were Miss Havisham's orphaned niece but if the truth came out,' he shuddered. 'It would mean ruin, the complete collapse of everything I have hoped and worked for all these years. I am no longer a young man, I have worked hard towards this knighthood, made many sacrifices for what was to be the crowning achievement of all my work in the realms of medicine. There might exist those unscrupulous enough to use such information as blackmail to destroy my professional life.'

And I knew as I listened that my own dream was over. He would never marry me now. Never. Almost with compassion I listened to his lame excuses, his feeble explanations: 'We have always been perfectly frank with one another. Should your background become public knowledge then my children too will face ostracism by society. We stand to lose all, to be shunned by even those we call our friends. Harry is growing up, a clever lad and by

all accounts headed for a brilliant future. In a year or two
Judith and Jane will be eligible for presentation. You must
realize that it is not merely for myself or for mere selfish
gratification, but also what I owe to my children. The girls
will be quite heartbroken if I do not get my knighthood.
They have set such great store by it. Oh dear, oh dear –'

He slumped into a chair before me, suddenly a tired
plain old man, pathetic and afraid. 'We will discuss it
tomorrow, my dear.' He consulted his watch. 'I am very
tired, and so are you. I have an operation to perform at
eight o'clock, so I must retire. Tomorrow we might think of
some way round this appalling circumstance.'

He did not take me in his arms as usual but turned from
me abruptly as we settled down for the night, nervously
keeping as much of the bed as possible between us, as if I
was likely to contaminate him.

When he returned home late the following evening, I had
already made up my mind. I tried to tell myself that I
understood his motives, as his duty toward his family. I
tried to tell myself by way of consolation that it was one
thing for a respectable doctor who had Her Majesty's
favour to marry the widowed Lady Drummle, but quite
another to marry the daughter of a convicted murderer and
murderess. It would have been cruel of me to insist that he
keep his word, and with pride outraged to threaten breach
of promise. Cruel and useless, for tears of recrimination
would only kill his love.

Better to leave with some shreds of dignity, knowing that
although my heart would no longer break, I was sorely
disappointed in his feet of clay. The fragment of Pip I
recognized in him had led me to false expectations that he
would love me with all his heart and hold staunch that love
against all the world, that he would be noble and gallant,
instead of humanly fallible.

Even as I grieved at leaving this house where I had hoped
to spend many happy future years, at parting with his
children, who had grown so dear to me, my imagination
always ready to look with optimism upon everyone, raced
ahead. As I rehearsed the decision I must take to him, I

heard him crying out at the thought of losing me, swearing that he could not live without me. What was a knighthood, what even his dear children who must find their own way in the world as he had done, what indeed was a social position weighed against his love for me?

He uttered no such words, there was no tearful tender reunion, clasped in his arms. Such tenderness was now unthinkable, laid aside for ever. He merely nodded, said quietly with more than a trace of relief: 'You must do as you think best, Estella.'

And sickened, I knew that he had resolved to lose me and was prepared for the outcome, indeed, had thought it out most carefully and had already decided the course he must take.

'Is that all we have to say to each other?'

He bowed his head. 'Is it not enough for you, Estella. Why prolong the agony?'

But had he asked me to remain as his mistress, then I would have done so. I took his hand and held it to my cheek: 'I have been happy with you and to have had a home for Angela and myself. It would not worry me one whit – to stay as we are – lovers –'

He pulled his hand away almost violently. 'Out of the question now, Estella. Absolutely out of the question.'

'I understand,' I said and stood before him, hands clasped demurely, like a dismissed servant. He did not need to add the words that the approaching knighthood also made the presence of a mistress inadvisable. The ranks of respectability must be tight closed against all eventualities.

'I will leave immediately,' I told him.

'There is no need for that. Another governess must be found. Feel free to stay until then,' he said somewhat unconvincingly and when I shook my head, suddenly blinded by tears, added gently: 'Where will you go?'

'I have the Dower House, remember. I will live there and as I have a small income, I shall not starve. There is much to do to put the house to rights.'

'Then let Angela remain with us – yes, I insist, until

everything is ready. You will work much faster without an active child at your heels.' He seized my hands. 'Estella, she may remain with us as long as you like. This is now her home, we are happy to have her with us – always, should you find some situation where a child is burdensome.'

I regarded him amazed. Did he understand nothing of the joyous burden that foster-motherhood was to me? 'It is very good of you, but I want my daughter with me,' I said trying to keep my voice level. 'She is mine, all I have in the world. As you know I am unlikely to bear a child again. With such parentage as mine, perhaps that is just as well.'

He bowed his head and said: 'Should you change your mind, Angela may have a home with us for the rest of her life. I will be happy to adopt her even.'

Not as long as I live, I thought, hurrying from the room. Angela was bewildered and wept, upset at Mama taking her from Judith and Jane and her boon companion Jessie, whom she would most miss.

'We are going to have a nice new home, all our own, where Mama lived when she was a little girl like you. There we will stay for ever and ever.'

How much of this was understood by her, I had no idea, but tears dried as I prepared to pack my trunk, I left her already bidding farewell to the inhabitants of the Faverley's doll-house and informing them of our new plans, scolding one doll and smiling upon another. As for those three girls in the schoolroom, so dear to me, Justin must tell them himself, make excuses for which I had neither heart nor adequate words and my distress would only make it harder for all of us to bear.

Unwilling to risk a further encounter with my mother, I wrote to Mr Jaggers. His reply applauded 'the good sense' of my decision, (dear God, what *that* had cost me!) and enclosed a letter written by Jim Skiffins and signed by Flora (who was learning her letters): 'We do well in Virginia and now have a growing family of two sons and at last a newly-arrived daughter. We wish to call her Estella and would be honoured if you would consent to be her godmother.' I would indeed, I replied, delighted that Flora

Jolly had found her hard-earned happiness at last.

At the Dower House there was much work to be done, especially for a woman single-handed, given that her hands and wrists were exceptionally strong and I had long since abandoned the vanity of wearing gloves upon every occasion. Considering my heritage, large hands seemed the smallest of my problems and I worked with a will each day and fell into bed exhausted each night, glad of the physical labour which absorbed mind and body and left little time for brooding upon the sorrows of a bruised heart.

Always a pretty little cottage, the Dower House had been sorely neglected and I planned to restore some of the handsome furniture which had escaped the fire in Miss Havisham's apartments and had lain long in an outhouse. The difference wrought by paint and polish was remarkable and soon I was hanging bright curtains to offset the old oak panelled walls. In the pretty bedrooms with their dormer windows, while I worked, at my side Angela mimicked each action for the solemn instruction of her own small family of dolls.

Sometimes as I paused to ease my aching back I looked out on the grass-grown ruins where Satis House had stood. The contractor who bought the property had gone bankrupt, the villas unbuilt. It seemed so wasteful. Such were my thoughts on sad melancholy days, and there were a few, as I remembered all those I had loved who had travelled far from me, lost beyond death's barrier.

Miss Havisham, whose misguided – perhaps even mad – influence upon my warped early years had been counterbalanced by Bessie Maydie's loving kindness. Sometimes I fancied Bessie's presence still, that she was not far away from Angela and me. A trick of sunlight that threw a shadow over the doorway, a breeze that rustled a starched apron: imagination perhaps, but as I smiled to what I could not see, it pleased me to think that she watched over us. I could still weep for Bessie whose hand I was unable to hold in her dying hour and for poor sad Rose

Harne, whose brief friendship and foster-motherhood of Angela had ended so tragically.

There were others I tried not to remember. Drummle and Flint and most recently Justin Faverley, and the bitter lessons of life these three men had taught me. And I knew that I was almost healed when I found it difficult to recognize the Estella of the past as the same woman who sang as she worked out of sheer gladness of heart: gladness for the child at her side, for this pretty cottage, two hundred and fifty pounds a year, and my few remaining jewels from Miss Havisham. But mostly for blessings, too many to count. These included new acquaintances, the promise of friendships, having soon discovered that a young child is a marvellous introduction into any society.

As for the Nightmare, from that moment when I fitted the last fragment of my father's true identity into the puzzle, it had gone for ever, its evil power vanquished. My living mother, I had long since forgiven but we would remain forever strangers to one another. A stranger too, my dead father, Pip's convict Magwitch, who had so hurtfully chosen to give his fortune to the blacksmith's boy in preference to his own daughter.

No matter, no matter …

As for Pip. Where was he now? Did Cairo agree with him? And had he found a loving wife to take away the bitterness Estella had planted in his heart? I most fervently hoped so and if I permitted myself one regret, it was that in my life I had known only one man's true love and had refused to recognize that what I held was beyond gold. Our roles had now been reversed. Tormentor had become tormented: Pip had returned to tantalize me from Aaron Flint's eyes and in Julian Faverley's smile. Dear God, would I ever cease to mourn those precious wasted years of my youth when I might have been Pip's wife, thrown away for the dross of an empty title, the lure of wealth and fine houses.

Pip. I smiled. How inescapable he was, still haunting the ruins of Satis House, too. One of many poor ghosts, I thought, as with Angela asleep and the twilight gathering,

I rested my head against the cool window-pane.

But there was a strange man walking out there alone ...

Strange, yet familiar too ...

I raced downstairs. Please God, please let it be him, don't let him be just another part of the dream.

'Pip?'

'Estella?'

In the eleven years since our last meeting, he had broadened in physique. Boyhood long vanished, Pip had become a very attractive man, with a look of prosperity and content. But in that first shy greeting, I saw it was a lie, and that his eyes were haunted by the pain I had put there long ago, and by loneliness equal to my own.

How warm and strong his hands, how gentle his smile. 'The years have been kind to you, Estella.' His voice too, always one of his most attractive features had deepened with the years. 'But I hear also that you are a widow now. I am sorry.'

'Spare me your sympathy, Pip. Estella got the husband she deserved. We were very unhappy together and so much for my breaking his heart, he succeeded in breaking mine and almost taking my life with it. It is a long story.'

'Some of which I have heard from Startop.'

'Ah, Startop again. We met in Derbyshire. I went to visit Bessie. She is dead, alas.'

'I am truly sorry, for she was a dear good soul.' We stood in silence and then he said, 'Come it is chilly, let us walk round the garden as we did long ago.' And I took his arm as if this was the most natural thing in the world, glancing shyly into his face, a well-beloved face indeed, as we walked. 'A pity you have no children.'

'Ah but I have. Not to Drummle, but an orphaned child, Angel – great niece of Bessie. I am to adopt her legally. She is asleep in the cottage at this moment.'

Pip smiled. 'Strange that you are to follow in the tradition of Miss Havisham.'

'Oh no, Pip, far from that. I am bringing her up, my little Angel – Angela is her real name but the resemblance does not end there – to love all the world, although when she is a little older, she is scarce three, I will teach her all the things to avoid, like trying to break any man's heart.'

Pip gave me a wry smile. 'I would love to meet your little Angel for although I am an old bachelor now and most unlikely to ever marry, it seems, I still relish the company of small children.' He laughed in the way I remembered, throwing his head back as if he had not a care in the world. 'Pip the blacksmith's boy, Estella, remember him? Well, he has never quite died inside this somewhat ageing exterior.'

'You do well, Pip, I hear, and you look well too. A wife should not be hard to find for you.'

I was aware of the intensity of his gaze and of how his arm trembled against mine before he replied sadly: 'I am difficult to please in that respect, remember, having made up my mind too firmly long ago. However, I work hard for a sufficient living, and therefore – yes, I do well, as you say.'

'I have often thought of you,' I said shyly.

'Have you indeed?' He seemed surprised and pleased too.

'Of late very often. I still treasure the book of Tennyson's poems you gave me long ago:

"All precious things, discover'd late,
To those that seek them issue forth;
For love in sequel works with Fate,
And draws the veil from hidden worth."

There was a long hard time when I kept far from me the remembrance of what I had thrown away when I was quite ignorant of its worth. But I have had ample reason, since we last met and walked here together, to bow my head before the bitter knowledge of the truth of those words.' I paused to look at him and whisper: 'Your poem has had a very special place in my heart, Pip.'

'Do you remember how "The Arrival" continues' he said and continued in that low vibrating voice, that many an actor would have envied:

"He travels far from other skies –
His mantle glitters on the rocks –
A fairy Prince, with joyful eyes,
And lighter-footed than the fox …
He stoops – to kiss her – on his knee
'Love, if thy tresses be so dark,
How dark those hidden eyes must be".'

There was a sudden silence before he added: 'You have always held a place in my heart, Estella.'

Our walk had come to an end and we sat on an old bench near the Dower House, I looking down at my folded hands. 'I must go indoors in a moment, Pip,' I smiled somewhat stiffly. 'Is it not strange that here on this very spot with so many memories, we two should part again?'

'Are we then to part again so soon, Estella? To me parting is a painful thing. To me, the remembrance of that last parting has remained through the years, ever mournful and painful.'

'But you said to me that day, God bless you, God forgive you. And if you could say that to me then, you will not hesitate to say that to me now. Now when suffering has been stronger than all other teaching and has taught me to understand what your heart used to be. I have been bent and broken but, I hope, into a better shape.' Timidly I put my hand on his arm. Suddenly I wanted very much not to lose him. 'Be as considerate and good to me as you were, and tell me that we are friends.'

'We are friends,' said Pip, bending over me as he rose from the bench.

'And will continue friends apart?'

'Is that all the hope you can offer me, dear friend?'

'Hope?' I repeated, feeling tears rising. 'What hope can such a one as I offer you? I, who have a murderess for a mother and a convict – your benefactor Magwitch – for a father? Can you look into my eyes, Pip, and say that makes no difference, and you will love me, in spite of it all?'

For answer, Pip took my hands and holding them tightly gazed deep into my eyes. 'I have known of your parentage for many a long year, Estella, and never thought the worse of you for what you could not help. I learned then to pity your mother and as for the man who was my benefactor and your father, I regret only one thing, that I was almost too late to love him, as you might have done had fate exchanged places with us. I held him in my arms when he died and was able to tell him that his daughter was alive and was loved. And he blessed me for it, having grieved long for your death. Yes, Estella Havisham, I can look into your eyes with pride and say that I love you – now, this moment and for ever. And that nothing in this world or in the next will ever change me.'

I knew then what my heart had always known, that he was all the real world to me, joys and sorrows too. I loved him and would continue to love him until there was no more time left in this world for either of us. As once in this garden, an uncaring child, I had kissed his cheek, now as a loving woman, I kissed his mouth.

How dear those lips, and how long this hour awaited. We could not smile, we could not say one word but we saw the answer in each others' eyes, that we were already one person, one love, one life together.

And we went out of that ruined place and into the pretty house that waited to welcome us, where all was comfort and hope and love, with a little child asleep.

As the morning mists had risen long ago when I first left Satis House, so the evening mists were rising now. But in all that broad expanse of tranquil light, there lay no shadow of another parting.